QUETZALCOATL DREAMS

TERRY ANDREWS

B&H Bennett & Hastings Publishing

ISBN 978-1-934733-53-0

Library of Congress Control Number: 2009941537

QUETZALCOATL
DREAMS

ACKNOWLEDGMENTS

This book was made possible by a grant from the universe, which ended my job. The generous gift of time left me free to write. If we allow it, the universe will help make all our dreams come true. If we look with eyes of wonder we will see the spark of magic that makes this happen. And if we walk our authentic path, the universe will sing to the rhythm of our feet.

I wrote my first novel to create something that I wanted to find—people who had kept ancient wisdom alive in order to provide guidance for those of us heralding a new age. The novel was called *Dance of the Jaguar*, and right after it was published, a group of Q'ero shamans from the high mountains of Peru came into my life. The Q'ero are the last of the Inca, and for hundreds of years they have tended the teachings passed down to them from the lineages of wisdomkeepers. From them I received the gift of a light body, my conveyance to the new time.

The Q'ero were told to protect the ancient teachings and keep them alive until they could be passed on to the West. My heartfelt appreciation to those keepers who passed this wisdom on to me.

This is a work of fiction, but it is based on the whisperings of those who dwell just beyond our range of seeing, beyond the veil. They show me pictures of the coming time, hieroglyphics from the future, which I have translated into a story.

With *Quetzalcoatl Dreams* the story begun in *Dance of the Jaguar* continues. While it can be read alone, those who read the first book will find the familiar characters have returned. Every generation creates its own myths, and this is especially true now as we enter a new age of our own making.

❦ I ❦

Right now, we are awakening to our true nature. We are connecting to the mystery held deep within and discovering the dormant power we have never used. The seeds were planted long ago. Our destiny is here.

Aurora stared at the letter she had just received. It was written in Spanish, but she translated it without thought. The truth of the words went straight to her heart, like an arrow shot from an ancient bow that had squarely hit its mark. A shiver ran completely through her as she realized who had written it.

His name was Francisco Ix. Don Francisco, he was called. She had met him years ago in the small city of Taxco. He was a stranger, but he said he had been waiting for her. She had no idea what to think. Her experience at that time with the world of shamans was limited. But she had dreamed about a pair of silver earrings in Taxco, and he knew about the dream; indeed, he had dreamed it too.

She moved to the open window, where a slight breeze played in the jasmine, and inhaled deeply of its calming fragrance. "Our destiny is here," she murmured, touching a white blossom. She had anticipated this moment; she had known it would come.

Pulling herself back to the present, she returned to the letter that seemed to have floated into her hand a moment ago.

No one knows how the awakening will manifest. We have the indications, but not the answers. This is the time to begin to share what we have never said. We can no longer live in the land of our ancestors. The transition is before us, and we are sailing into it in this ship we all share, the beautiful planet we call Earth.

Looking out over the placid, aquamarine water of the swimming pool, she felt a wave of excitement move through her. Her destiny—indeed the destiny of everyone on the earth—hung in the balance. She had prepared as much as she could. There were still things to do, but perhaps her list would never be completed. It was time to honor her future by readying herself for change. She plucked a solitary jasmine flower. As she dropped it into a small bowl of water on her desk, she heard a splash in the pool.

Steven's dive sloshed water on the concrete walkway. As he swam the length of the pool underwater, Aurora felt a tinge of trepidation. Their world, like the tranquil surface of the pool, was about to be disrupted in ways that no one fully understood.

But it was the last line of the letter that surprised Aurora the most. *I am coming to talk to you about an important matter.* As she placed the letter in her desk drawer for safekeeping, she wondered when he would arrive. He didn't say. As a shaman, Don Francisco lived outside the structure of traditional time. He came and went according to the unseen turnings of the great mystery.

His timing, however, was impeccable. The new session of the Ancient Wisdom School, which Aurora had founded several years earlier, was beginning this morning.

⚜ 2 ⚜

Before saying a word, Aurora Luna surveyed the familiar faces in the room. Almost every student from the Level 1 session had returned. This was good; they now had some experience under their belt, experience they would need, she knew, for what lay ahead. "Good morning," she said, happy to see them. Her smile was serene as she began with a few introductory remarks about procedures for the current session.

Then she dropped an unexpected bombshell. The Level 2 class, she told them, was heading in an entirely new direction. "I hope you are prepared for an adventure," she told them, "because this session is going to require a leap of faith. We are heading into uncharted territory."

The group erupted with excitement, but Roger drew back abruptly. As a Level 1 student at the Ancient Wisdom School, he had struggled with some of the techniques. Aurora knew he was beginning to worry, but she would explain later. For the meantime, it was enough for them to know what was in store.

Angela, however, sat bolt upright. "Are we going to help Martha?"

Anticipation filled the room and all eyes focused on Aurora. The morning sun, full of promise of a beautiful day, streamed through the windows. In the distance, a dog barked at some unknown provocation. The other noise from the street—a truck being unloaded, the honk of a car horn, people talking—evaporated into the air above the profuse pink and red bougainvillea vines blooming on the wall surrounding the school. Inside the classroom it was so quiet you could hear a pin drop.

"We will know the details soon enough," Aurora replied. "For now, all I will say is this. It is a puzzle, and each of you holds a piece. You will thus be required to work together as perhaps never before." As they began to twitter like a flock of finches, she beamed a wave of energy in their direction to create a calm, receptive state. Immediately it was quiet, and she continued. "This will be our most important Level 2 session ever," she said, letting the words sink in. "We covered a great deal of information in Level 1, but now…well, when you finish this you will look back and not believe how much you have taken in. For the believers," she added, "the wind is at your back."

Taking this in, Roger wilted in his seat. *What was the puzzle? What was his part? How would he discover it?* He wondered if he was in over his head.

Outside his window, just beyond his view, steam rose from Popocatepetl. At almost 18,000 feet, it was Mexico's second highest summit and part of the chain of mountains creating a monumental geographic necklace around Mexico City. Popo was one of the most active volcanoes in Mexico, which was why the ancient Aztecs had named it "Smoking Mountain." It was a beautiful snow-capped peak, picturesque on a summer day such as this, drawing tourists, hikers, and climbers interested in adventure. But no one knew when it might erupt again.

Aurora walked around the room, connecting with each person present. "I want you to approach this class in the same way you approached Level 1—with trust, enthusiasm, and courage. None of you when you first came here knew how to use portals. And yet you were soon navigating through them with confidence and ease. In this class, we are going to make another quantum leap. We are going to take you out of the three-dimensional world that you call home and into the expanded system. We will be moving through the information quickly. Thus your personal responsibility is to master it. Feel free to work outside of class in small groups to do that."

As she spoke, her voice became more songlike. "I mentioned that as believers you will have the wind at your back. And while it may be tempting to let the wind carry you, I am going to ask you to turn to face the wind." As if summoned, a breeze arrived through the open windows and almost in unison they turned toward it. "Close your eyes and envision for a moment," she instructed. "Listen to the voice of the wind as your eagle body grows. Sense how light you are, how powerful." She watched them visualize. "You will use the wind as you become eagle, unafraid to fly. When you are ready, you will lift your wings and soar. We will be going to new heights in this class. As I mentioned earlier, you will be flying into uncharted territory in order to create the life you wish to live."

There was a crash in the back of the room as Roger toppled over. Aurora hurried to help him as Sheila, recovering from her surprise, jumped out of her seat. But Roger was unhurt and got up almost immediately. "Sorry," he said. "That was so vivid, I lost my balance." He brushed off his shorts and sat back down. "But I will master eagle," he said. "I know it. This feels like what I was born to do." He smiled with unusual confidence, and the room erupted in spontaneous, supportive applause. He bowed his head in appreciation.

Aurora, touched by their camaraderie, realized this group had bonded more deeply than any other group she had taught. "This work requires great courage," she said as Roger settled in, "and a belief that there is a different way to live. You are all to be commended. Not everyone can do this."

Once again they clapped, this time for themselves. She could tell they were with her. As Level 2's, they would be learning to master very important skills, and there was no time to waste. Her only regret was that Martha wasn't here. The class would not be the same without Martha's unusual—albeit unpredictable—gift and her willingness to explore the wisdom of the ancients and the infinite realms of energy.

Martha. Aurora had not forgotten her first contact with Martha. Lost in the rainforest after having stepped through a portal, Martha arrived at the Cloud Forest House hoping someone could help her return to her home in Oregon. She did not realize that once the portal was activated, there wasn't a way to go back. Martha had stepped into the mythic realms that had begun to stir in the ancient lands of the Maya and the Inca. In doing so, she had become a part of the awakening that was occurring as powerful waves of energy flooded the planet. And because she had picked up the quetzal feather, she had answered the call to help usher in the energies creating a new earth.

Aurora brought her attention back to the class and described the first exercise they would be doing, which was designed to help them shed their limiting beliefs and ideas. "As you create the life you wish to live, you will consider every action," she explained. "Does it contribute to creating this life, or take you away from it? We are moving through the great shift, evolving into a new kind of human, which we might want to think of as *homo numinous.*"

Noticing a couple of frowns, she quickly explained. "*Numinous* means filled with the presence of divinity—and mystery. We are stepping into a new way of being in the world, a way that will utilize our inborn gifts and allow us to forge deep, sustainable, and meaningful connections with ourselves, with others, and with the natural world that is our home. Humans will come to see all living creatures as cocreators on this planet, and we will recognize that to live in harmony with all is our highest state." She paused, giving them a moment to absorb her words.

"Now, lest you think I know everything, there are still many unanswered questions. Martha, as most of you know, is going in search of the answers that we need. We will all be holding a space to encompass her journey and serving to anchor her return." She looked around the room as she explained that more details would follow. Then they began with the first exercise. For the next two hours, they worked in pairs while she quietly observed.

For a few minutes, she watched the new student, Will, as he worked with Roger. He seemed capable, a good balance for Roger's worry. Will had expressed a strong desire to join the Level 2 class and seemed prepared. And due to a last-minute cancellation, there was an opening. Besides, Ned was coming in as a Level 2 as well. Steven had offered to tutor both of them in any areas where they needed help. They could support each other as they worked to catch up, so that neither would feel overwhelmed.

Martha stood in front of a striking stone temple on the top of a hill with the sun warming her back. There were no other buildings in sight, no sign of civilization at all, and questions raced through her mind. *Who had built this? How had they done it? What had happened to them?* Surveying the massive stones, she wondered where she was. Everything felt familiar.

On the ground she spied a round stone shaped like a donut. The moment she picked it up, it began to vibrate in her hand. She carefully affixed it to the necklace she wore, realizing it was supposed to be there, but that somehow it had been lost. Immediately she understood the ancient teachings that were held in the stone.

She walked toward the temple. At the base of the temple stairs was an enormous stone serpent with a jaguar head. She traced the incised lines with a finger, struck by the details of the carving.

Nearby, she was drawn to a large square stone with rounded corners. As she studied it, the figure carved into it began to slowly unfold, shaking off centuries of inactivity. She watched in awe and disbelief as she recognized who it was. A moment later, the feathered serpent stood before her in full regal attire, looking every bit the king.

Quetzalcoatl was a deity from Mesoamerican mythology. Martha had learned about him at the Ancient Wisdom School. As Aurora had shared from her most recent visions, he represented the universal mind awakening in humans, allowing them to consciously orchestrate their manifestations in the physical world. His return had been predicted long ago, and Martha had assumed it would be metaphorical, showing up in the dawning of a new age.

She had not anticipated that he would unfold right in front of her after ages of lying dormant in the stone. The ancient place, it seemed, had come to life to reveal its long-held secrets. Martha wondered if she should speak to him.

Without warning, jaguar eyes flashed. The serpentine body uncoiled, lifting the head high. Majestic wings were spread to beat the air. He went from human form to the dramatic creature that towered over her.

"We come to finish what was started," he intoned. The words surrounded her like fire. She breathed them in and felt the heat expand her heart. "It is time to dream the world into being."

Where would she start? She felt the answer rise within her.

"We hold within us everything we need. We are masters of energy whose wisdom comes from the stars. We are awakening to discover the new time is upon us. The world of our making is near. We are the dreamers of a new earth."

Surprised to hear the words coming from her own mouth, Martha breathed in the clouds of fire and stared into the deep eyes, which were ever so close. Her heart burned in her chest with the light of love as Quetzalcoatl awakened her inherent knowing.

"Opening the heart begins the journey," he said. As the voice cascaded through her, stirring wisdom encoded in her cells, Martha became aware of something she needed to do.

Inside the heart of humanity was a hidden secret. It had been put there long ago so that in the future a new world could be created. She had come to do that.

She was here to be part of humankind's transition. The belief structure that had long kept the human vibration low was being shed. She had come to complete the work of bringing the new world into being.

"You are letting go of your past in order to bring in the new energy. As well, you are releasing your density," Quetzalcoatl told her. "You are growing a body made of light."

Martha was galvanized. A powerful sense of purpose permeated her being. She needed to begin at once. But she found herself unable to move. Her feet seemed to be stuck to the ground. *How could she begin if she couldn't move?*

A ringing phone pierced her awareness. Martha reached for it to silence it, but she felt disoriented. She put the receiver down, but then she heard yet another voice, which sounded faraway. When she finally realized it was coming from the phone, she held it to her ear.

"I woke you up, didn't I?" It was Ned, always an early riser.

Martha rubbed her eyes but decided not to open them because the room was too bright. "I am at the pyramid," she told him. "How did you find me?"

"I'm next door," Ned replied. "How about if I bring you some coffee?"

"Quetzalcoatl is here," Martha told him, not worrying if she was making sense. "I have some work to do."

"Sorry to disturb your dream," Ned said. "I bought chocolate croissants at the bakery, too."

"It was so real," Martha insisted, slowly beginning to transition back into the third-dimensional world she had awakened to and letting go of the ephemeral images of the ancient cultures. "What time is it?"

"Eight o'clock," he told her. "I have great news. And the caffeine will help bring you back to the planet."

Martha reluctantly pulled herself out of bed. She could tell that whatever Ned was coming to tell her was important. She put on a robe and went to unlock the door, then returned to her room to dress. By the time she emerged a few minutes later, the aroma of coffee and warm croissants greeted her. "This is a treat," she admitted, sitting down at the kitchen table. "So what is the news?"

"Steven called. I've been invited to join the Level 2 class. They have their first session today, but he's going to tutor me on anything I don't know so that I can be a part of it."

"That's fabulous," Martha replied. "How soon do you have to be there?"

"In an hour. Steven wondered if you could drop me off on your way."

"On my way?" Martha looked up from the croissant she was about to bite into.

"You know, to where you're going. I thought you were leaving today."

"Not in an hour," she said. "But I can take you and come back. That's not a problem. I was planning to leave about noon."

"I got us something," he said, producing two new black backpacks from a bag next to the table. "Look at all the pockets. And try it on. It's really comfortable." He held one up for her, and she stood and slipped it over her shoulders.

"Very nice," she said.

"Your old one didn't have the padded straps," he said. "And look, I put a little hummingbird on yours so we can tell them apart." Martha turned the pack around to see. Then, with her index finger, she cradled the beautiful silver trinket, less than an inch long, hanging from one of the zipper pulls. "Hummingbird travels far and wide," he added. "Just like what you're going to do. I thought it would be a good symbol."

She was moved by his gesture. In the short time she had known him, Ned had emerged from an emotional slump and come to life. He had been stepping out of his patterns and investigating many new things that she had introduced him to. They had both been widowed at middle age, so the fact that in some ways their lives were a mirror was not lost on Martha. "It's wonderful," she said. "Hummingbird makes an amazing journey, so it will be a good reminder. Hummingbird can inspire me."

For Martha, life in the last few weeks had never been more interesting, challenging, and fun. She did not regret for a moment the adventure she had stepped into, but it continued to surprise her and call for her to be courageous. At times she had wondered if she could once again summon the necessary courage for what she needed to do. More than ever, she wondered that now. But she smiled and thanked Ned for his thoughtful gift. "The hummingbird is a good reminder," she said, "not only of making the seemingly impossible journey, but of doing it with joy. Hmm. Does this mean I should take a lot of sugar with me?"

Ned smiled, happy that she was happy. "Oh, Olivia asked if you could stop to see her while you're at the school."

"Then let me get ready now. I probably am not going to have time to come back." She finished the last bite of her croissant and went to shower. Afterwards, she tucked everything she needed into the new pack. Taking a deep breath, she took a quick glance at her familiar surroundings and told herself she was as ready as she would ever be.

Making her way back to the kitchen, Martha mulled over the dream. It seemed prophetic. She felt like she had visited the mythical Lost City. Perhaps Aurora would know. And what about the incredible message from Quetzalcoatl? As she waited for Ned, she made some notes in her journal. *We are the dreamers of the new earth. We are masters of energy.*

A solitary orb floated in the cloudless sky, and it seemed to drift with no timetable. But that was only because it came from a world beyond time, a world of ancient heralding. In the fire circles of long ago, under the shifting stars, an age of peace and abundance was foretold, a world of pure intention, beyond the belief system of the existing powers. It was not a return to civilizations of the past, it was an entirely new creation. The vibration of the earth itself was increasing, for the first time since the pyramids were created. The veils between the worlds were disappearing, and thus the orb had emerged in the realm of planet Earth.

Ned, hurrying over to Martha's house, didn't see it floating just above his head. He was excited about heading to the school. His sister Carol and her husband Joe had gone on a long-anticipated cruise, so he didn't have to worry about what he would tell them. For the first time in a long time, he found himself looking forward to things. His early retirement had been spent trying to fill his days with one activity or another in order not to feel the void. But all that mindless activity had given way to learning about a whole new universe, as different from the one he was used to as it could be. The scientific system he had immersed himself in for so long was being replaced with something he could only describe as inexplicable. Martha called it mystical, but he usually referred to it as "magic carpet stuff." To him it was the perfect way to describe what he saw as a world beyond what he had always accepted as reality. Martha, of course, liked to argue that whatever he was experiencing was reality, but he was stubborn. "Once I am used to it, it will be my reality," he had said recently. "Once I can tell my sister Carol about it, then it will be really be my reality," he had added.

"That might take a while," Martha had replied. "I wouldn't rush it if I were you. I can't tell my son yet either, and I certainly can't tell my friend Liz, even though I wish I could. I know she senses something, but she's not open to hearing the few things I have told her."

"Or she's not able to hear them." Ned was thinking of his own situation. "But it is curious why some people are interested in knowing more and some aren't."

"According to Aurora," Martha had told him, "all of us are going to be shifting at some point, probably sooner rather than later."

Ned had become a believer, but he was taking it slow, looking for proof. So far, everything he had experienced had convinced him that something was going on; he just wasn't sure what. Thinking about it, he smiled as he let himself into Martha's house. What made this especially interesting for him was Martha herself. He found her both compelling and intriguing, and she possessed a spirit of aliveness that was very attractive. "I'm ready when you are," he told her, finding her in the kitchen putting a few things away.

"I am as ready as I will ever be." Martha shouldered her new pack. "Let's go before I lose my nerve." She took one last look around the kitchen to make sure everything had been put away.

Ned picked up his pack as well. "I can't tell you when I have ever been this excited. Maybe never. And I'm just going off to the school. I can't imagine how you must feel."

"I'm trying not to focus on it," Martha replied. "I still can't believe I'm headed somewhere and I don't even know where it is."

※

The second class of the morning got underway at ten-thirty. "We're going to begin with impeccability," Steven said, surveying the group in front of him. "Jaguar teaches us to live with impeccability, and to be unafraid. Jaguar has no enemies. This is the way we must go into the world. We have no time now for grudges or agendas. As Level 1's you learned how to manifest and how to use the portal. We are going to expand on that now, and begin to communicate telepathically." He instructed them to break into twos for an exercise. "Each of you will move to a remote location on the school grounds, somewhere away from everyone else. From that spot, you will establish telepathic communication with your partner, who will be at least one hundred feet from you. Your partner will send you the answers to these questions. Decide who will go first." He handed each one a sheet of questions as they left.

Taking his sheet, Roger groaned. "This sounds impossible."

"As I recall," Steven gently reminded him, "that's how you felt about manifesting chocolate."

"I'd like to do some more of that right now," Roger said, visibly brightening. "You're right, I'm still doubting myself. It's a pattern I haven't shaken yet."

"We can do some more weeding of the garden later, if you need that. For right now, focus on this exercise. I'll see you all back here in a half hour," Steven said, waving them off.

"Aurora was talking to us about our routine habits and patterns creating density," Angela said to Roger as they walked to the far end of the gardens. "It's the density that keeps us from being more aware."

"I've definitely got some density issues," Roger replied. "But tell me I'm making progress."

"I see progress," Angela said. "I notice you didn't take notes this morning."

Roger shrugged. "That's because I forgot my notebook." He pulled a pen out of his pocket. "You know, I keep thinking about Martha. Has anyone heard from her lately?"

"Not that I know of," Angela told him. "But I know she's alright. At least I hope she is. I wish we could go through the portal to check on her. Who's your partner?"

"The new person," he replied. "Will."

"Find out if he has a girlfriend," she instructed quietly. "But don't tell him I asked."

"I'll add that to my list of questions," Roger said, sighing. "Not that I'm going to get any of the information on this page."

Angela headed off to a private corner. "Good luck. See you in a bit."

✺ 3 ✺

Immediately after teaching the class at the Ancient Wisdom School, Aurora left for the Cloud Forest House. She had told Olivia and Steven of her plan to meet Martha there for the final preparations before Martha's journey. There was much to do, and using a portal she arrived quickly.

The Cloud Forest House was her home away from home. The rainforest sanctuary was a refuge, a place where she could find the solitude so essential to connecting to the energy of nature and the earth. It was this connection that not only taught her but sustained her. She had been looking forward to it, and after putting her things in the house she went for a walk.

The world of the rainforest, away from calendars and telephones, was a tapestry woven of connection and relationship. Each living thing communicated, not in the sense of speaking, but in the sense of communion, and not just the animals and the insects and the birds, but the plants and the trees, the stones and the streams. If she needed a particular herb, she simply thought of it and she would hear it respond. She would follow its energy to where it was located. By listening to plants, she had learned of their healing properties. She taught this class at the school, and students were always surprised to discover that a plant could communicate. They were even more surprised when they learned that they could understand this communication. "We are intimately connected to the earth," Aurora would tell them, "simply because it is our home. We are not separate from it, even though we may believe we are. But we have lost this connection by moving into cities and forgetting who we are. The reason we feel so good in the natural world is that we are attuning to its frequency. This frequency supports our health and well-being."

Students were never the same after these classes. When they discovered their inner beauty and their innate power, when they were able to call the power they had given away back to themselves, their lives changed in positive ways. She loved teaching about the retrieval of lost abilities.

But lately, however, the situation on earth had changed. It was no longer enough to learn about lost arts. Now people needed to learn to use their abilities to create the lives they wanted to live. In essence, they were going to have to pull those lives out of the realm of potential.

This was a very advanced class, and Aurora discovered that she needed time to herself in order to be ready to teach such classes. The Level 2's would soon be learning the basics of how to do this. And Martha! She was headed to the Lost City to bring back the information they all needed to complete this process.

Aurora pulled herself back to the present. Her mind had wandered, and she had walked farther than she intended. She paused to take stock of where she was, and in doing so she suddenly became aware of the silence.

In the remoteness of the rainforest, silence could be louder than sound. Accustomed to hearing birdcalls and monkeys chattering, Aurora always stopped to listen when everything grew quiet. *What was it?* She was a part of this world and accepted in it; she moved among the birds and animals as one of them. The silence meant a foreign presence.

Normally she saw no one when she came here because few knew the location of this retreat. But occasionally someone appeared—usually lost or off course.

Some distance away, a branch snapped. With the stealth of a jaguar, she moved toward the Cloud Forest House. The dense canopy of foliage blocked the mid-morning sun, but when she reached the edge of the clearing, she pulled on her wide-brimmed hat. The trail led down, then up, then down again, and a few minutes later she stepped into the hut, which was nearly hidden by the vines she had planted. She had seen no one.

She began at once to make preparations for the ceremony she was having later. As the sun descended she would make a fire in the outdoor fire pit and she had laid the sticks carefully. Foremost on her mind was Martha's safe journey. It was hard to believe that the time had arrived. She chose some sage to burn. The ceremony would be powerful, and she hoped Martha was ready. The ultimate outcome of the journey lay in Martha's ability to follow her destiny. *Could she do it? Martha had unusual power for someone so new to this process. And she had been chosen to make this journey.* Aurora understood this; she also realized it was beyond her own power to change the soul path of another. All she could do was offer support and guidance. Ever since Martha had shown up at her doorstep, this had been her directive.

The ancients had mapped the time to come, Aurora believed, based on what they knew. They spoke of being from the stars, and their wisdom came from many places—the mountains around them, the realm of nature, the stars, and the world of spirit. Hundreds of years ago they had lived in ways that to this day were not completely understood. Many contemporary people assumed that the ancients had the answers to all of life's mysteries. To Aurora, the wisdom from the past was essential. This is why she taught it to her students. But the planet continued to evolve, and it was necessary to stay abreast of the changes. She was continually bringing in new information and adding it to the foundation. *We are birthing our future on a daily basis, with every thought that we have,* she had told Olivia recently. *We are the creators. We live in connection with the world around us. It is essential that collectively we wake up and become aware of this. What the ancients understood was that the universe is responsive. That makes us responsible for creating the world we want to inhabit. We are powerful, and this is within the realm of our power.*

It was simple when she thought about it. Once people became aware of their thoughts, they could see how what they thought about appeared in their personal world. Still, something was missing. Using the information that was available was like putting together an important puzzle without all the pieces. The ancients had predicted that one day there would be a great shift. Aurora wondered how it would come about. *What form would it have? How would they transition? What were the missing pieces?* Her hope was that Martha could discover the answers.

Suddenly sensing someone nearby, Aurora wondered if Martha had come early. When she moved to the window to look, she spied a man approaching, his face shaded by his hat. He was alone. She studied him for a moment, knowing that something was familiar. Then she went to the door and stepped out.

Given the two-hour time difference between the Oregon coast and Cuernavaca, it was almost noon when Martha and Ned arrived at the Ancient Wisdom School. The day was clear, and to the east they could see Popocatepetl, the active volcano that towered over the Valley of Mexico. True to form, it sent a plume of vapor and ash into the blue sky. "We'd have a front row seat if it ever erupted," Ned said.

"It has erupted," Martha told him. "A few years ago they evacuated a lot of people from the villages around it."

"We'll hope that it stays calm while we're here." Ned reached over to knock on a wooden doorframe for good luck, then gave Martha a quick hug and said he would see her later. He was eager to begin his studies and went to find Steven.

Seeing Martha, Sheila and Angela immediately hurried over. "What a wonderful surprise." They spoke almost in unison, greeting her with hugs. "We didn't know you were coming." They were so excited to see her appear, they bombarded her with questions.

"How soon do you go?" Sheila asked. "Do you know where you're going?"

"Aurora told us we're going to have an adventure," Angela interjected. "Does it involve you?"

When Martha finally had a chance to get a word in, she explained that she had brought Ned to the school so he could join the Level 2 classes. "Otherwise, I would already be on my way. I am relieved to have an excuse to delay it. And no, I still don't know exactly where I'm going."

"Are you nervous?" Sheila studied her. "I would be."

"Nervous doesn't describe it," Martha confided. "I wish I wasn't going alone. That's the only part that doesn't make sense. It would be so much better if I had someone to go with."

"Then let's tell Aurora," Angela said. "I'll go with you to talk to her for moral support. If you do this trek solo we'll all be worried sick."

"Aurora's mind is made up," Martha said.

"I'm good at pleading. It's worth a try. Sheila, since I will miss the afternoon class, take notes for me. You'll have to tell me everything Olivia says."

"You guys are so going to get busted," Sheila said. "But I'm in. You do need a companion, Martha."

Martha frowned. "But who? Seriously, it has to be someone who really can be helpful."

"I'm thinking tall, dark, and handsome," Angela said with a smile. "You might as well have fun."

"This is not a romantic getaway," Sheila countered. "This is very serious, and Martha has to be focused."

"She can do both," Angela said. "What's better than a really good-looking guide? It'll make the time go faster. In fact, you might want to stay longer." She grinned.

"What's better is a really smart guide," Sheila said, emphasizing the need to be sensible. "Somebody who really knows how all this energy stuff works and can make sure Martha gets to the right place."

Angela frowned. "And he can't be both?"

Martha noticed Olivia approaching and she called out a greeting.

After warmly saying hello, Olivia went straight to the point. "I know Aurora is waiting for you at the Cloud Forest House, but I wondered if I might have a word with you."

"Certainly," Martha replied, as her two friends moved a short distance away to give the women privacy.

Olivia hesitated for an instant, then began. "I know this is a momentous occasion. I know you will honor the signs of your destiny. Your journey will awaken the power in all of us to dream the new earth into being."

Martha felt her knees grow weak. She tried to smile.

"But I wonder if I can make a request?"

"I guess so," Martha said.

"Bring me a stone from the Lost City, something that holds the energy."

Martha agreed, suddenly remembering the stone she had found in her dream. She reached up to her neck, half expecting to find it—but, of course, she had only dreamed it.

Sheila and Angela ran over as soon as Olivia left. Sheila said, "OK, you two better get going. And stick together. Wait!" She pulled out her digital camera. "Let me get a photo."

The two friends, framed by a wall of bougainvillea, leaned together as Sheila snapped a picture. They were both smiling happily. Sheila took one more picture of Martha by herself and then checked to see how it turned out. Despite her nervousness, Martha looked radiant. "Beautiful," Sheila said. "And look, there's a hummingbird above you. What a good omen! Like Aurora said, the hummingbird is fearless about making its impossible journey." As soon as she uttered the word "impossible," Sheila wished she could take it back, but it was too late.

"Ned gave me a totem so that hummingbird can inspire me," Martha mused as she glanced at the picture. "That's twice the hummingbird has shown up today. I wonder if this means I'll be flying over the Gulf of Mexico."

Francisco Ix sat in the Cloud Forest House with Aurora. Her initial surprise at seeing him was dissipating, but she studied him keenly. *Had it been twenty years?* That would put him in his fifties but his dark hair and youthful appearance belied his age. "What is your secret?" she finally asked.

"Ah, my secret." His eyes flashed in the way she remembered. "It's very simple. To live outside of time." He nodded. "But it's not a secret, it's a practice."

"In the years I studied with you, you didn't teach me that," she said.

"I didn't know it then." His eyes surveyed the room. "But I know it now. It is part of why I came." Then, because he wished to talk about that later, he segued into another topic. "So this is your retreat."

"Yes. I do most of my work here," she explained, intrigued by what he had just mentioned. "I have been coming here for some time. I am fortunate to have this." She made a decision to serve him lunch and let him relax for a while. He had come for a reason, and he would tell her soon enough. First, it was important to catch up. She put out the sun tea she had just made and the *empanadas* she had brought with her, as well as a sliced papaya.

"'Oh, I remember these fondly," Francisco said, placing one of the small meat pies on his plate. "Your grandmother taught you to make them."

Chaco eyed the stranger from across the room. Awakened from a catnap in the open window, he flicked his tail a few times to voice his silent opinion—*¡Ay-yay-yay!*—about being interrupted. He then remained watchful in a discreet way. If Aurora needed his help, she would let him know. *So this was her teacher.* Chaco knew the story; Aurora had told him. She thought about it too now as she and Francisco ate their lunch silently, appreciating the food. It began with an unusual experience in the ancient silver capital of Taxco.

She was a young woman buying earrings in a silver shop in Taxco when a stranger had approached her and asked the oddest question she had ever heard: "Do you know why you are here?"

She had drawn back, at first considering him only bothersome. But there was something compelling in his serene manner, so she answered what was obvious, that she was there to buy jewelry. As he began to walk away, something made her ask him the same thing, "Why are you here?"

His answer shocked her. "Your grandmother sent me."

She stared for perhaps a full minute. The shopkeeper wrapped the earrings in paper and told her the price. She quickly opened her purse and handed him some pesos. Then she left the cool interior of the shop.

The stranger was waiting outside. The sun was bright, the air was dry. Red bougainvillea cascaded down the hillside in a sea of color, echoing the emotions that were churning inside her. "My grandmother is dead," she said quietly.

"Yes," he acknowledged in a respectful way. "But she has been coming to you in dreams. She sent you here. She sent me to meet you. You want to know many things." His voice was calm, and she felt unusually drawn to him without understanding why. "I can teach you," he said.

Aurora's heart pounded. The situation was outside any that she had ever experienced, and yet the man was utterly believable. *Who was he?*

"I am Francisco Ix," he replied as if he had heard her thinking. "And you, you are the beautiful and headstrong Aurora Luna, currently feeling dissatisfied with life and unsure what you want to do. Yet you hear a calling. You have heard it for some time." He turned and began to walk away.

"Wait," she said. "How do you know this?" When he didn't stop, she ran after him. "How do you know about me?"

"I can read what is in your heart," he said.

Recalling how her journey of discovery had started that day in Taxco, Aurora knew that meeting Francisco had changed the course of her life. She quit her job teaching Spanish to Americans in Cuernavaca. She said goodbye to her three boyfriends, who did not understand her and demanded too much attention. She told her family she had decided to continue her studies. But really, she wanted to find out what Francisco knew. *What was the voice that had awakened in her and seemed to be singing the most remarkable song to her soul?*

She moved to Taxco to apprentice with Francisco, living in a tiny house on his property and tending the vegetable garden for her keep. Almost immediately, it seemed as if she had returned to the magical world that her grandmother, a *curandera*, had introduced her to. Evelina had died unexpectedly when Aurora was away at a university in Texas, and Aurora felt the loss sharply. There was so much she still wanted to know, but there was no one to ask. After a time, her grandmother began to appear in vivid dreams, teaching Aurora about the nonphysical world. In one of those dreams, Evelina had told her to go to the nearby town of Taxco to find a pair of silver earrings. Surprisingly, Aurora found the exact pair, and they became her favorite. But more important, she encountered Francisco and began to follow the path of her soul's journey.

❧❦❧

"What was the most important thing you learned from me?" Francisco asked, pulling her back to the present as he helped himself to another *empanada*.

"You redirected my fire," she said. "I can't thank you enough for that. You made me see that I was a woman of power. You helped me reconnect with my purpose on this earth."

"You give me too much credit," he said quietly. "You did this yourself, simply by looking at your reflection in my eyes."

Aurora nodded, knowing the depth of his dark eyes and the power of that reflection. "But in terms of specifics," she continued, "you taught me to track the energy of every moment. I saw that creation is an active process. By remaining fluid, we can manifest what we wish to create."

He patted his mouth with the cloth napkin she had provided. "You have done this well," he said. "I have heard many good things about your school."

"We have never advertised," she said. "But students continue to find us." She waited. She knew there was a reason he had asked her this question.

"But there was something even more important," he finally said.

She dropped into her heart, searching for the answer to the most important thing he had taught her. "To align myself with truth," she said. Chaco flicked his tail, as if to add emphasis.

"Ah, truth. Yes, that is very important." He helped himself to a bit of papaya. "And what is even more important?"

Aurora felt flustered. It had been a long time since she had been through this process of uncovering what lay beneath the surface, waiting to come out. *Why didn't he just say what it was?*

"It is there," he said. "I can see it."

At the same moment that he spoke, she felt it, the one thing that she had learned from him that had changed her more than anything else. *How could she have forgotten?*

"To never go against myself," she said.

"Exactly." They were both silent for a few moments.

Aurora felt her color rise as she considered the implication of this. "Are you saying I am going against myself in some way?"

"That," he said, "is why I am here."

The shock that Aurora felt shot through her body from head to toe. She was glad she was sitting down. Taking a deep breath and closing her eyes, she took stock. *After all this time, in what way was she going against herself?*

She trusted Francisco, but she also trusted herself. At some point, the student always leaves the teacher. It is simply the way it is. They must both be ready for the release. This had happened years ago. The moment Aurora had been ready, Francisco released her, and like an eagle fledging, she soared high. How was she going against herself? What did he mean?

"You can't see it yet," he said. "You will."

Again they were both silent for a few moments. Aurora poured more tea. The aroma of Celestial Citrus helped to ground her. She had collected these leaves herself.

"You and I both know the monumental importance of this journey," Francisco began.

"You're talking about Martha!" Aurora was unable to hide her surprise.

"I can offer invaluable guidance. I need to accompany her."

"My vision," Aurora said firmly, "showed me that she would go alone. The spirits of the animal world will provide guidance, in the same way that they guided her here."

"Yes, this guidance is valuable. Your own guidance has been valuable as well," he added. "You have been able to teach her the art of navigating the unseen world that she will enter." He paused, putting his hands around his cup of tea as if he was encompassing an idea. "But only a jaguar shaman can show her the map."

Aurora considered what he said, but some part of her resisted. "She has done amazingly well thus far."

"In many ways she's still a novice. You have taught her to call her power back from the places she gave it up to. This is good. But now she needs to know how to build that power. She will need immense power for this journey."

"I believe she was chosen to do this," Aurora said quietly. "I believe she has the skills she needs." Again they sat in silence. Chaco watched with keen interest, sitting motionless so as not to call attention to his presence.

"This is where you are going against yourself."

But Aurora couldn't see it. *How was she doing this?*

"When we first worked together, your biggest challenge was...?"

"My willfulness," she acknowledged. "But I cleared that. I dealt with it."

"I will leave you for now," Francisco said. "If you are supposed to see this, you will. I cannot change what does not wish to be changed."

Aurora was nearly beside herself. She had been reliant on her own wisdom for so long that she trusted it implicitly. *Why was it not working for her now?*

"Take your time," he suggested. "It will come to you."

"I really can't see this," she said, following him to the door.

"You will see it when you are ready."

"I don't have much time," she said.

"Yes, that is why I came in person. It was important to let you know."

And then he disappeared, walking off he way he came. She wanted to call him back to help her with this, but she also needed time alone to digest what had just happened. It had been years since she had doubted her own guidance. It would be helpful to talk with her close friend, but Olivia was teaching a class. She was left to ponder on her own.

Aurora was pacing back and forth when Martha arrived with Angela. Martha had, in fact, never seen her so agitated, but she was hesitant to ask what was wrong. Instead, she fumbled in her backpack as if she was looking for something, wondering if she should be concerned. She looked around for Chaco, but he was nowhere in sight.

But Angela was undaunted by this unusual display from their teacher. "What's up?" she asked. "Normally you are the epitome of calm."

Aurora stopped in her tracks, looking first at Martha, then at Angela, as if she had just noticed Angela was there. "What are *you* doing here?"

"It's a long story," Martha began.

"Wait," Aurora said. "Don't tell me yet. I don't need any more surprises." She resumed her pacing. "We may have to delay things for a day," she told Martha, moving the lunch dishes from one side of the counter to the other.

"Well, that's good news." Martha sighed with relief. "I'm practically a nervous wreck." Looking at the pile of dishes it dawned on her. *Someone had been there for lunch, but who?*

Aurora was not ready to share what had happened. "Let's do this tomorrow. An unexpected visitor came today and the preparations aren't finished."

Martha felt a sense of knowing come over her, almost as if she could see what had happened. "Did he give you some upsetting news?" Martha wasn't sure why she had said *he*, but that's what came out.

"You are becoming remarkably intuitive," Aurora told her. "Yes, my visitor was a man, and it was news that I did not anticipate."

¡Ay caramba! Chaco had appeared. He walked through the room and jumped into the chair by the window. *Are you all loco? There are no secrets.*

Aurora's face suddenly broke into a smile. "That's absolutely right! Did you hear Chaco? He just reminded me of something important. There are no secrets. We are all intuitive. Thus we are all required to live in truth, and to share truth. It is the only way to create change. It must begin somewhere."

She began twirling around the room, and at first Martha had no idea what was going on.

"You don't have to say anything you're not comfortable sharing."

"I get it," Aurora cried out happily. "I understand what he meant."

She grabbed Martha's hand, and they wove in and out of the chairs in the room. Chaco took cover beneath a table as Angela took hold of Martha's hand.

Aurora was completely giddy. "I was so serious about this venture you're going on, I was getting in my own way. I couldn't see what I needed to see."

Martha still wasn't sure what she was talking about. "Maybe you could start at the beginning," she said as they all came to a stop.

When their laughter subsided, Aurora said, "There is no beginning, because everything is a circle."

Martha was beginning to feel as confused as the first time she visited the Cloud Forest House, when she had learned that she had somehow opened a long-dormant portal and used it to travel almost instantly from Oregon to Central America. "I'm lost," she told Aurora. "I am as lost as I was the first time I came here and you were telling me things beyond my comprehension."

"You'll understand shortly," Aurora said, still in the grip of the giddiness that had seized her. "Allow me my moment of euphoria. I finally understand what he was telling me."

Turning to Martha, Angela shrugged. "Don't ask me. Just go with the flow. We should have brought Ned and Sheila. They'll be sorry they missed this."

Martha, who had had her own experience with the way that the release of blocked energy could affect someone—in tears or peals of laughter—surrendered to being patient. She didn't like the suspense inherent in waiting, but her choices were limited. For once, it wasn't about her. *We're all learning*, she thought, pulling out glasses for sun tea. Her own nervousness had vanished, and for the first time in days she felt ready for what awaited her. At that moment a feeling arose in her that she knew was true. "I'm not going alone," she announced suddenly. Her words surprised all of them.

A few minutes later, without discussing the purpose of his visit, Aurora was sharing the story of seeing Francisco for the first time in twenty years. Chaco, relieved that the dancing had stopped, watched from a windowsill.

"I can't even imagine that," Martha said when she had finished. "I hadn't really thought that there might come a day when my work with you is…finished." She had trouble getting out the last word.

"We won't focus on that now," Aurora said. "There is too much to do now." She pushed back from the table, stood, and walked to a desk across the room. She pulled a photo out and brought it over to Martha. "Here. This is my teacher, Francisco Ix." She spoke with respect. "His last name"—she pronounced it "eesh"—"means jaguar. He is a jaguar shaman, from the lineage of jaguar shamans, going back hundreds of years. He is the most powerful person I have ever met."

Angela leaned in to see as Martha studied the picture. "I think we have successfully called in your traveling companion," Angela said. "He appears to be exactly what we were looking for."

But Martha sensed something beyond the physical attractiveness. The deep, dark eyes spoke of worlds she had not yet experienced. Even in the photograph he radiated intense, otherworldly energy. Looking at the photo, it dawned on Martha why Francisco had come to visit, and she turned to Aurora for confirmation.

Aurora nodded.

"I'll come back tomorrow morning," Martha said with new confidence. "I want to get an early start."

"First," Aurora said, looking at both of them, "tell me why Angela is here."

Angela jumped in quickly. "I helped to manifest her traveling companion. Wait till I tell everyone. This is exactly what you were talking about, how we would start to create what we need in our lives. I never knew it would be this easy. Or this much fun."

"Taking the initiative," Aurora said, "shows your developing ability and increasing power. However, please remember the importance that each of us will create what we need."

"But if someone is hesitant, what's wrong with helping?" Angela asked.

"Each person must learn the technique. It's all right to help one another occasionally in the beginning, as long as this doesn't become a habit."

But Angela persisted. "Aren't we supposed to begin to work as a community?"

"Yes, that's what we talked about in class this morning. But remember that community begins once each has mastered individual power."

Angela, wanting to celebrate their victory, gave Martha a high-five, and the two of them began to dance like children as Martha released the nervousness she had held in her body. The gleeful energy from earlier seemed contagious, save for Chaco, who disappeared out the window in search of a quieter spot.

Using the portal, Martha and Angela returned to Cuernavaca in time for Angela to make it to the afternoon class. She slipped in and sat down next to Sheila, giving her a big grin and a thumbs-up. She promised to reveal the details later.

Martha, meanwhile, decided to have lunch at her favorite Cuernavaca café. She settled at an outdoor table in order to watch the parade of passersby. Her pale skin made her an obvious tourist, and she rolled up the sleeves of her shirt in the interest of tanning. Basking in the abundant afternoon sun, she tried to silence the chatter in her brain about everything that was going on. For the first time in weeks, there was nothing that she needed to do. The brief interlude free from the pull of obligations felt almost like a vacation.

She pushed her hair back. *What a luxurious feeling to be idle,* she thought. *How rarely we let ourselves enjoy doing nothing.* The air was balmy. The temperature in the City of Eternal Spring was a predictable seventy-two degrees.

Cuernavaca was the place where her training had begun, and she had not forgotten her first visit to the Ancient Wisdom School. The doors to a new way of looking at the world had been opened when she arrived. Although it was just weeks ago, it seemed like ages had passed. Sitting in the café, she thought about her experience at the school with a certain amount of awe. She had learned phenomenal things. In just a short time, she had become a different person. No longer was she the woman who resisted change, due to fear and limiting beliefs. Because of the school, she had stepped into the magical realm of understanding and working with energy.

Soaking up the sun, Martha took a deep breath and exhaled. She'd worn hiking boots in anticipation of her trip, and she wiggled her toes, wishing she could take the boots off. In fact, because she was wearing jeans, she was overdressed for the warm day, but she should have been on her way by now.

But she wasn't, and she let herself relax. For a few hours, she was a tourist. She could forget about the journey she was about to make to who knows where, which felt to her like jumping off a cliff blindfolded. Her rational mind struggled with the idea of giving up control. On this trip, she felt like she would have very little control of anything. The good news was that she would have a guide.

She reached into her backpack to get her notebook. Even though Aurora had told her it wasn't necessary to take notes at the Ancient Wisdom School, Martha had written down the details of several things she'd learned, just in case she forgot them. But the notebook was not in her pack; she must have left it on the kitchen table.

Her heart sank. Now what?

The waiter appeared and took her order, *sopa de ajo,* a chicken sandwich, and fresh fruit. Garlic soup and mango, she decided, would get her off to a healthy start and compensate for some of the snacks in her backpack.

Martha enjoyed a leisurely lunch. When she finished, she ordered a latte and began to think about Aurora's teacher, the jaguar shaman. *What did a jaguar shaman do,* she wondered. *What did he know? What would he teach her?*

The waiter reappeared with a steaming latte. She thanked him, and with a quick smile he moved to check another table.

Martha pulled the cup closer, caught up in her questions. *But mostly, would he take into consideration that she was fairly new to all this? Would he cut her some slack? Or challenge her with things that she had only read about, like shapeshifting?*

It took her a moment to notice the drawing in the latte. There, where normally she found a heart or a leaf traced in the foam, was a jaguar head. For several seconds, all she could do was stare at it. Even so, she couldn't believe what she was seeing. She looked around, wondering if Francisco was going to magically appear at her table.

Finally she pulled out her cell phone to snap a picture as proof so that she could show everyone, especially Aurora, who had introduced her to synchronicity. Surely this was a sign. *But of what?* It gave her an odd feeling to know that it showed up as she was thinking about the jaguar shaman.

All of our thoughts, Aurora had told her, go out into the world as energy. It is as direct as using a cell phone to make a call. "This is why we need to be aware of what we are thinking," Aurora had said. "Just as you wouldn't push random numbers on your phone to make a call, your thoughts should not be random. What you are thinking about attracts that energy in the universe, bringing it to you, especially what you are thinking at the deeper levels of your subconscious, the habitual thoughts."

Looking at the jaguar, Martha got an odd feeling of lightness, so she took hold of the table just in case and smiled nervously when the waiter came back to check on her. She managed two sips of her latte before she knew she was in trouble. This had happened to her once before, at her first dinner with Ned. That night, despite holding onto her plastic chair, she had lifted an inch or so off the ground. Only the sturdy table had kept her from completely floating away.

Without further ado, she decided to return to the school. She picked up her pack, glad to have the weight on her shoulder, paid her bill, and made her way across the street and into the square. Each step was deliberate, and she thought, *I can do this. I will take my time. I am just fine. I am not going to float away in the middle of the main square, with all these people around me.*

And then she lifted slightly off the ground.

She kept moving her feet in a walking stride, but she could tell her movements were exaggerated. When she looked down, her feet were about four inches above the sidewalk. She was still several blocks from the school. She walked faster, but it made no difference. Her feet were not making contact. Not wanting to draw attention to herself, she continued with the motions of walking.

At that point the entire thing began to feel hilarious. She knew from experience that if she even so much as snickered she would dissolve in a sea of uncontrollable laughter. She fought it for a full minute until she snorted with the effort. The snort threw her over the edge just as she rounded a corner. Unbelievably, there was no one in sight.

She surrendered to the feeling of flight, soaring up above the buildings like a helium balloon released from a child's hand. It felt so good to fly that she almost didn't care where she was going. It was exhilarating. Lately, she'd been too busy to practice. But feeling the lightness in her being, she vowed to practice more.

On the opposite side of the street, she noticed a woman on a balcony. The woman's face held a look of astonishment. Not knowing what else to do, Martha waved. She saw the woman's knees slightly give way. Martha knew she was supposed to be careful about her powers, but there were times when she was still not in control of them. This was one of those times. Even with the ballast of her backpack, she had floated away. At some point, she thought, she did need to be in complete charge of her abilities. It was something to discuss with Aurora.

Martha pulled herself into a ball so as not to attract undue attention. With her arms wrapped around her legs, she floated like a puff of cottonseed. She felt so relaxed that it was several minutes before she looked down and realized she had no idea where she was.

⚜ 5 ⚜

No one knew where Martha was. When she failed to show up for dinner with Ned and the others as promised, they grew worried. Finally they consulted with Olivia and Steven, hoping their teachers at the Ancient Wisdom School could be of assistance.

Steven asked the obvious questions. "So the last time you saw her she was off to lunch? Do you think she went home?"

"She said she'd be back at six." Ned looked helplessly at the rest, wishing he had more to offer.

"She's only a half hour late," Olivia said.

"Martha is prompt," Ned said. "In the short time I've known her, she's never kept me waiting. It's not like her. She had a powerful dream this morning about beginning her journey, so I hope she hasn't gone without telling us."

"I'm not sure what we can do," Olivia said, "without having something to go on."

"I hope nothing has happened to her." Ned's shoulders drooped as he began to worry.

"Aurora is due back at any moment," Olivia told them. "We will consult with her."

"In the meantime, I think we should nibble on something," Sheila said, beginning to feel hungry. "I'll go and get some food." But the others, caught up in their thoughts, scarcely noticed that she left.

⚜

The street was noisy. Sheila decided to head to the café where Martha had gone to have lunch. She planned to do her own espionage work while the rest of the group waited for Aurora. She walked the six blocks quickly. The café was not crowded, although it would fill up as the evening diners arrived due to its popularity. Sheila showed the wait staff the photo she had taken earlier to ask if any of them had served Martha, and a young man recognized her. She had been there for lunch, he said, and she'd left at about two, headed toward the central plaza.

It wasn't much, but at least it was something, and Sheila considered it as she sipped a glass of sparkling water and waited for her order. *Martha had been here at two o'clock.* That fact was somewhat comforting, and it was something she could share with the Ned and the others. She watched the people passing by. Most of them were headed home after work, but one couple strolled leisurely arm in arm, making Sheila wish she had a beau. She kept an eye out for Martha. *Perhaps she'd gone shopping and lost track of the time.*

The wait seemed endless, and she wished someone had come with her for company. As she fidgeted with her napkin, an attractive man about her age approached. He was an apparent tourist. "Are you dining alone?" he asked. "Perhaps we could eat together."

Sheila invited him to sit, but explained that she wouldn't be staying. Sliding into the chair across from her, he introduced himself as Mark. He had a friendly, open manner, one that invited conversation, and Sheila felt an immediate rapport. She also realized that she was experiencing something she had learned at the school. She had created this situation by thinking about it. That was why Aurora told them to be aware of their thoughts. This was something she still needed to learn.

Sheila introduced herself in return, and asked if he was traveling alone.

He nodded. "I'm taking a Spanish intensive at the Language Institute. What about you?"

She told him she was also taking classes, and they chatted for the next several minutes. Mark was curious about the Ancient Wisdom School, and Sheila gave him a quick synopsis. "In the beginning we learned how to manifest things," she said, "in order to show us how to utilize our power." She smiled, remembering some of the things that had happened. "It was absolutely amazing to see that each of us was able to do this. Then we learned about the ways we give our power away, and we also learned that we need to practice awareness at all times in order to stay out of trouble." She laughed and her eyes sparkled. "Let's just say we needed all the help we could get."

Mark smiled. "This sounds a lot more interesting than what I'm doing. I've been conjugating verbs."

"It's very hands-on," Sheila said. "There haven't been any dull moments. And now, because of the energy shifts going on, everything has been accelerated and our learning has been intensified." Surprised by how much she was sharing, she ended by telling him that they were helping to bring in a new world.

He leaned forward, intrigued. "I'm very drawn to all of this." His voice was quiet but excited. "You have no idea what's been happening to me. But I have no one to talk to and I'm not sure where to start." He paused and looked around to see who was in earshot. "I've been having strange dreams about being in Mexico a long time ago. That's part of why I came to learn Spanish. I was hoping I would begin to understand what I am going through."

"What kind of strange dreams?" Sheila felt the energetic charge that comes when a spiritual connection is made with another person and she wanted to know more.

"I dreamed that I lived here—right in Cuernavaca—a long time ago, but there was a pyramid here. There was an ancient civilization that I was a part of."

"There is a pyramid here," Sheila quickly told him. "When Cortes came, he built his palace on top. Many of the temples were taken down so that the rock could be reused. But there are still some structures visible." She went on to explain what Aurora had talked to them about, how one belief system had been superimposed on another. "This is part of how we lost the ancient teachings," she added.

Mark shook his head. "I can't believe it. I dreamed about that as well. To me, it feels like the dreams are real. But I don't know why I am having them."

"We are all waking up," Sheila said. "We are beginning to connect with our ancient pasts and with the energy that is helping us to make this shift."

"How lucky that I decided to talk to you," he said. "I almost didn't."

"Maybe it wasn't luck," she said. "Maybe you were drawn to me for a reason. These kinds of things are happening to all of us."

Mark nodded, studying her. "So this is an example of what I've read, that there's no coincidence. I did feel drawn to approach you." He grinned. "It was almost like I was being pushed by something…or someone."

Making a quick decision as her food arrived, Sheila invited him to visit the school. "You will find the answers to many of your questions. There is so much to learn and we are running out of time."

"Are you talking about the Mayan calendar?" he asked.

She stood to leave. "We are undergoing a global shift in consciousness. This is a time of major transition. We are evolving as humans." She wanted to stay and talk, but thinking about Martha she knew she needed to go. "We can talk more later, but right now I have to run. Sorry."

"I'm only here for a couple more days," he told her. "Then I head back to Tucson."

Sheila shook her head in disbelief. "That's where I live."

"Then here, take this." He reached into his wallet for a business card. "I'm definitely interested in checking out the school. Maybe tomorrow." He waved goodbye as she set off with her bag of food.

Crossing the central plaza, Sheila had a sudden intuitive feeling that Martha had gone this way. Tapping into the feeling, she moved across the plaza and down the block. There it seemed to grow fainter. She stopped to look around. There were no doorways that Martha might have turned into. Had she gotten into a car? Sheila debated momentarily, then continued on her way.

At the next corner, she moved past two women who were conversing in Spanish. When one of them gestured at the sky with her arm in a very animated way, Sheila glanced up. There was nothing overhead, but she had a sudden realization that they were talking about Martha.

In one of her classes at the school, Aurora had taught her to recognize and trust the images that came through intuition and the third eye. Looking up, Sheila got a clear picture of Martha and knew that she had flown over this spot. That was the reason she had lost Martha's trail. But why, she wondered. *Why would she fly in the middle of the day, in the center of the city?*

She raced back to the school as quickly as she could. Ned was in the courtyard. "Aurora is here," he said. "She just arrived."

They all gathered around a table on the veranda, talking quietly. Sheila and Angela unpacked the food and Steven helped them serve it. Chaco appeared and jumped into one of the empty chairs.

Sheila caught her breath enough to talk. "I think I know—" she began and then stopped herself. "Wait. I got a picture of what happened." Starting at the beginning, she told them what she had learned. "I wish I knew more," she finished.

"So two blocks from here a woman saw her fly overhead?" Ned was astounded. "Where was she going?"

Olivia and Aurora looked at each other, shaking their heads. "My guess is that she didn't choose to fly," Aurora said. "But for some reason she did. Her unusual abilities got the best of her. Something must have triggered the flight."

"Oh no." Ned was growing more concerned by the minute. "What do we do now?"

"We wait," Aurora said. "Until we know more, there's nothing we can do."

Ned appeared to be worried by these words, and Sheila put her arm around him.

"Martha will come out on top," Angela said. "I know. I've traveled with her. Do you remember the time she and I got lost in the portal system? She kept her cool. She's very level-headed."

Ned pushed his food away but Sheila urged him to eat. "We have to be strong," she said. "And ready."

"I just wish someone was with her," he said.

"Let's not worry," Aurora cautioned. "Knowing Francisco and how much he wants to make this journey, he will probably find her."

"Francisco?" Ned's curiosity got the best of him. "Who is that?"

Aurora explained that Francisco was a university-trained anthropologist and one of the country's leading shamans. "He left the university after a few years," she said. "He received his training and then returned to the land of his ancestors." She went on to say that he had published an important book and was in demand as a teacher and a speaker, but he chose to live quietly. Few knew his whereabouts, and he surfaced when he wished. "He has crossed the bridge from the old ways to the new," she said. "He is one who stirs the pot of the new world. If there is anything Martha needs to know, he will be able to teach her." As she spoke, Aurora realized that Francisco was essential to the journey. No wonder he had come to find her. Just as she had said in class earlier, everyone held a key to the puzzle.

"If he finds her," Ned said darkly.

Aurora quickly took charge. "I had planned to have Martha's send-off ceremony in the morning," she told them, "at the Cloud Forest House. But we will have it here instead at eight o'clock tonight. Let everyone know. Be prompt. This is important."

When Martha finally landed she found herself standing by the temple she had just dreamed about. She stared at it, feeling a disconcerting sense of deja vu. She expected the plumed serpent to come to life at any moment, and she felt completely unprepared, like Dorothy transported to Oz. She tried to remember the details of her dream. Things were happening too fast, and out of sequence. Time was being jumbled. She hadn't yet had her ceremonial send-off with Aurora. She hadn't met with Francisco. *What was going on?*

"I really am not ready yet," she said out loud to no one in particular, hoping that her bargaining would work. "I want to do this well, and if I have to do it like this, I am going to make a mess of it." She waited, but nothing happened.

"Can you hear me?" She cautiously looked around. "Is anyone here?" she appeared to be alone, and after a few minutes she decided to investigate. The first thing she did was to approach the temple and touch the stones, as if to make sure the structure was real. She stood in front of the door, wondering if she should go in. The interior was dark; she squinted in the bright sun, trying to see inside. She hesitated to step into the darkness. *Why was there no one here? Surely, as beautiful and ancient as this was, it was a tourist attraction. But there was no sign of tourism here.*

It was a large structure, perhaps forty feet square. She walked the circumference, watching her step on the dusty ground. There were intricately carved stones around the base; the repeating patterns formed the body of a serpent. Tracing one of them with her hand, she wished she understood the significance. Nothing made of stone moved or spoke, as in her dream, but certainly there was much to be known if only she could make sense of it. She remembered what Aurora had said about the serpent: it represent-ed shedding the past. *In the process of coming to know ourselves we shed our old ways. We let go of the dry skin of who we were. We move into our becoming.*

At last Martha decided to enter the temple. She took a deep breath and stepped into the dark interior. Letting her eyes adjust to the light, she scanned the inside. There were tumbled stones, perhaps the remains of an altar. As she moved toward it, she heard a strange sound. Startled, she turned, not sure where it had come from. At first, she couldn't even identify what it was. But then it dawned on her. It was a hiss. Somewhere in the darkness a serpent had awakened. Slowly, she backed up toward the doorway.

She was unprepared for the strike. It seared through her body like a lightning bolt. Stunned, she staggered outside and fell to the ground. After a minute she pulled herself up and tried to run. She wanted to get as far away from the temple as possible.

A short time later she stopped, very winded, to catch her breath and take her bearings. Hunkered over, hands on her knees, she wondered if she was going to die in this remote place. Her heart raced.

Whatever had happened to her, she realized, had been far more powerful than a snakebite. In fact, in checking herself, there was no sign of a bite. Instead, the strike had pierced her awareness, and she found it hard to think. She still wasn't sure what had happened to her.

Because she felt sleepy, she curled up on the ground with her backpack for a pillow and closed her eyes. For some reason, she had an odd thought: it hadn't been a real snake. What she had done was awaken an ancient serpent.

A moment later she fell asleep and began to dream. In the dream, an enormous serpent uncoiled from the base of the stone temple and wrapped itself around her as she stood quietly. Transfixed by the beautiful, intricate pattern of its scales, she didn't think to escape or even move. She knew that what was happening was part of a cosmic plan, and she felt no fear. The serpent coiled up into the sky as high as she could see and she felt her genetic structure begin to change, although she didn't know how she knew that, except that her cells tingled, as if something inside of her was waking up.

What was happening now had been planned a long time ago. Martha felt the truth of that. Her very being was changing, and excitement raced through her that she was part of this historic time. And then, unbelievably, her old skin fell off and she was bathed in fresh skin that seemed to shine with newness. She stared at her old skin for a brief moment, as if it was completely normal for it to have fallen away. She stepped out of it, stroking her arms and remarking on how beautiful they were.

Martha awakened just as she wondered what would happen next. She felt exhilarated and filled with energy, as if she had been renewed and recharged. Thinking that the dream was responsible for that, she stood up, brushed off her clothing, and put her pack on. She needed to return to the school. The thought was so strong that a moment later she was there. Emerging from the portal, she made her way to the circle of familiar faces.

Ned was the first to see her and he ran toward her, calling her name. "Where have you been? We were worried sick." His emotion surprised her as he hugged her.

She tried to speak, but no words emerged because she still didn't understand what had happened to her. She wondered how long she had been gone.

"You were supposed to meet us a couple of hours ago," Ned told her.

Martha looked at the circle of students and wondered what was going on.

"It's your send-off ceremony," Sheila told her. "Aurora has been calling in the energy for the past hour."

Just then, Aurora appeared. "What wonderful timing," she said to Martha, touching her arm. She stopped and studied Martha closely. "Come with me to the office for a moment."

Aurora told the others to tend the fire until she came back, and Martha dutifully followed her into the office. Closing the door, Aurora spoke quietly. "Your energy is very different. What happened?"

Martha took a deep breath. She knew she could speak if she took her time. She felt Aurora's support, and she relaxed. After a little bit, she was able to relay what had happened, and once she began, the words tumbled out. When she finished, she began to cry. As the tears streamed down her face, she felt relief—and something else, a new sense of her own power emerging. "It was so powerful," she managed to say. "I thought I had been struck by lightning. I was sure I was dead. But then I dreamed about the serpent coiling around me."

"The Temple of the Serpent." Aurora's tone was more serious than usual. "Here, sit down while I explain." Martha settled into one of the chairs opposite Aurora, not sure what she was about to hear, but hoping Aurora would be able to shed light on her experience.

"Everything has started," Aurora told her. She sounded far away. "Your journey has begun. There is no stopping it now. Once you have activated the serpent, you must continue. I wish I could tell you more, but beyond this I have few answers. What I do know is that the serpent represents the opening of the new energies. The serpent has to do with the activation of our DNA as well. Scientists have always felt that most of our DNA was not being used, and that our lives would change when it was activated. This is the beginning of us becoming the new humans. At this point, anything can happen at any time."

Martha's mind raced with questions and her heart pounded with excitement. "I definitely felt something begin to happen," she said. "It was very real. In fact, I almost can't tell what's real and what is a dream."

"Consider it all to be real, "Aurora said gently. She fell silent for a moment. When she continued, she spoke with reverence and love. "You have begun the process. At this point all you can do is summon your courage and trust yourself completely." She smiled. "Most important, always remember to breathe."

Martha, sitting on the edge of her chair, was grateful for the reminder. She drew in a few deep breaths to calm herself.

"Your journey is of utmost importance. You will be accessing wisdom from the ancient lineages as well as wisdom from the time to come." Aurora's voice was soothing. "You will come back with knowledge to share with the rest of us, so that we will know what we need to do." She took both of Martha's hands to reassure her. It helped to bring Martha back to the present moment, and her remaining fear dissipated. "Nothing will ever be the same for you, or for any of us. This is the beginning of what we have been waiting for," Aurora told her. "This opens the doorway to the new earth. It also begins to anchor the new earth in our current reality so that the rest of us can access it more easily." She pulled her hands back and put them on her heart, taking a deep breath of her own. "You," she said, looking directly at Martha, "have already gone through. It is written in your eyes. They are luminescent."

Martha felt a chill run up her spine. "I still don't have a clue what I'm doing," she offered.

"You know more than you think," Aurora responded. "Far more. You have indeed called back some of the power you need to make this journey."

"I wish I felt more confident."

Aurora smiled in a reassuring way. Then, almost as an after-thought, she spoke again. "Perhaps you should know one more thing. This is the lightning path to transformation. You have been given the lightning tool. Use it carefully."

"The what?" Martha's question was more of an exclamation.

"The lightning bolt that you felt activated your DNA. It began a process of change within you. You can now pass this on to others. You can also use it if you need it. Use it carefully," she cautioned once again.

"What would I use it for?" Martha was perplexed, and a frown formed on her face as she tried to imagine a possible need.

But the only thing Aurora said was that she would know. "You have worried about everything, and worry is basically useless, especially now. Now you must learn to simply be, to make decisions as they need to be made. You must realize that you are a woman of power—in the same way that we are all becoming powerful—and to use that power wisely and actively. The ancients worked with the energies of the universe. They tapped into the natural rhythm to create a magical dance with those energies, and we have forgotten how to do that. This knowledge is being returned to us now, because, if we are to survive here on earth, we must begin to use it."

After a few more minutes, the two women headed back out to the courtyard.

⚜ 6 ⚜

Torches blazed in the courtyard of the school. The Level 2 students who were participating in Martha's send-off had gathered in the darkness to take part. Two had been appointed Fire Keepers and their job was to tend to the needs of the fire. The others began singing to the fire to give it energy. Several were drumming.

Martha ate the dinner that Ned had saved for her, talking quietly with him while she did. She had noticed that Ned was connecting with her differently. He offered support without asking for anything in return. He listened attentively. When she had first met him, a few months ago, he had been lonely and needy, wanting to be with her in order to not be alone. A retired engineer, he had been defending the positions he had long held of science and skepticism. But that seemed to have fallen away. Lately, she had not heard him remind her that by training he was an engineer and a person who relied on things he could measure and document. She was happy about this.

But also, she no longer felt a need to convince him otherwise. She simply carried on with what she needed to do. For the first time, she was feeling empathy from him, and that felt good. He wasn't resisting with his statements of "I'm having a hard time believing that." It was a refreshing change.

"Do I seem different?" she asked Ned.

"A little," he said, "but I couldn't tell you why. So what happened? Where did you go?" He listened as she briefly explained and then told her that he wasn't surprised. "I'm actually beginning to believe there is something very powerful going on with all this magic carpet stuff." He paused. "I think I will stop using that term. It's not very respectful, is it? I need to take this seriously."

They talked a bit more and then he fell silent.

"What?" she asked.

"Nothing," he replied. But she could tell it was something, and he wasn't ready to share. "We should join the others." He offered her a hand up and they walked over to join the group.

Martha found Aurora by the fire. Ned squeezed in next to Sheila. Steven appeared with Olivia. "It looks like everyone's here," he said. "Shall we begin?"

Aurora scanned the group, as if she was looking for someone. "I was hoping—" She stopped in midsentence.

A solitary figure made his way confidently through the darkness. He had a regal quality, and indeed everyone fell silent watching his approach. A moment later he stood next to Aurora, who made the introductions. Francisco Ix, her teacher, had come to accompany Martha on her journey to the Lost City.

Francisco had a charismatic presence, and everyone seemed to breathe a collective sigh of relief when he began to speak. But then he reminded them that no one, himself included, had ever made this journey or knew exactly where the Lost City was. "But I have heard about Martha, and if anyone can do this, she can." There was nervous laughter from the Level 2's, who all knew about the things that had happened to Martha since the day she managed to step through a long-dormant portal and show up at the Cloud Forest House. Martha was capable of doing unexpected and even amazing things with great aplomb, surprising even herself.

Francisco had such presence and charisma that he magnetized the entire class in the dark courtyard. "Martha can be an inspiration to us all." His voice was resonant. "She has stepped through fear into a completely new way of being. She has connected with her authenticity and why she is here on the earth. Even now, she is doing something she knows very little about, but she has learned to trust and follow her intuitive guidance. She has tackled some of the biggest hurdles by simply being willing."

Martha was astonished. *How did Francisco know so much about her?* But more than simply knowing about her, she felt transparent, as if he could see into her soul. He was also speaking about her in a way that allowed her to see herself with new eyes. She shook her head, trying to take it all in. Her life had changed so dramatically. And now it was going to change even more. Sometimes she could scarcely picture the woman who had been a devoted wife and mother. Right now, that person seemed like someone from another lifetime.

Her memories were clear, but as she reflected on them, it seemed the person she had been was simply acting a role. She had done what was expected of her. But now that she had tasted writing the script, she wanted more of that. She was excited to have a part in such a grand endeavor. She had secretly dreamed about making the world better, but never knew how to do it. This was her opportunity. Was it really possible? Optimism and excitement surged through her, replacing the nervousness that had been dogging her earlier. Everything had clicked into place. The cosmic plan that she was a part of suddenly felt right. She was filled with a sense of confidence so satisfying that she actually smiled. *This was the most amazing thing that had ever happened to her.*

The celebration after the ceremony lasted well into the night. New Fire Keepers took over to tend the fire. Ned enthusiastically took his turn. The fire was a living being, Steven told him. It had to be fed and tended. "When you work with fire as a living being, the fire works with you. Fire is a powerful entity. We will learn more about it later. But just begin to think of it as alive."

Francisco told of the importance of keeping the vibration of the energy high as long as possible. Several students with drums kept a rhythmic beat that was matched to the pulse of the earth. Francisco talked to them all about listening to the earth. "She is going to make it possible for us to be here, and we are going to help her. It is an interdependent relationship. As her vibration increases, so does our own. We have forgotten about the rhythm of nature.

Our ancestors lived by it. We now live by artificial rhythms created by clocks and calendars. We are tuned into our music, television, cars, and cell phones. This is killing us slowly. We need to attune to the natural frequency, the song of the whales, of the salmon, of the eagle, of the jaguar. This is the way we connect to the frequency of the earth. The song of the earth will sustain us."

"How do we attune to nature?" Angela quietly asked Olivia, who was standing next to her by the fountain.

Olivia answered with a question. "Do you hear the sound of the water in the fountain?" When Angela nodded, Olivia said, "Spend time listening to natural sounds, like water cascading over rocks, ocean waves, birdsongs, fire burning in the fireplace. Even silence carries the natural vibration. It is simple. You can sit quietly and listen to natural sounds or to the silence. Fill your being with those sounds rather than human-made sounds. For instance, when you are driving in your car, turn off your music."

"Turn it off?" Angela seemed shocked by this idea. She contemplated it for a minute and then said, "It's a challenge, but I'll give it a try."

The last thing Francisco talked about was the approaching shift. "All the indigenous peoples are preparing for it," he told them. "Many of them are sharing their knowledge at this time. It is why I have come here. We must all come together. We have never been through anything like this, and no one knows exactly what will happen. But the earth will be different and we will be different. With all of us working together, it is hoped that we can create a time such as we have never seen before of peace and abundance. This is the new dream, for all of us to transcend our judgment and our anger and to move into joy and love. We are leaving behind the old world to move into the new one."

"That is a tall order," Angela said to Olivia.

"It is coming. We can each choose to be a part of it, or not. The reason you were drawn to come to the school is to be a part of the new dream. A part of you, deep inside, knows about truth. This is the part that is guiding you now."

The flames lit up Francisco's face as he spoke again. "So let us call in our helpers from the spirit world," he said, as the drumming grew louder. "Call on them to be a part of this magnificent time and to assist us in creating it." It seemed like everything—the earth beneath their feet, the plants around them, the fire, and even the stars above—was pulsing with the energy of possibility, of what could be created. "We are all creators of the new time." Francisco's voice rose above the drumbeat. "Now is the time. Each one of you will summon your gifts. We will all join together to dream a new earth." And then he sang in a clear voice in a language they didn't know, and when the song repeated they joined in, and their voices became a prayer that was carried off by the smoke for all of creation to hear.

❧❦❧

The coals from the fire were still smoldering at four o'clock in the morning when Aurora awakened Martha. "You'll be leaving shortly. I have tea and fruit waiting." Martha wanted to sleep about three more hours, but she pulled herself out of bed to get ready. She was excited to be going with Francisco and even though the hour was early she began to wonder about the things she would learn from him.

A few minutes later she found Aurora on the terrace. The two of them talked quietly while they waited for Francisco.

"I am glad he came," Aurora said, "It will be good for you to have his help."

"I am very grateful," Martha said. "It gives me a new sense of confidence."

"Eventually you will feel the confidence at all times. Your body will relax enough for you to be aware of it," Aurora told her as Francisco approached and settled into a chair.

"Good morning," he said. "Whose idea was this?"

The women both laughed. "Good question," Martha said, wondering why she hadn't asked it herself. "Is there an answer?"

"Ah," Francisco said, studying her. "We will come to that."

Martha found it impossible to read him. He was a blank screen. She wondered why that was.

"You will discover the answer," Aurora said, and Martha wondered if she was addressing her question or her unspoken thought.

"The answer may not be important," Francisco said. "Sometimes all we need is the question. It is what sends us on the journey." Not to be rushed, he ate slowly.

Martha, who had finished her own food, began to notice his process. It was almost ceremonial. He seemed to be paying attention to each bite, chewing with reverence, savoring the flavors, and swallowing before he took another bite, as if he had all the time in the world. "But aren't we looking for answers on this journey?" she asked, still studying him with interest. She had never met anyone with such a calm, compelling presence.

She moved her plate away. It occurred to her that she had eaten in order to accomplish a task, so that she could move on to the next task—pulling out her notebook in order to write down what Francisco had to say. Perhaps this was something she would learn in her time with him, how to be present when she accomplished routine actions. "Am I not supposed to bring back answers?"

"We have no idea what you will bring back," Francisco said. "If we knew, you would not have to go."

Martha's mind began to go blank, as if she was once again losing her ability to track, which frequently happened when Aurora spoke to her.

"I am not really following," she told him.

"On some level you are. When you drop out of your mind, into your heart and into your intuitive senses, it feels as if your mind isn't tracking. But actually you are using your other faculties to get to where you need to go. This is good." He moved his plate to the side and reached for his tea.

"Ah, a new blend," he said to Aurora. Martha hadn't realized it was different.

"I wondered if you would notice. It is indeed a new mix for the journey. Herbs that will help you with what you need to do."

"And the name?" Francisco knew that Aurora was very careful with her teas, and each was named appropriately.

"I haven't named it," she said.

Francisco's silence spoke volumes. "I see," he finally said.

Martha was fascinated by their interaction. The student-teacher relationship had dissolved, but there was something between them that she couldn't quite put her finger on. Obviously they knew each other well and respected one another, but they had an unspoken language that Martha was not a part of, which had evolved in their years of working together. She watched them look at each other as if they knew something they hadn't shared.

"What?" Martha asked. "Tell me."

The other two sat silently for a moment. Then Francisco spoke. "Do you know about Quetzalcoatl?"

"He spoke to me recently in my dream."

"You must tell me about that," Francisco said. "So he is in communication with you then." He folded his hands together. "Things have been ahead of schedule for some time."

"Meaning?"

"The Mayan calendar has indicated that two thousand twelve is the year of the great transition. But things are accelerating, and most of us feel it is happening sooner than that. In fact, it is already underway. The signs are clear."

Once again, Martha wondered if she would be able to make sense of all this. It was like learning a new language.

"The legend of Quetzalcoatl tells us that one day this great ruler will return. I call him the Ancient One because that is how he has appeared to me. Many people believe he will return in person, but I feel he will come back as energy. It is his energy that will guide us into the time to come. You see, some of the interpretations are based on our best guesswork. We have had to make assumptions about exactly what will happen, and when it will happen. We are working with only a partial map."

"You are speaking now as an anthropologist." Aurora offered more tea. "What if you speak as a shaman?"

"When it's time," he said, politely declining a second cup. "Speaking of time, shall we go?"

Martha stood up. "I am as ready as possible. Do we leave from the portal?"

He replied that they were taking the bus.

"The bus?" She was incredulous, having heard stories of bus travel in Mexico. "Why?"

"First rule of shamanism," he said. "Don't question the teacher."

Aurora studied him without saying anything.

"But what if—?" Martha began to protest, but stopped cold as Francisco shape-shifted into a jaguar in front of her. Her jaw dropped. She jumped behind a chair as the large cat moved toward her. "Help. What do I do now?" Her voice was barely audible.

"He is a master of many things," Aurora told her. "This is why he will be helpful to you. If he wants to take the bus, he has a reason. As you see, he has many means of travel at his disposal."

Francisco reappeared as a man. He spoke in a voice that was both matter of fact and clear, not mincing words. "This is all about doing. You do your part, and I do mine. We are collaborating. We must completely trust each other."

Martha immediately agreed. But she felt bewildered as they headed out.

"Second rule of shamanism," he said. "Don't believe everything I tell you."

Martha took a deep breath, remembering one of the first things Aurora ever told her, to trust herself. "I will do my best," she said. But she was thinking, *this is crazy. What am I getting myself into?*

The street was dark. There was no traffic, and no sign of life at all. Aurora waved them off from the doorway of the school. "Safe journey," she called. "Be in touch if you can." She closed the gate and said a silent prayer for them, for herself, for everyone that she knew, and then for all beings everywhere.

As they moved quietly toward the main plaza, a figure came out of the shadows and followed them. Francisco stopped to listen. "One moment," he said quietly. "I must see who it is."

But when he turned, the figure was gone.

7

Their first day started according to plan. Francisco and Martha took a crowded bus from Cuernavaca southwest to Taxco, where Francisco lived. Martha sat by an open window, and above the noisy engine, just before daybreak, she heard a lone rooster crow. And then slowly, light came to the countryside, and she was able to see an arid landscape of rolling hills dotted with small trees and brush. As they neared Taxco, the terrain became more mountainous. It was a place Martha had wanted to visit, and she found herself focused on taking it all in as the bus bumped along. The silk scarf around her neck blew in the breeze, and she might have been easily mistaken for a tourist on a romantic holiday.

Francisco was quiet on the trip, choosing to keep a low profile. When they arrived, Martha clambered off the bus and followed him to a small café. He ordered *huevos rancheros* for both of them, but the breakfast was so spicy that Martha was unable to eat hers. The waiter graciously offered to bring her eggs without the salsa, and she was grateful.

After breakfast they walked through the old town, which dated back to the Aztecs. The temperature was mild, and the morning sun threw long shadows. Martha was giddy with excitement at her opportunity to sightsee. Taxco, the silver capital of Mexico, was built on a mountainside. Picturesque and punctuated with cobblestone streets, its whitewashed houses with red tile roofs cascaded down the hillsides like lush flowered vines in the plentiful sun. Martha wanted to look in the interesting shops selling tinware and silver, but Francisco kept a steady pace. She stopped finally to pull out her sunglasses and sun block; Francisco waited patiently for her to apply the lotion to her face. The day grew warm, and she tucked her scarf in her backpack.

Reaching the outskirts of town, they walked for almost an hour on a dusty road. Finally she spied a walled complex hiding a house, surrounded by a grove of low trees. She was relieved when Francisco turned in and made his way down a path to the house. Stepping out of the hot sun, they passed through a gate and into the beautiful, well-maintained grounds, planted with flowering trees and shrubs. The gardener greeted them cheerfully in Spanish as Francisco pushed open the old, intricately carved wooden door and led the way into the house.

"Is this where you live?" Martha surveyed the large, comfortable room with its adobe walls and *vigas*, the heavy rafters supporting the roof that were common in Spanish architecture. There were tan and brown Mexican rugs on the Saltillo tile floors and simple furniture covered in white cotton, creating a restful feeling. The house was spotlessly clean.

Francisco was impassive. "It is my house. I visit from time to time. The gardener and his wife live here and tend to everything. I do not have a permanent residence."

He led the way to the comfortable chairs on the terrace. "If you'd like to freshen up," he told her, "the guestroom is down the hall."

She found a very pleasant room at the end of the hallway. There were fresh-cut flowers on the table. The window was open to the garden, where she could see a yucca tree. Greatly relieved, she put her things down, closed her eyes, and said a small prayer of thanks. Since Francisco had chosen to travel via bus, she had not known where she would be staying.

When she returned to the terrace, there was a glass of fresh lemonade on the table. Very thirsty after their walk, she drank it all; it was sweet and tart and refreshing.

"There's more," Francisco told her, and a short, smiling woman named Esperanza, who wore her black hair in a long braid, appeared with a pitcher. Martha was still taking in the garden. A jacaranda tree shaded the terrace on one side. In the spring it would be ablaze with lavender blue flowers. She had seen one at the school.

"You are probably curious about my plan," he said.

"Very much so," Martha told him, although she was enjoying the unusual nature of their trek.

"In due time," he replied. "First, some things you should know. This journey will require you to use everything you know and have learned at the school." He stared into the distance at the low mountains. "You will also be using what you don't know that you know. This will require that you open to your creative and intuitive capacity. You are entering new territory. You are encountering the unknown."

Martha frowned. "Are there ways you can help me?"

"I can teach you everything I know, everything the ancestors have taught me," Francisco said quietly. "I wish for you to succeed in your journey to the Lost City. It is a place of legend."

"And you believe it is possible to go there?"

"Yes. We have been waiting for this time. Everything tells us it is now."

"Such as what?"

"Ah," he said. "One very important thing. The earth herself is changing. Her vibration is increasing. She is working with us to evolve. She is sending up vortexes of energy. We can use these to do our work." He spoke in short sentences, and Martha tried to listen without asking questions. But she did not know how she would use the energy he spoke of.

"How much time do you think this teaching will take?" One hand cradled her glass of lemonade.

"That depends." Again he stared into the distance, as if divining information from the mountains themselves. "We no longer have the luxury of time. In the past we could spend years learning what we needed to know. Indeed, it often took years to learn these things. Now, we have to learn very quickly. We have to assimilate much in very little time."

"I see," Martha said, not really sure that she understood but willing to learn as quickly as necessary. She wondered anew why she had been chosen for this as she took in the giant elephant ear plant nearby and the delicate orchids hanging overhead. A row of palm trees lined the pool.

Francisco, born and raised in Taxco, had trained at the university as an anthropologist. But he had also learned at the feet of his grandfather to be a shaman. As a shaman he lived in direct contact with the visible elements of the natural world and worked with the powerful unseen forces of the energetic realm. His story unfolded slowly.

As a boy he had an experience that impacted him deeply at Xochicalco, an archaeological site not far away. "My grandfather told me," he said, giving her some background, "I was going to be shown something important. Once I knew it was coming, I waited for that day. When I was fifteen I went to Xochicalco, and on this visit I was standing by the pyramid of the Feathered Serpent. I reached my hand out to trace the stone carving of a bird and instantly everything came to life." He turned to face her. "It was as if the world I was living in had vanished and been replaced by an ancient time, and yet there was also a sense of timelessness. I didn't know exactly the time period I was in." She was surprised that he was telling her about his early life. According to Aurora, this was not something he shared with people.

"I heard a voice," he continued. "It was the Ancient One. He spoke to me that day. There was no one else around." Again he stared out at the mountains. "I haven't yet written about this," he said, not looking at her.

She did not want to break the thread of the surreal story he was spinning; he was offering a gossamer filament connecting her to an unspoken mystery. He too had experienced things beyond the realm of normal understanding. Although he didn't say it, she knew he was speaking of Quetzalcoatl.

"I was given a sacred message."

Martha was spellbound. She sensed she was hearing something he had never spoken of.

"What I am telling you is not to be shared," he said. "This is the way of sacred things. Their power must be protected."

"I understand," she stated. She was scarcely breathing. For the first time she realized that Francisco had his finger on the pulse that was sending its resonant heartbeat into her world. And for whatever reason, she was also walking down the path over which the feathered serpent flew. It was Quetzalcoatl who had brought them together.

"The message was that I was a wayshower. When the time came, I was one who would help to show the way into the new time. I did not understand this message then. But I understood its importance. That was all that I needed at that time."

He fell silent. Martha sat quietly on the edge of her chair as if struck by lightning. His words had gone straight to her core. As they rippled through her awareness like waves across the surface of a lake, she tried to absorb the fact that she was sitting within inches of someone who had been told he had the power to change the world. That meant he was quite literally an architect of the new time. It was the closest she had come to realizing that what she had embarked on was truly momentous. It was real. For the first time it hit her that she had been entrusted with an awesome and enormous responsibility. She too was a wayshower. The very idea sent an electrifying chill up her spine.

Aurora pulled a journal off the shelf. It had been years since she had looked at it. It was a record of her studies with Francisco twenty years ago. She held it for a moment by her heart, then opened it and began reading. She had recorded everything faithfully in order to not forget the details.

Today we went to nearby Xochicalco, which means "the place of the House of the Flowers." This ancient temple-city dates back to 200 B.C. yet not much is known about it because it has not been excavated. It is not known how the massive granite stones were moved or carved. Francisco feels that most of what is said about this place is largely conjecture. "We are trying to interpret a civilization from the standpoint of today," he told me. "Through our mechanistic eyes. These eyes cannot yet see the truth." The Pyramid of the Feathered Serpent especially intrigues me. Quetzalcoatl, he said, transcends our ability to understand him. "He is an invisible force, and we have no way to comprehend his meaning," he told me. "But there will come a day when we can. When that day comes, things will happen very quickly."

Sitting on the hillside above the ball court by herself, Aurora had experienced what felt like a flashback. An ancient time had suddenly come to life. People were moving about engaged in activities. *Can you hear us?* they asked. *Can you teach what we know?* But she was unable to understand what they were telling her at first.

Francisco later told her that the energy of another time can remain strongly in place, and to those who are sensitive it can become visible. The experience stayed with Aurora, and she thought about it over the next several days. Finally, Francisco had asked her a pointed question: *Would she accept the responsibility?* She would have to listen carefully and faithfully record what they said, he told her.

This is what had led to her school.

She had left Xochicalco with a deep feeling of being propelled forward by an idea that she did not completely understand. Somehow the ancients were willing and able to share their information with her. In turn, she began to share what she had learned and what she would continue to discover with others who wanted to know. Thus it came into being, the Ancient Wisdom School, which met initially in a house in a remote area of Morelos. Students came to her by word of mouth, wanting to learn about the ancient arts, until there were so many that she needed a larger space. It was then that she made the converted bishop's palace in Cuernavaca the school's permanent home. And it was then that she realized that she had formally accepted the responsibility to teach the ancient wisdom to a new world.

Life is mysterious and compelling, Aurora thought. It calls us to the dance, then sweeps us across a floor of experience, whispering, cajoling, encouraging, leading, and supportively following our lead.

She closed the journal and put it back. Things were happening very fast, she realized. Twenty years ago there was ample time to assimilate all the information. But now, time seemed to be speeding up. To Aurora, it felt like everything she had learned so far was being funneled into a narrow opening, and that she herself, and everyone she knew, would need to pass through the eye of a needle into a new era, leaving their past, and their old ways of being, behind. She knew it was coming. She could feel it energetically. She was obviously part of a bigger plan, and her role had been to reintroduce the ancient ways. She had taken part in preparing those who wanted to learn. She had worked with the earth and with those who were aware of the shift.

But now, what else could she do besides pray?

She said a prayer for Martha and Francisco, wondering where they were. She did not spend time wishing she had been chosen to go. It was important to focus on what was taking place and the kind of earth she wanted to create.

Olivia poked her head in the door at lunchtime. "May I bring you some food?"

"That would be lovely." Aurora wanted a bit more time to herself before the afternoon class. She was feeling some stress, which she had not anticipated, about Martha's journey.

Intrigued, Martha thought about Francisco's story, so different from her own. The world he had grown up in was the world she was just learning about. She had taken an afternoon siesta, and then a shower, and she came out on the terrace with damp hair to find Francisco sitting quietly. Esperanza was in the kitchen preparing the evening meal, and her husband Clemente was gathering some oranges.

Martha settled into a nearby chair and asked Francisco about having taken the bus early that morning. "It is the way I like to travel," he said. "No rush. Sometimes," he added, "I like to be a part of the way things are. It is a good reminder of the three-dimensional world to travel in it or to do some shopping."

Martha was surprised. "You mean you did it on purpose?"

"Yes, with intention," he replied. "I spend a great amount of time in other worlds, so taking the bus keeps my feet on the ground, so to speak." He smiled. "There is something you have probably heard from Aurora, but I will mention it in case you haven't. We are what we believe."

"Yes, I have heard that. The challenge seems to be discovering what we believe."

"That's true," he said. "Much of it is unconscious belief that lies just out of reach, but impacts what we do every day." He closed his eyes for a moment, as if he were thinking of something, then repeated his earlier words. "We are what we believe. Do you know how we say that in Spanish?"

Martha shook her head. She had learned no more than a few simple phrases.

"*Somos lo que creemos.* We are what we create."

"Oh!" Surprised, Martha absorbed the slightly different meaning. "That seems more instructive."

He laughed. "Tell me about you," he said.

"Judging from what you said last night at the ceremony, you already know quite a bit about me," she began. "I'm not sure what I can add to that."

"Why do you think you are here?" His voice was as soft as the warm air, and Martha felt lulled by it.

Martha picked up her glass of iced tea, took a sip, and put it back on the table. "Here with you or here on the earth?" she asked, unsure what he was getting at.

Francisco, who had just jotted something on a slip of paper and put it in his wallet, turned to look at her. His face was a question. "Which one would you like to answer?"

"Whichever one you're asking," she replied. She felt slightly off-balance.

"It seems that you've needed to please people in your life," he said. "You don't need to spend any time pleasing me. In fact, it will be a waste of your time."

It became clear to Martha that she could answer whichever question she was drawn to.

"Exactly," he said. "Each of us must take responsibility for our own happiness."

As Martha thought about that, she realized she was drawn to answer the second question, even though she didn't have an answer. "I never realized I might have some greater purpose," she said. "It never occurred to me. And because of that—I've never said this before—I was afraid of dying. But as I have begun to learn from Aurora, we are all here for a reason. That's made me want to find out why I am here. It's taken me past my fear of death because when we are truly living…"

He held up his hand. "I don't need the whole history," he said. "A simple answer will do."

At that moment Martha became aware of the fact that she was hesitant to express her power in the face of someone she considered powerful. She had been beating around the bush, trying to soft-pedal her answer. As this sank in, she knew exactly why she was there.

"Ah," he said. "Now we can begin."

☷ 8 ☷

Ned sat in a shady spot in the courtyard with Steven, learning about manifestation. The others were enjoying a half hour break after lunch. "It's becoming easier than it used to be to manifest," Steven was saying, "because the energy has shifted. It won't take you long to learn this." A hummingbird buzzed by, just inches from Ned, headed for the wall of brilliant red hibiscus. "That is a good reminder," Steven noted as he watched the iridescent bird hover nearby, "that we are designed for this process. Before we lost our power, before we stopped relying on our instincts, we knew how to create. Be clear about what you want."

The hummingbird reminded Ned of Martha, and he thought about how easy the process seemed for Martha.

"She's a good example," Steven commented, picking up on his thoughts. "You've watched her manifest what she needs."

"I have," Ned admitted. "But I am still trying to learn how to ride that particular dragon of our wishes becoming our reality."

Steven nodded. "Let's quickly run over the basics," he said. "First, we don't *try* to do anything, we simply do it."

"Good point," said Ned. "I need to break the habit of thinking like that."

"Second, we make it easy for ourselves. We shed any beliefs that don't support us."

"Help me with that one." Ned gave Steven a perplexed look. "I didn't believe I could fly until Martha took me flying with her. So now I know I can fly, but I still don't believe it, if that makes sense."

"That means you haven't been able to fly by yourself then," Steven said.

Ned nodded, letting Steven know he was correct.

"So think about changing that belief."

"You say that like it's easy. How do I do it?"

"It's a choice. The first step is becoming aware of what you believe. Once you become aware of a belief, you can make a choice to change it. In this case, you can realize that what you think about is what comes into being. Listen, it's easier than riding a dragon, to use your metaphor. Think of something you want to manifest."

Ned grew pensive. "I'd like to manifest a relationship."

"My advice is to start with something small. At the school, we always start with chocolate. If you start with something too big, you'll give up before you get the hang of it."

"What about licorice?" Ned asked.

"It's one of my favorites." Steven grinned. "Make sure you show it to me."

"Will do," Ned said. "I didn't bring any with me and I really want some."

Steven reminded Ned to be aware of his thoughts. "In other words, if you don't think you can do it, you won't do it," he said. "So pay attention to what you are thinking."

"OK," Ned said, mulling over his challenge. He looked at Steven. "Where will it come from exactly?" he asked, referring to the licorice.

"It's always a surprise," Steven replied. "That's part of the fun."

Angela appeared, waving as she passed. Roger went by a couple of minutes later.

"It's time for the afternoon class," Steven said, standing up. "I'll check in with you later. Relax and have fun with this. It doesn't have to be serious. Oh—before I go. It's not time for you to manifest a relationship yet."

"Even if I'd like one?" Ned asked.

"Not yet," Steven said. "It's not time." He headed off without explaining what he meant.

Ned sat in the courtyard for a little while, wondering how to manifest some licorice. He wanted to do it, and he worked on it according to what Steven had told him to do. A couple of times he looked up, just in case it fell from the sky, because he didn't want to get hit in the head. When he realized he was going to be late for class, he grabbed his backpack.

"Wait," Sheila called, hurrying to catch up with him. "Will you hold my bag for a minute? I've got something in my sandal." She thrust a plastic bag at him, but he fumbled as he took it. It dropped to the ground and spewed its contents like a broken pinata.

"Sorry," Ned muttered, bending down to pick up the tooth-paste, hand lotion, gum, and candy and put it back in the bag. There was a lot of candy, and Sheila explained that she bought treats for everyone. "Fortunately they're all in wrappers," she said. "Or you'd be in big trouble." But Ned wasn't paying attention, because underneath a package of tissues and some chocolate, in a black and yellow wrapper, was a licorice bar.

"You just made my day," he told her, meaning every word of it.

"That's for Steven," she said.

"I know it is," Ned replied. "It's my very interesting cosmic science project."

Walking into class, Ned had a grin the size of Australia. Immediately, Steven knew what had happened. "Here you go," Ned said triumphantly, handing him the licorice. There was applause as he settled into a chair.

A moment later Chaco, who rarely went to class, arrived and sat in the open window. No one bothered him, but they wondered why he was there. He was already a Level 3.

"We are going to do something a little different today," Steven said. "We're going to talk about two things that are important to this work, personal responsibility and using filters." He waited while Chaco jumped down and walked across the room. Then he continued. "Everything begins with personal responsibility, so we will start there. Chaco is going to help."

¡Ay-yay-yay! Chaco exclaimed. *I must be loco.* It was one of his favorite expressions and everyone laughed. Ned, who still couldn't hear the cat when he talked, asked what he had missed.

"Chaco," Sheila said, smiling. "Sooner or later, you will hear his commentary."

"I can't wait," Ned said. "Right now I am still enjoying my success at manifesting something. This is almost as much fun as flying."

As soon as he mentioned flying, he thought of Martha again. He wondered how she was, and where she was. She'd only been gone a few hours, but it seemed like much longer. He sent her a silent message of support and then brought his attention back to the class.

Steven explained that personal responsibility in the ancient wisdom tradition referred to self-management with integrity. "It is about learning to live with impeccability," he said. It also meant the alignment of words and actions. "This means doing what you say and saying what you do." He was a relaxed speaker who used his arms and hands very naturally to make a point, and it was easy for students to relate to him. "You will become aware of your actions and your reactions," he continued. "You will want to turn reactions into responses—in other words, work towards cocreative solutions rather than continue to engage in reactivity, which just creates more reactivity. We can all model this. You have had some practice with this already, and we are going to deepen your practice to make it a part of who you are."

Ned wondered how Chaco would help with this.

As if on cue, Steven explained. "Chaco will be assisting all of us by judging how we do. Because he is a Level 3, he is able to monitor several situations at once, so he will be observing and reporting on what he sees."

Several of the students turned and smiled at each other, not having worked with Chaco before. He flicked his tail in response and looked at them without expression. Then, noting that the group was still smiling, he hissed. He wanted everyone to know that despite his generally calm demeanor, he was as fierce as his relatives in the wild, and not to be underestimated. It was the first time he had displayed such behavior, and they drew back—the exact response he wanted. He taught people to treat him with respect. No one ever said "Hi, kitty," to him twice.

"I've never seen him bite anyone," Sheila whispered to Ned as they broke into small groups to practice an exercise related to personal responsibility. "But I think he would if he needed to."

Sheila had volunteered to help Olivia in the office. Olivia wanted her to answer emails and to send out materials to prospective students. "We are getting more and more interest from people," Olivia told her. "If it keeps up like this we will outgrow this space."

"I can't imagine having the school anywhere else. This space is perfect," Sheila said. "Maybe you should keep the school small."

"It's hard to believe that Aurora started with just two students. Now we have thirty."

Sheila spent an hour answering emails and sending materials to those who had requested them. Queries had come from all over the world, and she wondered how they knew about the school. Finally Angela came to see if she wanted to have dinner. "C'mon, the gang's going."

"Sit down for one minute. This is the last one," she said. "It's from England." She began to read: " 'I am interested in coming to your school. I wonder if you have scholarships available, as I don't have much money for travel.'" Sheila looked up at Angela. "That is a long way. I'll have to ask Olivia about scholarships."

"Then let's go," Angela said, standing by the door. "You can answer it tomorrow."

"Hang on for one more second. Let's see. Where was I?" She went back to the email: "'I met two students from your school, Martha and Angela, when they…'"

Angela nearly flew across the room. "Let me see that," she exclaimed in disbelief, leaning in over Sheila's shoulder to view the computer screen. "It's from Mary Bole! The woman Martha and I met in England when we got lost in the portal and went all over the world trying to get back!" She was practically jumping up and down. "I wish Martha was here. We have to get Mary a scholarship."

"I said I would ask Olivia," Sheila said. "Tomorrow." She closed the email account and shut down the computer. "OK, let's go."

"Wait, I have an idea," Angela said.

Sheila studied her. "I'm not sure I want to hear this."

"Except it is a fabulous idea." She looked to make sure no one was around.

"Tell me later," Sheila replied. "Where are we meeting everybody?"

"At the café. Listen. I think we should go get Mary."

"Absolutely not." Sheila led the way out of the office and closed the door behind them. They walked across the courtyard, rich with the scent of jasmine.

Angela, putting on her sunglasses, was insistent. "We can bring her here through the portal. That way it won't cost her anything." They left the school and headed out into the evening traffic. A bus rumbled by, discharging a cloud of diesel fumes.

"I always forget about the traffic," Sheila said. "It's lucky that we don't hear the noise in the school." It was a balmy evening, and they walked quickly. Sheila soaked up the beauty of cascading flowers on the adobe walls that protected the private homes behind them.

But Angela persisted. "Seriously, what do you think?"

"No way."

"Mary will be so surprised if we go and get her."

"Olivia will be surprised, too. It's not how the school operates."

Angela searched for a convincing argument. "Martha gets to do all kinds of special things."

"Martha *is* special," Sheila said. They were almost at the café. "Look, there they are." They headed for the table where Ned and Roger were sitting with Will, the new student. Angela immediately smoothed her hair with her fingers.

"Will you at least think about it?" Angela whispered, almost pleading.

"We're not going," Sheila said firmly. "End of discussion."

The others welcomed them, and Ned stood and pulled out chairs so they could sit. Roger had been sharing some of his exploits while they munched on chips and fresh salsa, and he immediately launched into his favorite story, when he had accidentally emerged in the outfield during a nationally televised baseball game after using a portal. "It was a close call," he said, "but I managed to hold onto the baseball I caught."

"I remember," Sheila quipped. "You wanted the baseball for proof. You didn't realize you were on TV and millions of people saw you appear out of nowhere."

"They finally decided I ran out on the field to catch the hit. Luckily I got away with a warning."

Will had been listening attentively, not saying much. Angela took a chair across from him, and she twirled a lock of hair with her finger. "So, Will," she said, "tell us about you. How did you end up at the school? Have you been studying somewhere else?"

He seemed uncomfortable with the questions about himself, and he shrugged them off. "This was where I was led. You know how that happens, right?" He gave her a wistful glance.

Angela tilted her head. She stopped twirling her hair and instead stroked the side of her neck in a flirtatious way. "Whereabouts do you live?"

"Colorado," he said as the waiter took their orders.

It was obvious he wasn't going to share much about himself, and so the conversation changed direction. Ned wanted to discuss the filters. "I like the idea of that and I am hoping it works with my sister."

As Steven had explained, the idea was to picture a filter that surrounded your body, straining out negative comments. "It's just like an air filter on a furnace," he had told them. "Without that filter, the furnace would get clogged. Your system is the same. It doesn't function as well when it's trying to digest negativity. So the idea is, filter it out so it doesn't get in. It's an energetic filter, one that can be replaced any time you wish with a new one. Visualize that happening as well."

"I already put mine in," Roger said. "It's big. I put in the best model I could imagine." Everyone laughed. "I love the idea that it is capturing stuff that would normally get in and fester inside us."

Angela gave a mock pout. "Does that mean we can't use guilt to get what we want?"

Ned smiled. "Yes, that's part of the personal responsibility that Steven talked about. We are supposed to be monitoring the way we are in the world." The waiter brought their soup. "Of course, you can still use guilt, but our filters will take care of it."

Angela crinkled her nose.

"That won't work either," Ned added.

"I am loving my filter," Roger said. "I can actually feel it working."

Steven had also told them about the strainer. For things that were already in their system, they could use another technique: imagine running every cell in their body through a strainer. The cells flow through easily, but the strainer catches foreign material, such as anger, past hurts, and judgments. "In this way," he had told them, "you can begin to purify your system of what is not beneficial to you. Imagine everything passing through the strainer and returning purified and revitalized. This technique," he had added, "separates out what isn't you from what is you, so that you can begin to get in touch with who you really are."

He had reminded them to work at the energetic level. "Until you experience it, just imagine it. Visualize that what you are doing is happening."

"I strained out some things," Will volunteered. It was the most he had said so far, and they waited, but he didn't say anything else.

"I think the most important thing is personal responsibility," Sheila said. "We especially have to be responsible for our own happiness. That hit home for me."

Going back to the school, Sheila walked with Roger and Will, Angela with Ned. Ned was feeling a sense of confidence because of the licorice, and he mentioned being eager to see what else he could do.

"There's a lot you can do," Angela said, still contemplating her idea. "How game are you?"

"What do you mean?" Ned asked.

"I need some help with something," Angela told him.

"Of course I'll help you," he said. Not only was she Martha's friend, but it was his nature to willingly help people who asked.

"Meet me in the courtyard at ten," she said without further explanation.

That night Francisco stayed out under the stars for a long time. His grandfather had told him that his ancestors came from the stars, bringing their wisdom. Their star was of blue light. His grandfather remembered being there, in another lifetime, and he described the vision he had of it. There was peace and harmonious connection. They moved by flying and also by relocating their consciousness. Life was very advanced compared to what humans experienced on the earth. "We knew each other then," his grandfather had said. "We come back into form to experience all things."

Francisco often called on his grandfather—the *abuelo*—and his other ancestors. They were his guidance system. As he did this night, he called them to the council, which was a gathering of the ancients. All information, Francisco knew, came from light in all its forms, including the sun and the stars. The stars played a great part in what was taking place. As if to affirm that changes were afoot, a meteorite blazed across the Milky Way, a brief, unmistakable sign that the cosmos was in concert.

Francisco ambled out to the area where he did ceremonies. One by one he called in the energies that he worked with, the four directions, the ancestors, the earth and all her creatures, the sun, the moon, and the stars, and the unnameable one that was the source of everything. He asked for guidance and support. He asked to be shown what needed to be done. He offered prayers.

From the darkness of the terrace, Martha watched. She could see the outline of his body against the night sky. The energy of what he was doing encompassed her. She was caught up in its power.

She expected he might shapeshift, but he didn't. He remained in human form, silhouetted against the sky between heaven and earth with arms outstretched. Overhead, the stars danced like fairy lights, as if they were in on the secret, pulsating with the rhythm of the new energies awakening on the earth.

Right then, it dawned on Martha what she wanted: to dream like Quetzalcoatl, to dream a beautiful new world into being. And because the veils were thinning, she saw her ability to do that.

☰ 9 ☰

Angela was waiting when Ned arrived at ten o'clock. Before he could ask any questions about what she needed, she told him to follow her. They threaded through the darkness to the far side of the courtyard. As soon as they settled into two chairs, she spoke in a hushed voice.

"A while ago Martha and I met a woman who wants to come to the school. She doesn't have much money, so I want to go get her."

"No problem," Ned said. "Where does she live?" The warm night air was thick with the sweet scent of flowers. Ned inhaled, taking it in, wishing Martha was there.

"England." She said it matter of factly, in the same way that she might have said, "just across town."

"England!" Ned's voice rose at least an octave. "I've never gone that far."

"Shh. Keep you voice down. It's not that far if we use the portal."

Ned shook his head. "It sounds too challenging."

"It won't take long," Angela insisted.

"I don't know." Ned struggled with a decision, wanting to help but not wanting to get into trouble.

"Please?" Angela pleaded. "Otherwise I have to go alone."

"You can't go alone," Ned responded. "But I wouldn't be much help."

Angela continued to plead, and in an effort to accommodate, Ned gave in.

"We need our passports and jackets," he told her.

"Not in the portal." Angela's confidence got the best of her because she had become good at using the portal between the school

79

and her home. Lately, she'd wanted to do something more exotic. But she didn't relish going alone. Having Ned along for companionship would be perfect.

"Mary will be so surprised," Angela said. "Shall we go?"

Mary Bole was cooking breakfast when she heard a knock at the door. Wondering who would be there at that hour of the morning, she wiped her hands and went to see. She found a man and a woman, and at first she didn't recognize either one of them, until Angela introduced herself.

A few weeks earlier, Martha and Angela had ended up on the farm by accident. They'd gotten lost when they simply tried to go to Martha's home from the school late one night. For several hours they had bounced around the world, emerging in one remote location after another, until they finally were able to get back. One of their unexpected stops was the English farm.

"I saw your email," Angela explained. "We came to get you. This is my friend Ned. He's Martha's friend, too."

"Come in," Mary said, leading them into the kitchen. "Have you had breakfast?"

"No thanks, it's about ten-thirty at night for us," she said. "But pack a few things. We're taking you to the school."

"Oh dear," Mary said. "I'm not at all ready." She seemed flustered, and Ned looked at Angela.

"Why don't we come back at a better time," Ned suggested.

"Sit down a minute," Mary said. "Let me think. This is all so sudden."

Her husband came in from the barn for breakfast and was surprised to find them there. "Not you again," he said looking at Angela. "Did you crash your spaceship?"

"Good morning," she said. "We don't have a spaceship."

"What are you doing here?" He looked at his wife for clues.

"Just a visit," she told him. "Right?" She glanced quickly at Ned.

"Right," Ned said, beginning to feel uncomfortable and wishing he had asked more questions before agreeing to help. He did not enjoy being asked to lie. It seemed to him that they should be ambassadors of goodwill at the very least, and that they should represent the school in a positive light. Yet he understood that it was not always possible to talk openly about such things.

William looked at him. "Who are you?" he asked suspiciously.

Ned introduced himself and offered his hand, but William declined to shake it. "We're busy here as you can see and you should probably be on your way," he told them.

"I was thinking the same thing," Ned said, moving toward the door.

"Wait." Angela turned to William. "Mary is coming to our Open House. She won't be gone long. We will have her back before you know it."

"What Open House? Where?" William shifted his weight as he waited for an answer.

"At the school," Angela told him. "She's our guest. This is a surprise." What she said was partially true, but it failed to include all the details.

"I don't know." William's hedge gave Angela the opportunity she needed.

"Grab your purse," she said to Mary. A few minutes later they were off, with William watching from the porch as they walked out to the field.

"He'll have a heart attack if he sees me disappear like you did last time," Mary said.

But after waving one more time, William disappeared into the house for his breakfast, and the three of them quickly moved toward the portal. "Just hold onto Ned," Angela instructed. "And don't forget to breathe."

"How does it work?" Mary asked.

"It sort of stretches everything around us taut, like the skin of a drum. It eclipses distance so that it becomes two-dimensional in that moment." Angela was surprised that she remembered so clearly what Aurora had taught them. "We step through into where we want to go. Don't be distracted by the sense of the ground disappearing beneath your feet. And whatever you do, don't panic."

Landing roughly, Ned found himself on the top of a hill. It was pitch black, and the terrain was dry and rocky. He heard Angela call his name and he stumbled as he made his way over to her. "Where's Mary?" he gasped. He looked around, calling her name.

"I thought you had a hold of her," Angela said, trying to see in the darkness.

"I did." Ned, realizing Mary was not there, was in a state of shock. "I don't know what happened." He kept looking around, certain Mary would materialize at any moment. "She was right next to me." He stood helplessly. "She has to be here." He called her name again, listening in vain for a response. The silence was deafening.

"Where could she possibly be?" Not having anticipated anything like this, Angela was on the verge of becoming hysterical. She shouted Mary's name.

"Wait," Ned said, silencing her. "I hear something." They were both silent for a few seconds, straining to hear. In the distance, a pack of coyotes yipped, giving them hair-raising chills.

Angela immediately freaked out. "We're going to be eaten," she said. "We have to get out of here." She grabbed onto Ned.

"We have to find Mary," Ned insisted. "We made a promise to her husband."

"Let's come back when it's light," Angela said, clutching Ned's arm tightly.

"You're cutting off my circulation," he said.

Angela loosened her grip and Ned rubbed his arm. She called for Mary again. "We need a flashlight."

"Well, what was that you said about not needing anything in the portal?" He stopped, deciding not to blame her. After all, he had gone along with her terms, so their lack of preparation was equally his fault. His voice softened. "Maybe she's still in England," he offered. His voice raised at the end of his statement, suggesting it was really more of a hopeful question.

"Or in the portal." Angela began to hyperventilate. She was at a loss for what to do, and tears quickly followed. "We're in trouble," she wailed. "I should have listened to Sheila. I don't know what made me think I could do this." Finally she broke down, sobbing. "You...have to...fix this."

"Fix this? I'm a beginner." Ned, on the edge of losing his composure, walked about thirty feet away, trying to get a sense of where they were. He felt at the end of his wits. He was not good at dealing with emotion.

"Don't leave me," Angela pleaded, wiping her eyes with her hands.

"I'm not leaving. I'm thinking," he said, looking up at the stars in an attempt to orient himself. "It's important to get a grip," he finally told her. "I can't do this alone."

Angela continued to cry.

"I'm serious," Ned told her. "Do whatever you have to do to regain control. You can't lose it. We need to find out where we are, and then decide our best course of action." His prompting finally seemed to have an affect on Angela, and she began to calm down. He walked back over to where she was.

"OK," Ned said. His ability to take charge in a crisis kicked in. "First, we have no idea where Mary is." His pronouncement made Angela choke up again, but Ned put his hand up to say stop. "Second, and perhaps almost as disturbing, we have no idea where we are. Third…" He paused for a minute, thinking. "We need to make a plan." But Ned couldn't think of what to do. Try as he might, his mind was blank.

"I simply can't think," he said to Angela after a few minutes. "Can you?"

"I'm too upset," she replied. "I wish you had talked me out of this."

Ned sighed. "Let's not go there."

They stood on the hilltop for a while. Ned wanted to pace, but the ground was rough and uneven. He didn't want to risk breaking an ankle. "I really have no idea what to do," he said after a bit. "Can you get us to the school?"

They tried a few times without succeeding.

Ned checked his watch. "It's late. I vote we get some sleep and then make a plan first thing in the morning." He hoped that things would look different in the light of day.

"What about the coyotes…or poisonous snakes?" Angela's voice sounded small as she surveyed the dark ground around them.

"You can sleep next to me if you want to." Ned patted the ground, and Angela gingerly sat down next to him. "There's a wall here we can lean against." He closed his eyes, and even though Angela was leaning up against him, his mind was elsewhere. He was thinking about Martha, wishing she were there. Martha always had a plan, and somehow, in her presence, he was very good at coming up with ideas and suggestions. Martha, he realized, inspired him.

Not for one minute did he let himself think about what he wished he had done when Angela asked for his help. It was too late for that. Now that he was in the situation, there was only one thing to do: figure a way out.

At daybreak, he hoped they would discover they were close to civilization, because the darkness was making him feel a million miles from anywhere.

⚜

Martha woke with a start, not sure where she was. It was still dark, and she looked around the room to get her bearings. Then she remembered: it was Francisco's house. She pulled on her clothes and went out on the terrace. The first hint of light in the east appeared. Soon the sun would come up over the hills.

"Ahh. You're up. We'll have breakfast and begin," Francisco told her, returning from a walk. "The ancestors sent a dream."

They ate on the terrace. It was already warm; there was no wind. Esperanza brought them eggs and toast and the freshly squeezed orange juice that Martha craved. "So tell me about the dream," Martha said, putting some fresh salsa on her plate after Francisco's assurances that it was mild, in her honor.

"It was a dream of the Pyramid of the Feathered Serpent."

"That sounds like the dream I had," Martha said.

"They said we must go there to begin the journey. Yes, they also sent you the dream."

"Where is the pyramid?" Martha asked.

"Close by. We will go after we eat, before the tourists."

Martha was excited. She had yet to visit a pyramid except in her dreams. She was glad she had brought her camera. She couldn't believe she had dreamed about a place so close to Francisco's house. "Did they tell you anything else?"

"That the temple itself holds a secret."

"Do you have a car?" she asked.

"No, we will take the bus. Many people don't have cars," he said, as if that explained something.

"Of course," Martha said. The salsa was so good that she helped herself to more.

"Walking creates connection with the earth," Francisco told her. "Above all, we want to be in contact with the earth now, to receive her energy and her messages. When you are in a car, you lose all sense of that."

It made sense, even though Martha had never thought about it before. Cars were convenient; she used her car without thinking. Otherwise it would take her forever to get everything done. She had noticed that Francisco was never in a rush.

"I thought it might save us time, was all," Martha explained. She was trying to eat more slowly, to notice the flavors of the food, and to feel appreciation for it.

"I am teaching you awareness," Francisco told her. "This is one thing you will need. Your awareness needs to be as complete as possible. If you are taking anything for granted, you may not notice something important."

"I see," Martha said, thinking how different Francisco was as a teacher from Aurora.

"We are all different," he said, hearing her thought. Martha was embarrassed, having forgotten that in the world of energy, everything was visible. "This is good," he said. "After a while, you can send me what you are thinking and I can answer you with my thinking. We will not need to speak."

That will feel very odd, Martha thought.

No, you will become used to it. You will see. Then you can choose, conversation or thinking. He laughed. "Consider the dolphins," he said. "They commune. This is the way they share thoughts. It is a beautiful process. If you experience it, you will like it very much."

"How can I experience it?" She leaned forward, very curious.

"One way is by dreaming. We call it a lucid dream, because you are not asleep. You were part of a dolphin kingdom in the past. You can revisit this place. You will feel how effortless the communication is. It is simply by being together—communing—that it takes place."

Martha was so intrigued that she wanted to do that first. But he was clear about going to Xochicalco, and they left after breakfast.

On the walk he gave her an exercise, to stay very present and simply notice everything around her. "I will listen," he said with a smile.

Oh dear, she thought. She was used to letting her mind ramble, especially when she walked. *This would take discipline.*

"Yes," he said. "This is what you are practicing."

He also talked to her about intention. "Intention is a force in the universe. We line up with it to cocreate our experience."

"I learned a little bit about this from Aurora," she told him.

He nodded.

Of course, Martha thought, realizing she didn't have to explain everything to him.

He told her one more thing, and then he was quiet, allowing her to absorb his words and begin her practice. "You will use your heart to read situations," he said. "The heart is as intelligent as the brain. As you grow used do using it, you will discover how intelligent it us. Your life will become very simple."

The morning class began at nine. Students filed in promptly, and as Aurora took stock, she noticed some missing faces. She asked if anyone knew where Ned and Angela were.

"Oh no," Sheila said. Aurora asked if she had something to share.

"I'm not positive," Sheila said. "But Angela tried to get me to go to England with her last night."

"England!" Aurora exclaimed. "Why?"

All eyes were turned on Sheila as she explained.

"Is there a chance they went this morning?" Aurora asked.

"Ned told me he had to help Angela with something last night, about ten." That was Roger, who felt happy about being able to contribute useful information. "Wow, I had no idea what they were going to do." He looked around at everyone, and then something dawned on him. "Will's not here either."

"Would he have gone with them?" Aurora asked. But Sheila and Roger had no answer.

"I was hoping not to have to worry about anyone but Martha," Aurora told them. She sent Sheila to tell Olivia to contact Mary to see what she could learn.

"This is all my fault," Sheila said. "I shouldn't have shared the email with her. I feel responsible."

"It's important to stay focused," Aurora reminded them. "And I hope I don't have to repeat my earlier words to not try unnecessary things. Martha's journey is of utmost importance, and we may be called on to help her with it. I want everyone here to be ready if that happens." A hush came over the class.

Sheila returned a few minutes later to say that an email had been sent to Mary. They'd wait for an answer. Until then, there wasn't much that could be done.

The students were distracted by this event, so Aurora knew it would be difficult to teach what she had planned. On impulse, she decided to do something else.

"Let's talk about right relationship," she said. "It is important to be in right relationship with everything in our lives—our family, our neighbors, our community, the plants, the animals, the earth. We need to clean up whatever is not right. As we do this, we will lighten our load." They spent the next two hours sharing examples from their lives and clearing things out on an energetic level. By lunchtime, each of them had done some serious housekeeping. They felt lighter, more energized, and released from emotional burdens. "Continue to practice this," Aurora told them. "Our slates will need to be as clean as possible."

Martha found it hard to quiet her mind on the walk. Francisco told her that when a thought arose, to just let it be. "Don't jump on and ride it," he said, "to who knows where. Just observe it: there's a thought about doubt. There's a thought about Ned. By the way, who is Ned?" he asked. "You think about him a lot."

"You met him," she said. "He's a friend."

"Ahh. He's thinking about you, you're thinking about him. There's a virtual freeway of thoughts going back and forth. Practice letting your thoughts follow your intention."

"You can tell that he's thinking about me?" Martha was surprised.

"Only when I tune in," Francisco replied. "Most of the time, I tune out. But right now, I am working with you."

"So he's thinking about me. That's nice." Martha felt happy to learn that. Now that Ned was taking classes at the school, they had more in common. They were able to share things with each other that they couldn't share with most of the people they knew.

"Tell me what your intention is."

"To be present and aware of everything that is happening."

"Good. Let Ned know you're fine, you'll be in touch later."

"So thoughts are that powerful?" Martha asked.

"The same as words. It's all energy. Our thoughts impact the world around us." He bent down to pluck a leaf from a plant by the side of the road. "This action," he said, "impacts every other thing. There was a famous naturalist in your country—John Muir—who said that all things are connected: If you pick a flower, you jiggle a star. Everything is part of the whole."

Martha had admired Muir. He had founded the Sierra Club, urging people to experience nature for its spiritual nourishment. His innovative writings and philosophy had had a strong influence. He had once walked from Florida to Indiana—something she couldn't imagine as she made her way over this rugged terrain—and in his later years he had devoted himself to preserving wild and natural land, even camping with then-President Theodore Roosevelt in Yosemite to make his point.

She felt like she was on an adventure like that, but could it have similar impact? *Everything is connected. Every action has an impact.* She walked in silence for a time, mulling over the immensity of this. But it was too big to fathom, and she let it go.

Instead, she remembered something she had wanted to ask Francisco. "How do you shapeshift? Can you teach me that?"

"Right now we are practicing awareness. No more talking."

They walked in silence after that and Martha worked hard to stay present and notice everything around her. It was more challenging than she had expected. At first she focused on the rough ground, the shadows cast by the bright sun, and how far they had to walk. But after a while she began to notice how beautiful everything was. She started to feel connected to everything around her, the rocks and the bushes and the plants. She began to feel that she was no different than they were, that they were all part of the same breath of the universe. A feeling of peace came over her. Her mind grew calm. She felt fine just walking, just being. She had no sense of needing anything. The walk became effortless. She became a part of the flow that Aurora had talked about. But best of all, her worries vanished. She was suddenly moved to tears by the absolute beauty all around her; even the imperfections were perfect. She was in *communion* with everything. The minute the word popped into her mind, she knew Francisco had sent it to her to describe what she was feeling. This was what she had asked him about earlier, and now she was experiencing it for herself. The sensation was vivid. The plants were sharing who they were, as were the rocks and the scrub trees. They had opened to her, and she connected in response. It was the first time Martha had experienced this connection in such a profound, all-encompassing way. An overwhelming sensation of love and warmth flooded her heart.

After a few moments, Francisco spoke. "It becomes easier with practice. Like everything we do. That is why we practice."

A short time later they climbed on the bus. Martha worried briefly that the bus ride would throw her out of her peaceful state, but the worry buzzed by like a fly and she let it go. Not long after that they arrived at the ancient site called Xochicalco, Martha still in a serene state.

The site was at the top of some low-lying hills with a 360-degree view. The view, in fact, was spectacular—miles and miles of hills as far as the eye could see. Off in the distance was a lagoon. Francisco led the way up a small hill to the Pyramid of the Feathered Serpent.

Martha continued to quietly observe. Everything felt familiar. In fact, she was feeling quite subdued when suddenly she was jolted out of her serenity by an almost electric charge. She became aware in a heightened way, like an indoor cat that has just heard an animal sound outside at night. Her senses went into overdrive. *What was it?*

Francisco watched her from a few feet away. The moment she noticed him she was distracted, and the feeling dissipated.

"You felt it," he said.

"What was that?"

"That is why we were supposed to come here."

"But what was it?"

"I don't know. Let's see if we can find out."

The Pyramid of the Feathered Serpent was about seventy feet square. Carved in relief in the stones around the base was an undulating plumed serpent. There were also human figures and numerical symbols.

"I want you to notice something," Francisco told her. "Quetzalcoatl is three beings in one, serpent, quetzal, and jaguar."

"Yes, I saw that in my dream," Martha said, intrigued at the power of the dream world to bring in what she did not know with such accuracy.

He traced the carving with his hand. "The teaching of the jaguar is ancient. Jaguar wisdom represents all knowing. The jaguar can see in the dark; this is what we all want, to see into the unknown with ease. Quetzalcoatl encompasses three powers and three elements: serpent and water, quetzal and air, and jaguar and earth. The element of spirit is represented by the fire, here." He traced it with his fingers. "The elemental forces combine to achieve ascension to spirit."

A passing tourist, the first of a group that had just arrived, stopped nearby to look at the bas-relief. Francisco waited until the man moved on before he continued. "What I am going to tell you is not generally known," he said to Martha; those words sent another charge through her.

"I will tell you what my grandfather told me, and his grandfather told him. This has been passed down from antiquity. The ancient civilizations were set up by beings who came here from the stars. They gave humans the information needed for an advanced civilization. But as it turned out, the vibration of the earth was not high enough to hold the level of wisdom that was given and eventually the technology was lost. This is why no one remembers, and why no one has been able to figure out the meaning. It is beyond our capability to know." Francisco waited for more sightseers to pass.

"But we are coming into a time where we will once again know these things. In fact, these beings are again in touch."

"What do they say?"

"They are helping to bring in an era of harmony and peace on the earth," he said quietly. "Many are working with the energy of it. Your journey will connect you with them. They are the source for what you will learn."

Martha was stunned. "I thought it was something from the past—the ancient wisdom—that I was supposed to find."

"No," he told her. "This is very current. We had it a long time ago, and it is coming back to us again. This time, we have to get it right. What we learn will truly enable us to live in harmony, as our true selves, in thriving, peaceful, and supportive communities, in ways that nurture and respect the earth and all her creatures."

Martha was speechless. It was as if everything she had expected had been turned upside down. "This is a quantum leap for me," she finally said.

"Yes," he agreed. "But this is why few can know until the time is right. There is no understanding of this now. This contradicts what most people on earth currently believe."

She shook her head, trying to take in the enormity of what he had told her.

"Will I see these beings?"

"You will be in contact with them. Or they will be in contact with you. You are going to permeate the veil. You will pass through something that has never been possible for a human to do. This will be the beginning of rewriting history. It will begin a new future," he said. "We will be remaking, and remapping, our world, even the wisdom teachings. All of it is changing, because we are on the way to becoming universal beings." At that moment the cry of a hawk overhead pierced their awareness. It seemed to affirm his words. Cupping his hand over his eyes, he looked up. "The hawk can see the bigger picture," he continued. "The animals recognize what we are doing. You will find them aligned with you on this."

Martha, who thought she had begun to understand what she was going to do, now had even less of an idea than before. The crease of a frown formed on her forehead. She slowly shook her head, expressing some internal doubt that had been stirred. "Do you think I can do this?"

"Absolutely," he replied. "Because you are the one who has been led through the portal to this path. You came here at this time to do this. You must trust this."

Martha continued to shake her head as the doubt took hold. "Everything I have learned in the last several weeks is new. It's so much to take in."

"But if it did not feel right," he said, "you would not be here. You are here because your internal wisdom knows this is what you are supposed to do. We are all being guided. All we have to do is follow those feelings that are pulling us into something different. It's that simple."

"That feels so true," Martha told him. But she wished that she could be more aware of the guidance.

"You are aware," he said. "At some point you will accept that. Right now, it's still new for you. Continue to practice acceptance. Continue to accept guidance. The rest will be taken care of. You will see."

Martha agreed, but Francisco could see that she was not completely convinced. "We will talk about the Myth Maker," he said. "That will help you."

10

Once again, Martha had more questions than answers. She wanted to ask about so many things, but Francisco said he was going to leave for a short time. He asked her to explore on her own to see what she found. For a while she wandered around the grounds, looking at the site, but finally, not feeling any particular sense of connection, she decided to sit on the hillside and wait for Francisco to return. She did not know where he had gone.

Gazing out over the valley with its breathtaking view, Martha realized that the builders of this city had found an amazing location. The rolling blue hills in the distance seemed to go forever, disappearing finally into the hazy horizon. She felt quite at peace simply enjoying the panoramic view as she wondered about the people who once lived here and what their lives were like.

In the foreground the hills cradled a beautiful lagoon. And still closer lay the ball court, a rectangular area with sloping sides and two upright stones, one on either side, that looked like large wheels. Still closer were two gray-green maguey plants with their sharp spines. She knew that they had long been used for food, drink, and fiber.

Martha reached out to touch one of the smooth maguey leaves. "If you could just tell me what you know," she said. She picked up a small rock near her foot, remembering Aurora's teaching that everything is alive and has a spirit, even stones. "If you could tell me what you know," she mused, closing her hand gently around it.

All at once, she was surrounded by people. It was as if an invisible director had yelled "Action!" and the ancient set had come to life in a very realistic movie, with people who had lived several hundred years earlier carrying on their activities of daily life. She could barely take it all in. The pyramids were pristine, as if they had just been built. They rose up from the ground in geometric perfection.

A group of women came up the walkway below her, engaged in conversation. Martha strained to hear them, forgetting cultural and language differences. They were speaking of…what? If only they were closer. She stood up, but the maguey snagged the leg of her jeans, pulling her back. She leaned down to free herself.

A lizard skittered by just beneath her feet. Startled, she made a sound as she jumped out of the way. The women looked at her.

They could see her. *Think fast,* Martha told herself. *This may be the Lost City. I need to ask them.*

She started to walk down the hill toward the women, wondering if they would be able to understand her. She wished there was a handbook for this venture. Winging it was challenging and left her open to making mistakes. She was on a trip to an unknown destination without a map.

Lizard represents dreaming, Martha thought. *Am I dreaming now?* But she was awake. Somehow she was witnessing the events of another era, and about to participate in them. Briefly she thought about Ned, but then remembered Francisco's reminder to stay present. That meant watching her footing on the hillside so that she didn't tumble. But then she slipped, dropping the rock she had picked up. It bounced twice and came to rest nearby. When it landed, she could see markings on it, which she hadn't noticed earlier.

Picking it up, she discovered a jaguar head carved into its surface.

She stopped. The jaguar had started everything. She had found a jaguar mask hanging in the den of the house she bought. It had transported her to Central America when she put it on, opening a portal and introducing her to the unseen world of energy. This was how her journey had begun.

Now here was jaguar again, connecting her with an unseen force field. The jaguar seemed to show up everywhere. Francisco said it was tracking her, calling her to participate in the most challenging experience she'd ever faced.

Hearing her name startled her. Absorbed in the ancient culture that had come to life around her, it took a moment for Martha to realize that someone was calling her name. It began as a question of surprise, "Martha?" and then grew more insistent, trying to get her attention. "Martha! Martha!" It seemed to come from her contemporary world, and it took all her resources and immense power to return to present-day life in order to answer.

Turning, she saw Ned and Angela rise like apparitions from beyond the ball court and run toward her. She could scarcely believe her eyes. *Where had they come from? And how had they found their way into this long-ago time?* But when she looked around, the women she had seen were gone. The past had vanished into thin air.

Martha tucked the jaguar rock into her pocket, wanting to show Francisco. Ned, slogging up the hill, wrapped her in a big hug, and then Angela did the same. It was as if they had not seen her in two years instead of two days.

"You have no idea," Ned said, "how happy we are to see you."

Angela agreed. "We are positively thrilled." She was a sight; her mascara was smeared and there were bits of dry grass in her hair.

Knowing how careful Angela was about her appearance, Martha decided not to mention this. "What are you doing here? I can't believe you found me, especially since..." She began to explain, but stopped herself. The ancient set had dissolved, and along with it, the indigenous people. She saw only a handful of sightseers making their way through the ruins of the archaeological site.

But Ned and Angela were focused on their plight. "We have bad news," Ned said. "It was supposed to be good news, and a good surprise."

"But something went wrong," Angela finished. "It's my fault. You have to help us. Please." She was pleading as she smoothed her uncombed hair.

Martha hesitated. "I think you should go back to the school and ask Olivia. I'm in the thick of things. Francisco is helping me, and..." But looking at their faces she knew they really were in trouble. "What is it?" she asked.

A few minutes later, after hearing their story, Martha had no idea where to start. She shook her head, finding it almost impossible to believe they had gone to England to get Mary in the first place, and she could not imagine what had happened to Mary when they tried to take her to the school. Finally, they had ended up in what Ned had called "the middle of nowhere," only to discover, at daybreak, they were at the archaeological site.

"No wonder I kept tripping over stones when I tried to walk," Ned said.

"So you slept on the ground? But how did you find this place?"

"We have no idea," Ned said. "We just ended up here. As far as we know, it was a fluke." He explained that he had never heard of Xochicalco.

"Did you think about me at all when you stepped into the portal?"

Ned stared at the ground. "I might have," he said. "I remember wondering what you were doing, and where you were. We've all been wondering."

"That might explain how you got here," she said.

"But I thought about the school," Angela said. "Why didn't I go there?"

But Martha wasn't able to give her an answer. She looked up to see Francisco approaching, and his questioning glance spoke volumes.

"Ah, yes," he said when he was introduced. "I remember you both. So this is Ned," he added. "Is the whole school here?" Francisco looked around.

"Just us," Ned told him. "Kind of an accident."

"They need some help," Martha explained. "They were hoping that I could help them."

"I see," Francisco said, a faraway look growing in his eyes. "It is best to get help from someone from the school."

"They're not sure how to get there," Martha said. "From here."

"There's a bus," Francisco said. "If they walk out to the road, they can catch it. The school is not far."

Angela was aghast. "The bus? Don't you have a car? Can you drive us?"

Francisco shook his head, completely undisturbed by Angela's state.

"Francisco," Martha said, taking charge. "I would like to take my friends back to the school. It will take no more than a few minutes. It is important. Then I want to talk to you about an experience I just had." She pulled the stone out of her pocket and showed it to him.

He took it, examining it carefully. "So the jaguar has been awakened. We cannot ignore this message. Go, come right back. Time is of the essence." He handed Martha the stone and walked away without further conversation.

"Guys, don't do this again," Martha told them. "I really need Francisco's help. I don't want him to get upset and not help me."

They both apologized as Martha led them to a spot near the back of the Temple of the Feathered Serpent. "We'll try here," she said. "It feels right." She had made a decision that the smartest action was to go to the school and enlist the help of Aurora and Olivia. "That's really all I can do," she said. She was preoccupied with what had happened to her a few moments earlier, and she wanted to talk to Francisco.

Knowing Martha was taking them back to the school, Angela breathed a sigh of relief. "I will never do anything this stupid again, I promise."

"You still have to tell Aurora," Martha told her. "Everybody focus," she reminded them as they stepped into the portal. They were back at the school a moment later.

⚜

Olivia hurried over the minute she saw them, telling them how worried everyone was. She asked what had happened. Ned began to explain but Angela stopped him. "This was my fault," she said. "I need to take responsibility." She told Olivia what had happened, ending by saying they had lost Mary. "We have to find her," she said, "but I don't know where to start."

"Aurora will want to talk to you," Olivia said. "We will wait until her class is finished. For now, go get cleaned up, both of you. And just so you know, Mary is fine. After you left, she found herself standing alone in the field. She answered our email when we wrote to ask if you had been there."

Ned hung his head sheepishly. "Sorry for all the trouble," he said. He was greatly relieved about Mary.

"Aurora wants to talk to you, too," she said. "She is having second thoughts about letting you stay in the Level 2 program. You too, Angela."

"I agree," Ned said. "I may not be ready. I made a poor decision, not realizing the potential consequences."

Angela began pleading their case, but Olivia told them both she would see them at noon. Tears streaming down her face, Angela headed for her room. "I'm so sorry," she called to Ned. "Martha, thank you, and good luck with everything in case I don't see you."

Ned shook his head. "She's very dramatic. A little bit of that goes a long way." He looked at Martha. "Is everything going OK?" he asked. "With Francisco and all?"

"It's going well," Martha replied. "With luck, I will make my trip soon."

"I hope so," Ned told her. "I really want this to go well for you." He hugged her. "Since I don't know if I'll be here when you return... Well, I will see you when I see you. Good luck."

But it seemed like there was something else he wanted to say. Martha asked what it was. "I've just been wondering about something," he said. "Because I am starting to like you as more than a friend."

"We can't talk about this now," Martha said. "Really, it's not a good time."

He seemed dejected as he walked away, and Martha left the school with a heavy heart. It was not the way she had wanted things to go. It was much better to leave after a celebration than to leave knowing her two friends might get kicked out. She wondered why some times things went well, and other times there was such struggle.

But before she could leave the school, her cell phone rang. It was her son, reminding her about her granddaughter's birthday in two days. He wanted to tell her about the party and ask her to bake a cake. Martha, with everything she had been through, had completely forgotten. "You have to be there, Mom," Clark said. "She'll be very upset if you don't come. What on earth are you doing?"

"I'll try to be there," Martha told him. Quickly, before anything else could delay her, she stepped into the portal.

Will stepped out of his hotel, pulling his black baseball cap low on his head. He had tracked Martha to Taxco and lost her. He decided to spend a few more hours looking for her before heading back to the school. He also inquired about Francisco. He knew they had taken the bus here, but he did not know what they had done next.

Finally, from an old street vendor, he learned that Francisco lived outside of Taxco. Following the directions he was given, Will headed that way in his rental car. He got hopelessly lost on the dusty road, not finding the turnoff that supposedly led to Francisco's house.

Frustrated, he pulled the car off the road and opened his bottle of water. He climbed out of the car to see if he could see any houses in this area. Spying a verdant spot, he headed in that direction and discovered a path leading back to it. There was no road. He would have to walk.

Off he hiked down the winding path. Crossing a small ridge, he dropped down into a low area. He kept an eye out for snakes. As he drew closer, he could see a walled courtyard. The wall itself, about six feet high, was thick with flowering vines. It was too high to see over or climb, but there was a ladder leaning up against it. Someone had been trimming vines. He moved quickly. Looking both ways, he saw no one, so he ran to the ladder and scaled it for a look.

Inside was a large, beautifully landscaped area with a modest house. It was too risky to explore further now. He would have to come back later, when it was dark.

11

Deep within, Martha felt a dawning realization that galvanized her: she had something important to do. A growing sense of purpose had supplanted the uncertainty, because some part of her that had been asleep was waking up. A seed planted on earth, she was beginning to bloom in a beautiful way. It was deeply satisfying to have purpose, she thought, heading back to Xochicalco. It created momentum, like the force that sent waves to the shore. And all she had to do was surf it. She was a sunflower tracking the sun with her broad yellow face.

She arrived at the site without a hitch, but Francisco was nowhere to be found. Not knowing what else to do, she returned to the hillside and gazed out at the lagoon. It was almost noon and her stomach growled with hunger. She wished she had eaten something at the school. But she had promised Francisco she would come right back. *Where was he?*

She saw someone coming up the path where earlier she had seen the women. As he drew closer, she suddenly realized he looked familiar. It was the new student, Will. The moment she thought about his name, he looked up at her. Their eyes met in that moment of recognition, but then he kept walking. He didn't even wave, which struck Martha as peculiar. Even though the sun was warm, the hairs on her arms stood up.

He continued up the path and then disappeared behind a pyramid. Martha jumped up and ran to where she could see around it, but he had vanished. The experience left her feeling uncomfortable, but she didn't know why.

At that moment Francisco returned. "It didn't take you long after all," he said. "Let's get back to work."

"I just saw someone else from the school here," she said.

"Why am I not surprised?" he asked. "It seems that the students are ricocheting all over the place. It happens with some of those who are new to the process as they learn to master the energy."

"It made me feel uneasy," she said.

He studied her for a moment. "Ah, then pay attention to that. But put it away somewhere where it is not in the way of what needs to be done."

"He saw me but he didn't speak to me," she said. "Perhaps it's nothing. We were both surprised to see each other. Maybe he is exploring the area during the lunch break."

"That is a beautiful example of rationalization," Francisco said, using the opportunity to make a point. "Always trust your intuition and instinct first. You had an experience. It made you feel uneasy. Trust that instead of talking yourself out of it."

"All right," she said. "What should I do about it?"

"Right now, nothing. Just file it away. If it is important, we will find out. But we are not the only ones interested in what you are doing," he said.

"What do you mean?" Martha, who was finally at peace with the journey she was about to make, felt a new sense of concern.

"This is not new," he said, calming her. "Many have been interested in this possibility. Others have attempted to make this journey. You must be judicious in what you say and who you talk to about it."

"I have been," Martha assured him. "The only ones who know are the people from the school. Not even my family knows the details."

"This is good," he said. "Soon enough, they will know." Briefly, she thought about her granddaughter's birthday. She had never missed it before. Perhaps later she would mention it. It would be easy enough to return to Oregon through the portal for a couple of hours.

She felt a momentary pang of guilt about not making the birthday cake, but the details of the dozens of cakes she had made now escaped her. This experience, in contrast, was one she would never forget. She would have another opportunity to bake next year. But the opportunity of working with Francisco in preparation for the journey came around only once in a lifetime. And soon, she hoped she could share stories about it, if for no other reason than to relive the adventure. It would be wonderful to tell her granddaughter, who would probably become a trailblazer in her own right.

They ate a delicious lunch at Francisco's house while bees droned in the bougainvillea. Afterwards he pushed his chair back from the table and stood up. "You may have learned this at the school but I don't see you using it, so we will discuss it, because it is important." He walked a few feet from the table and turned to face her.

"We have a direct connection to the universe," he told her. "It is right here." He put his hands on his belly. "This is as direct as you can get. Focus your concentration right there and you will feel it. There's movement. It is a bit like roiling water. This is our power center. This is a very active place, a place of creation. In this place you are totally aware and present, not lost in thought." He waited for this to sink in, and Martha realized that while she had learned about this, she had forgotten to practice it.

Martha stood up, copying his stance. She closed her eyes. As she brought her focus to this area of her body, she noticed movement that she had not felt before. By putting her attention there, she felt connected to everything around her. She also found herself paying attention to all of it without effort.

"Our power center is alive," Francisco continued. "This is where the action happens. When we go into our head, we start to analyze everything. We end up pulling back from this connection.

We become busy being human, and then we forget. We hang out in our head with our thoughts—thinking, thinking, thinking."

Martha knew she was guilty of this.

"Sometimes we even check out of our bodies," he added. "We ignore them. We act as if we are a mind that can do anything regardless of what the body needs."

He had her full attention, and this time she would remember the teaching. "In this center," he said, "is where you can create what you wish to have in your life. This is where it happens. Feel the aliveness and the fluidity. This is power. Think about what you wish to create, perhaps a cup of tea, perhaps a relationship, whatever you need at the moment. Feel it. See it. Visualize that you are creating it from that place, in that fluid state. Make the picture and breathe love into it from your heart. Then release it and allow it to come in as it will."

Martha kept her eyes closed to focus fully on his instructions. When he stopped speaking, she felt what she had created leave her power center and connect with the universe.

"That's good," Francisco said. "You released it. What often happens is that we hang on to what we wish to create with wishful thinking. We are wishing for it from a place of powerlessness rather than creating it from our power center. This is a very important distinction. In the past, you have often used wishful thinking. Very little comes of that," he added.

Martha nodded, absorbing his words. She opened her eyes, squinting in the sun. The cloudless blue sky formed an infinite canopy above her. Her whole body felt powerful.

"This is how you will go to the Lost City," Francisco said. "You will create your connection in this way. Do you feel that you understand it?"

Martha nodded again. "Yes," she said. "But may I ask you why you keep mentioning relationships?"

"You believe you are wanting that," he told her. "I am telling you how to create it if that is what you want. But I would like to ask you to pursue relationship after you have gone to the Lost City. That way the relationship will not be a distraction."

It was so obvious that Martha agreed.

"I'm going to take a short siesta," Francisco said. "And then we will meet the Myth Maker."

Angela and Ned felt a sense of trepidation walking into the office to talk to Aurora after their escapade. Angela insisted on taking full blame for what had happened. It was her idea, she said, explaining to Aurora what had happened. "Martha makes it all look so easy. I thought it would be such a great surprise to drop in on Mary." Aurora listened quietly to her list of justifications.

When Angela was finished, Ned took his turn. "I take full responsibility," he said, looking down as he began in a show of regret. "I did not understand the risk involved, but I do now." He glanced quickly at Aurora. "I sincerely apologize for the problems I caused." It was heartfelt, and Aurora knew he meant it.

"We really can't have things like this happening," Aurora said. "It is enough that Martha is gone. We all need to support her endeavor. In addition, this is very serious work that we are doing. It is important to think about it in that way." She paused for a moment. "Ned, what is your lesson?"

He thought about it. "I'm not sure. I like helping people, but since it got me into this predicament, I wonder if it has to do with that."

"It has to do with *accommodating* people," Aurora said. "If you help in order to accommodate, that is not helping anyone. Your intention must be clear." Ned knew that he had had second thoughts about going along with Angela. "That is when it became accommodation," Aurora continued. "True help is coming to someone's aid. Accommodation is a willingness on your part to adjust your actions in response to the needs of someone else. Do you see the difference? Accommodation benefits no one."

"I see that," Ned said.

"It is important not to go against ourselves," Aurora said, her earlier conversation with Francisco still fresh in her mind. The lesson had hit home for her, and it was a good time for Ned to become aware of this. "This was a case of you going against yourself. I want you to consider this until you feel very aware of what actually happened and how it made you feel."

"I will," Ned told her, the subtlety of the information already sinking in. "I needed to learn this." His countenance changed as other examples of his accommodation came to mind. "Wow, I have done this a lot. It is helpful to see this. Now I can say no with a clear conscience." He lips formed a slight smile, mostly of relief. "This is a powerful lesson."

Aurora turned to Angela to ask about her lesson.

"Not to try to do things on my own?"

"No, there are actually many things you must do on your own. It's deeper than that."

Angela squirmed uncomfortably. She was not fond of learning these things.

"You are an instigator, but not an innovator. In other words, you know how to start things, but you don't know what to do with them once they are underway. You want someone else to take charge at that point."

"Is that good or bad?" Her face crinkled in anticipation of the answer.

"You can turn it into something good. I want you to begin to practice innovation. Bring me some examples tomorrow."

"But I'm not very creative," she said.

"We are all creative," Aurora told her. "But some of us have not learned to access our creativity." She reached into her desk and pulled out a child's set of watercolors with a brush, handing it to Angela. "Paint what happened to you during this episode. I think it will give you some clarity. Paint some other scenes that have happened to you. I think you will see a theme. It is important to call your power back in this area."

She looked at both of them. "I know I can count on you both to learn from this. I will be checking in with you. And I would appreciate no more disruptions. I know you understand how serious this is." With that, she sent them both off to have a quick lunch before class.

The afternoon class was about moving beyond linear time. Will arrived just as they began and took a seat at the back. Steven began by noting that it was one o'clock, but then pointing out that one o'clock was simply the way they had all agreed to name the moment. "Time as we understand it doesn't really exist," he said.

Sensing another challenge, Roger put his hands over his face, as if that would help. Ned glanced at the wristwatch he had worn for many years, all the while thinking to himself that he was in over his head. Angela wondered how she was ever going to make a painting of what she had just been through, and she fretted as she considered this new information.

"All I want you to do," Steven said, "is stay with me for a bit. I am going to show you how to step outside of time. When you do that, *anything* is possible."

"What do you mean by anything?" Roger asked as some of the color drained from his face.

"Just that," Steven said. "When you move conceptually from time to no time, you enter the world of possibility. Most of us dream about creating the lives we want to live, but we aren't able to do it. With this, you will be able to. But let's keep going, so that you see what I mean."

Roger wasn't sure what to write down in his notebook. He finally scribbled "Shaman Time." Ned knew that this would challenge everything he learned and used in his career as an engineer. He thought about the clockwork universe of Galileo and Newton. Never could he have foreseen for himself that one day he would be sitting in on a class about a timeless world.

"This is definitely new territory," Steven said, moving around the room as he talked. "But think about meditation. When we meditate and stop the chatter in our heads, we can experience timelessness. In that experience, we discover that the inner space in which thoughts float and the outer space in which stars float are the same physical space. Have you all had the experience of deep oneness with the whole universe?" There was a show of hands because all of them had experienced moments when they felt that they were a part of the universal pulse. "This is the space where our greatest scientific discoveries and our most beautiful works of art come from."

Ned noted that what Steven was telling them did have ties to science. Roger, meanwhile, had put his notebook away. He decided to try trusting what Aurora had told them at the beginning, that they didn't need to take notes, because they would absorb the information. Will focused his attention. He had a keen interest in this topic.

"Shamans journey outside of time, or ordinary reality, to the nonordinary realms of magic and mystery," Steven continued. "The shaman travels beyond the construct of ordinary reality to contact the spirit world to seek healing, knowledge, and power to help the individual and the community. This is what Martha is doing right now. This is what you will learn to do in this class."

There was an audible gasp from Roger, and Steven smiled. "You've already begun to do this, Roger, by using the portal," Steven assured him. "This is not as far-fetched as you might think."

Roger seemed unconvinced. It took all of his power not to take notes.

"What we will be doing is dropping the limitations imposed by the world of time to enter the living, creative pool of universal consciousness to dream and to create our lives. In this space we have access to all that is, to infinite possibility, and we can pull from the pool of potential that which we wish to use for the fabric of our lives. Once you begin to dream in this way, there is no going back. It will be as indispensable to you as the Internet. The Internet has not been around all that long, but try to imagine your life without it."

In a far corner of the garden, Chaco was busy. He had a table covered with small jars, about the size that spices come in. Ned wandered over to see what he was up to.

"So what are you doing with these empty jars?"

¡Ay caramba! They're hardly empty!

But Ned wasn't able to understand the cat's reply, and he stood with a puzzled expression.

"Check them out," Steven said, coming to get Ned for his tutoring. "They're full of starlight. It's something he came up with. I'm not sure what he's doing with them."

With a swish of his tail, Chaco jumped off the table, and disappeared into the bushes.

"Well, if there's anything I can help with, let me know," Ned called. "Seriously, I'd love to help." He picked up a jar and looked at it. Curious, he stuck it into his backpack, zipped the pack almost shut, then peered into the small opening he'd left. "Holy cow," he quietly exclaimed.

Unbelievably, the jar was glowing like the night sky.

12

Clark knew that his mother was taking classes somewhere, but being busy with the demands of work and family he had not asked for details. What he had noticed was this: She was traveling at the drop of a hat, due to her newfound hobby of learning more about the world. She was especially interested in indigenous cultures and had somehow picked up a smattering of Spanish. He missed having her reliably at home a few blocks away. Truth be told, her recent streak of independence had left him feeling somewhat rattled.

"It's not like her," he complained to his wife, Leslie. "She is behaving very differently these last few months." He flipped aimlessly through the mail that had come that day. "I can't believe she's not making the birthday cake."

"It's probably hormones," Leslie replied. "I wouldn't worry about it. Did you order the cake?"

"What if you bake it?" He made the suggestion hopefully, remembering a cake his wife had made the first year they were married.

"I don't have time." Without offering her usual explanation about her hectic schedule at work, she disappeared into another room and Clark let the subject drop. He pulled the phonebook out of a drawer. In the yellow pages he found the number for a bakery, and as he dialed, he thought, *how hard can it be to bake a cake?* His mother had always baked cakes for his birthday, and until recently, beautiful, delicious cakes for her grandchildren as well.

He hung up the phone, pulled a cookbook off the shelf, and opened it to cakes, scanning the recipe as the children opened the back door and came running in, excited from play.

"Daddy, can Kerrie come over now?" Melissa asked. "Her mom said she can." Matthew dropped his baseball glove on the floor and hurried to his room.

"Sure, baby," he said. "Matthew, put your glove away."

"Can we go get her?"

"Where does she live?" he asked, still focused on the recipe.

"In her house."

"Leslie, do you know where Kerrie lives?" he called, jotting down the ingredients he needed for strawberry cake.

After getting the address, he loaded Melissa in the car, planning to make a quick stop at the store. He grabbed his reusable shopping bag.

"Daddy, I don't want to go to the store," Melissa said. "I want to play with Kerrie."

"Five minutes," he bargained. "I'm going to get the ingredients for your cake. Did you forget about your birthday?"

"Of course I didn't," she said.

"How many candles do we need?" He backed out of the driveway into the street.

"Six! Right now I am still five and a half and three quarters. But on my birthday I am going to be six!"

"You're growing up in front of my eyes," Clark said, smiling at her in the rearview mirror. "What a smart, beautiful girl you are."

"Don't forget intrepid," she said. "I'm intrepid and I can fly."

"Intrepid," Clark exclaimed. "That's a big word. Where did you learn that?"

"Chaco said we have to be intrepid. Is Grandma coming to my party?"

"I hope so." Clark was still thinking about how the cat could have possibly told her anything about being intrepid. "I don't think most six-year-olds believe in talking cats," he added. "And unless you're Tinkerbell, you can't really fly. Humans don't fly. But it's fun to pretend."

"It's too bad you can't talk to Chaco," she said. "He might show you how to fly." For a moment she was quiet, then she said, "I know Grandma is doing something important."

"What's more important than your birthday?" Clark was puzzled.

"Chaco told me. She…has…to…do…something…very…important." She emphasized each word in order to make her point.

"Like what?" Even though Clark did not believe that the cat actually talked to Melissa as she claimed, his curiosity was piqued.

"It's a secret," she said. "But you'll find out. Maybe it will be on the news." She giggled.

"What?" Clark nearly went through the stop sign at the corner. "Sweetheart, what did Chaco tell you? If your grandmother is going to be on the news, I need to know about it."

"It's a secret," she repeated. "Just like my birthday present is a secret." She giggled again. Melissa, even though she was just going on six, was wise beyond her years, often surprising her parents with the things she said.

"If your grandmother is doing something crazy, you need to tell me." Clark's voice was firm.

But Melissa was singing a song and happily ignoring him. Clark sighed. He was not his mother's keeper, even though he had tried to fill those shoes after his father died. His mother's newfound independence seemed self-serving to him, but she was in her mid-fifties and perfectly capable of looking after herself. He decided not to worry about it. He pulled into the store parking lot and he and Melissa, in her white shirt and pink shorts, went in search of ingredients for strawberry cake with strawberry frosting. She held his hand, still singing her song, which she must have learned at school. Clark had never heard it before, and it didn't make much sense.

"Jaguar dances in the wind
To make the world new.
We are the ones we're waiting for.
This is the time to come."

Then she growled like a large cat. The next verse was similar, except she substituted quetzal for jaguar and made a bird call at the end.

"Honey, did you learn that at school?" Clark picked up a basket for groceries and then located a carton of fresh organic strawberries in the produce department.

"No, of course not, Chaco taught me," she said. "Now… don't…interrupt." Once again she punctuated the words for emphasis. "I'm helping Grandma."

Clark sighed as they headed to the baking aisle, wishing he had a better understanding of his daughter's private world. "How are you helping her?"

"By singing. How are you helping her, Daddy?"

"Helping her do what?" Clark still wasn't sure what she was talking about.

"Make the new world. We can all help, even if we're little, even if we're big." She said it as if it was the most logical idea ever.

"I'd love to help," he said, putting the items he needed in a basket. He checked his list to make sure he had everything. "Tell me what I can do." He wondered if finally he would get some insight.

"You can help me sing my song."

"All right. You teach it to me and I will."

They paid for their items at the checkout and headed off to pick up Kerrie. As they drove, Melissa taught her father the words to the song that Chaco the cat had taught her, and he happily obliged by singing them, feeling happy because Melissa was happy.

"Do you even know what a quetzal is, sweetie?"

"Yes, Daddy, it is a—" she struggled with the word—"a danger bird that lives in the rainforest."

"Endangered?" he asked

"Yes. What does that mean?"

"It means there aren't very many of them left."

"Why not?"

"People have moved into the areas where they live and cleared the trees," he explained. He never like having to tell his children about the way the world was changing in ways that were not good.

"See, that's why we have to make a new world. So the en...dan...gered"— she sounded out the word for herself, dividing it into syllables—"animals and all the jaguars can live there and be happy."

"That is a very good idea." He was touched by the humanitarian impulses of his young, still innocent daughter, and he liked to think she had a life of infinite possibility before her.

"You know what I want to do when I grow up, Daddy?"

"No, what." Clark played along, because he knew she would change her mind as she got older, but it was always good to dream.

"I want to fly and go all over the world, like Grandma."

"Do you mean you want to be a pilot?"

"No, I just want to fly."

"Honey, humans can't fly. Remember?"

"Yes they can," she insisted. "Grandma can fly."

"How do you know?"

"Chaco told me," she said with confidence.

"I see," her father said, deciding to let childish imagination reign supreme for a short while longer. Eventually, she would grow out of it. He almost couldn't bear to think that she had to grow up and learn about the problems in the world. He wished there was more that could be done to change the current global situation that the newspaper brought to his doorstep.

"You'll see," Melissa said. "And when I have a car I will fly in my car, and I won't need gas."

"That sounds great," her father said. "Can you teach me that?"

"Grandma can teach you. She knows how. They flew in Ned's car as high as a flying saucer."

"Oh boy," Clark said under his breath, hoping that his daughter did not say these kinds of things at school. He decided not to encourage her any further. She had had imaginary friends when she was younger, and then recently, the cat she called Chaco had been talking to her and teaching her Spanish. He shook his head at the idea of flying. It was so farfetched that it made him chuckle.

"What, Daddy?"

"I was just thinking how glad I am that you are my daughter." They pulled up in front of Kerrie's house. Kerrie ran out to meet them, climbing into the back seat with Melissa. Her mother waved goodbye as they drove away.

"Does Kerrie know your song?"

"No. I just learned it." She began to tell her friend about it and soon they were singing together, inventively adding more animals and sounds as they went.

Clark smiled to himself. What a nice idea, he thought, to make a new world. He wished it were so easy. He loved the fact that Melissa felt she was helping simply by singing a song. The optimism of children was a wonderful thing. *Too bad we grow up,* he mused, *and have to leave it all behind.*

He wondered if he had ever had imaginary friends or talking cats as a child. He made a mental note to ask his mother, and he hoped that she wouldn't think it was silly that he had asked. It would certainly be a fun way to learn Spanish, more fun than the way he had learned, in a classroom with a textbook.

After reading for a while in the hammock, Martha dozed briefly and began to dream. The jaguar appeared, beckoning her into the land beyond time. He turned to lead the way, and as she followed, she fell further and further behind, until she lost sight of him in the darkness. No matter how hard she tried to keep up, she could not make her feet walk faster, and she couldn't see in the dark.

She woke with a start, wondering how long she'd slept. Checking her watch, she discovered it was three o'clock. She'd only slept for twenty minutes. It should have felt restorative, but it didn't. It appeared that she was doing as much work in her dreams as she was in her waking hours. Rubbing her eyes, she pulled herself out of the comfortable hammock. Francisco appeared a minute later, looking refreshed. Esperanza brought out bottled water and a plate of fruit.

"How was your dream?" he asked, as if he already knew.

She told him about it.

"Ah," he said. "Walking is too slow. Perhaps next time you can fly. It is important to take advantages of these opportunities to learn as much as you can."

"I didn't even think about that because I was dreaming. I don't seem to be in control when I dream."

"You can learn to be more in control," he said. "I can show you. You have to be aware that you are dreaming."

This had not occurred to Martha, and she wondered if it was possible. Her dreams seemed to appear out of nowhere and have a mind of their own.

"You will see," he told her. "It is a new idea. But you are already considering it. This is the way to begin, to be open to the possibility."

Francisco had promised to tell her about the Myth Maker, something Martha didn't know about. She was curious. But because she had found the stone and then experienced the dream, he wished to talk to her about the jaguar. "In our history, the jaguar leaps easily and gracefully between worlds," he said. "The jaguar can lead you into the time to come. This stone that you found is a pathway to where you are going. Keep it with you."

"But in my dream," Martha replied, "I couldn't keep up with the jaguar."

"Then we must talk about this. It is an important dream. The jaguar is showing you what you need to do." Francisco leaned forward. "There are three choices. You can track back through the ancient time, which you saw at Xochicalco. You can track through present time. Or you can go outside of time. It is your decision. If you were unable to keep up, call to the jaguar. She knows her way through the dark very easily. Know that you can tell her what you need. She is here to help you. So are many others."

With his arms he gestured toward the surrounding terrain. His voice was reverent. "Call on the plants and animals to assist you in your journey if you need to. Call on the stones. Call on the wind." His teaching was etched with centuries of indigenous wisdom and experience. "Call on the stars. Call on the sun and the moon."

He pulled his hands back and placed them on his heart. "Call on all of creation." He fell silent, dropping his eyes. Then he looked directly at her. "We must move into who we are becoming without fear. We are in this cosmic journey together and always have been. This is why I will tell you about the Myth Maker. She is the one who helps to create what we believe."

"So this can happen when I am sleeping and when I am awake." Martha wanted clarification, thinking about her dream.

"Exactly," Francisco said. "Once you enter the world of energy, there is very little difference. Things can happen in many different ways, and all are valid. This is why you must learn to be aware at all times. Even when you are dreaming."

"I see." Martha fell silent to absorb his words. She had learned that she didn't need to understand everything for the processes to work. She simply needed to know that such things were possible. There seemed to be many options available.

Giving her some time, Francisco turned to their snack, putting melon and papaya on his plate. Martha ate a slice of papaya. Food helped to ground her, she had discovered, and the fruit sugar helped to revive her.

A few minutes later, Francisco finally got around to the promised subject. He was eager for her to learn, but he didn't push. In some ways, he was an enigma to Martha. He seemed not entirely of this world, in part because he was little interested in material things. As an example, even though this was his house, he had very little ownership of its contents. This was a space that he used, but did not claim. She saw no personal effects. It was comfortably furnished, but there were no collections of books or art—or even trinkets. The house reminded her of one you would rent for a vacation. *How could he not live anywhere?* Thinking of her own cozy home in Oregon, she found that hard to imagine. She liked to have a nest, somewhere she could burrow in and feel comfortable, a place full of her favorite things, personal mementos, and reminders of who she was. It gave her a sense of security. She liked being "home."

"Shall we begin?" Francisco asked politely, summoning her gently back to the work at hand.

Martha pulled herself from her reverie and he began. "The Myth Maker is the one we call on when we are ready to look at how we live," Francisco explained as Martha focused anew. "She helps to create your beliefs and your dreams. At the mythic level, the threads of your dreams are woven snugly into the landscape of your daily life. Your life becomes the same as your dreams, because you are dreaming your life into being. Everything you dream is based on what you believe."

Martha tried to take this in. She had never considered such an approach. She had always been discouraged from dreaming about what she wanted. She had learned it was pointless to wish things were different. So she focused on being practical and effective. For instance, she saved time by doing two things at once. That meant she sometimes returned phone calls while she cleaned up the kitchen. But no matter how much time she saved, there was never enough time to get everything done. Francisco seemed to be telling her to do the impossible. *How could she dream her life into being?*

"As you clear out what is unnecessary in your life, you will discover that you have all the time in the world." He smiled, picking up where he left off. "Once the door is opened to the mythic, everything makes sense," he said. "Everything you have wondered about falls into place. Your questions evaporate. The answers are apparent. It is a peaceful and beautiful place, and it exists outside of time as we know it."

Martha asked what this meant in terms of daily life.

"You can still live comfortably in the world," he explained. "Your life can be very much like it is now, except that it will feel completely different. But all of our lives are about to change," he reminded her.

"How do I call in the Myth Maker?" she asked.

"I will show you tonight. When we go to her," he added, "we learn why we are here."

Martha was intrigued. "I've asked that question," she said.

"This is sacred ground," Francisco said. "Soon you will understand. You will see your belief system, and the belief system of your culture. You will see the web of belief systems that are operating on the planet. You will need to step outside of all of this in order to make your journey." He was silent for a few seconds, considering something. Then he spoke again. "You have enormous courage, Martha."

Martha thanked him. "There is so much to learn," she finally said. "Can I really learn all this in such a short time?"

"You will need great power to make this journey," Francisco told her. "You are gathering that power now. Occasionally you still feel doubt. This is natural until the power integrates." He spoke without judgment or emotion, simply sharing the truth that he saw. It occurred to her that she was nearly mesmerized by him. He radiated innate power in the way that some people radiate charisma. It was something she had never encountered before, and it was hard not to stare at him. He was like a living work of art, classical, compelling, ethereal. She wondered if she could absorb some of his power just by being around him.

"Ah," he said, sensing her thoughts. "You will have to build the power that you need. I can help you. Also, those at the school will help you. We will build the power that is needed. In the interim, we will review the elements of impeccability."

She reached for her notebook so she could take notes. Everything he was saying was raising questions. She jotted down a few things. He waited, in no particular hurry.

"Going to the Ancient Wisdom School has accelerated your process," he said, "but the process began with an awakening inside you. It was the awakening that led you to the school. It also led you to me," he added.

Once again she looked at him, trying to take this all in. "You see, when we begin to awaken, the magic begins in our lives. When people first start down this road, often they think it is only their imagination. But imagination is a very powerful thing. The root word is *mage*, the same root word as in magic. The mages were ancient priests and magicians. To imagine is really to see the power of your own creation."

Martha felt her head begin to spin.

"What you are going through," he explained, "is the opening of who you think you are, to who you truly are, the *you* that exists beyond anything that you have learned or been taught about yourself."

Martha listened intently. She had stopped taking notes.

"We each have a doorway to our true self," he said. "When we are young, we go out through this doorway as we learn from our family and our school and our culture about the world and how they think we fit into it. As we get older, we have an opportunity to return through this doorway to discover our personal truth: who we really are. We can do this at any time, but usually we need to become aware that it is possible. Some people experience a dramatic event that shakes them awake. For many people, it doesn't happen until they die. But with the evolution of consciousness that is taking place, many of us are seeing this doorway open. We are facing a choice. We have an incredible opportunity to discover our truth while we are here on the planet." He fell silent, letting his words sink in.

Looking past the garden at the arid landscape, Martha thought about the responsibility she had accepted. Everything she was learning was so different from what she had accepted in her earlier life. And yet, it resonated with truth. It felt right. And it awakened within her a desire to finish what she was called to do. She was a part of something bigger than herself. Like Francisco said earlier, if you pick a flower, you jiggle a star. By making this journey, she would help to anchor in a new world. The shift would be felt everywhere.

After a while Francisco continued. "Let go of who you think you are, and what you think you want, and receive what has been cultivated by Spirit just for you. Everything is shifting into a higher order. Who you are on the inside is being set free. The butterfly cannot remain in the cocoon. It is designed and destined to fly."

Martha's heart began to grow warm. It felt like it was expanding to connect with her bigger life, to the life that was waiting for her just beyond what she could imagine.

"You have heard of the two roads," Francisco said, "and the traveler chose one."

"It was a famous poem," Martha said, "by Robert Frost. After long contemplation the traveler chose the less traveled road, because it was what he wanted for himself. I memorized it in school." She began to recite it, happy to have something she knew about, but he stopped her.

"You are traveling the third road, the road no one has traveled," Francisco said.

Again, Martha experienced what felt like a lightning strike. The words themselves seemed to sear through her consciousness to the core of her being. She closed her eyes and felt heat rise inside of her.

Francisco watched without speaking, knowing the message had been delivered.

After that, Martha needed to walk. She went out on the land behind the house for some distance, feeling the earth beneath her feet. Overhead, she watched a band of clouds scuttle across the sky. Her thinking mind had stopped, replaced by a sense of connection. She heard the wind speaking as it moved past her, and the plants she passed glowed with the light of their essence. *Who am I?* she wondered. *Why am I here? What is happening?*

A half hour later, she returned, feeling refreshed, even if she didn't have the answers.

Francisco was making some notes. "One more thing," he said, looking up. "On this path, when we shed our past we take flight, in a spiritual sense. We become eagle. Eagle cannot fly with more than she needs. She cannot fly with a suitcase of baggage." He looked at her as he spoke. He could see that she had undergone another shift on her walk. "When we fly, we achieve personal freedom. We find freedom from our past and the patterns that have kept us constricted. The process is straightforward. It is both release of the old and acceptance of the new. When we release the past and the energy that we had put into holding it, we become full of light. We encounter the new, and we begin to fly. Flying is a way of thinking and a way of being. It is who we are becoming."

That night, Martha sat outside on the terrace at Francisco's house, listening to the rich melody stirred up by the natural world. It crossed her mind that her decision to attend the Ancient Wisdom School had opened the door to a process that was both magical and mysterious, introducing her to the persistent and real power of ancient mysteries and magical creation.

All her life, she had been a part of the mystery and yet she hadn't realized it. Now that she did, she wanted to soak it up like a sponge. She sighed with simple joy, thinking, *How blessed I am to have this experience!*

It hardly seemed possible. Months ago she felt like life had passed her by, that her girlhood dreams of doing something special would never see fruition. *Where was the adventure she had hoped for?*

And what about the answer to her biggest question? It was something she had puzzled over a few times but never spoken out loud. *Why was she here?*

It was beyond her wildest dreams that this—what she was involved in now—could have happened to her. She wanted to pinch herself to make sure it was real. Inhaling the heady scent of gardenia, she was happy, at that moment, from her head to her toes. For perhaps the first time in her life, nothing else mattered but the fact that she felt truly and deeply alive. It lit all the cells of her being. She was on fire, like a birthday cake covered with thousands of candles.

13

The counter was covered with bowls and measuring cups, canisters of flour and sugar, and a large carton of plump, ripe strawberries. Melissa was standing on a chair in order to participate. Chaco had also come to take part. Clark, who was wearing one of Leslie's aprons, opened the cookbook to the recipe for strawberry cake and preheated the oven.

Melissa wanted to help measure flour and sugar. Holding a big spoon, she carefully transferred those ingredients from canisters to measuring cups. Every few minutes, she would ask, "Daddy, is this how much?"

"Almost."

Matthew ran in to see what they were doing. "I don't like that kind of cake," he announced.

"I know, but Melissa gets to choose, just like you did on your birthday."

"But what cake will I have?"

"We'll work something out. Maybe you can just eat ice cream."

"I want cake, too," he insisted.

"Matthew, I need to focus. Is your homework done?"

"I don't have any. It's summer vacation."

"Well, you can help or you can find something else to do. Your mom will be home any minute. Maybe you can set the table for dinner."

"I don't want to."

"I'd like you to," Clark said. "After dinner we'll play a game."

"Yay!" Matthew shouted.

"But you have to set the table." Clark pulled out plates and silverware for him; Matthew found placemats in the drawer and decided to use a different color for each of them.

"That's creative," Clark said, hoping Leslie didn't mind. He went back to checking the measurements. He had decided to measure everything and put it in bowls as he had seen done on television. That would make it easy. He pulled out the mixer.

"I want to mix," Matthew said.

"Melissa, do you mind if Matthew does the mixing?"

"I want to do it so I know how."

Clark sighed. He felt like he needed two heads and four arms. "We will cross that bridge when we come to it," he said, hoping Leslie would be home by then. He thought briefly about giving up and ordering a cake, but he didn't like to quit once he had begun a project. He was determined to succeed.

"Whoa! That's plenty of flour, young lady," he said, suddenly noticing the measuring cup overflowing onto the counter. "We'll do two cups and then another three-quarters. Then two cups of sugar in this bowl. Put the flour in here."

Melissa dumped the flour into the designated bowl, sending a cloud of white dust into the air. "Oh, I guess we need to pour it slowly," Clark said. Part of the flour had ended up on the floor, so he tried to calculate how much extra they needed to replace that. He went to get the broom.

Meanwhile, Chaco walked across the counter, inadvertently sending one egg rolling slowly to the edge. It hit the floor with a smack and splattered just as Clark returned. "Oh no!" he yelped. "Melissa, your cat needs to be off the counter."

"He's helping, Daddy. We're making a magic cake."

"He's not helping if he's knocking eggs off the counter."

"Can he sit on a chair?"

Thus Chaco ended up supervising from a chair at the end of the counter, standing on his back legs in order to see, his front paws resting on the edge of the counter. But within a few seconds he disappeared.

Clark asked Matthew to get the eggs out of the refrigerator. In doing so, Matthew dropped the entire carton on the floor, breaking all five eggs inside. Clark shook his head, wondering what he would do now. But it occurred to him that he could use a broken egg in the cake. He set the carton by the sink and consoled Matthew by telling him it wasn't his fault, saying it could have happened to anyone. But Matthew decided he was done in the kitchen and left. Clark mopped up the broken eggs with paper towels and used the back of his hand to wipe his forehead.

"Dad, look!" Matthew called from the other room.

"I can't right now, buddy. I've got my hands full," Clark answered. "What is it?"

But there was no answer from Matthew, who was watching Chaco attempt to open the desk drawer. The cat eyed Matthew intently as if he was trying to tell him something.

"What?" Matthew asked. Going to the drawer, he opened it, looked inside, and then pulled out his father's jackknife. Carefully, he opened the sharp blade. Eight years old, he had never been allowed to use the knife by himself. It was strange to feel like he had permission. Looking over his shoulder to make sure no one was around, he opened the sliding glass door and went out on the deck.

In the kitchen, Clark was absorbed in cutting fresh strawberries for a puree. Melissa, still helping, decided to open the package of strawberry-flavored gelatin. Ripping the paper on one end, she accidentally sent sweet, pink powder across the counter. Clark surveyed the scene. In the process of making the cake, flour and gelatin had settled on his dark hair like fairy dust.

Eyeing the counter, Melissa dipped her finger into the gelatin for a taste. She crinkled her nose and then, inspired by the potential of the sugary, floury palette in front of her, began to finger-paint.

Chaco, who had returned, flicked his tail in a defiant but satisfied way.

"Can we put everything in the big bowl?" Melissa asked, looking at the cat. "Chaco wants us to make the cake. He wants to put the magic in."

"Let's do it," Clark said, deciding to clean up later. Into the large bowl went all the ingredients. As he started the mixer on high, batter flew like a hurricane had hit. Melissa shrieked and covered her face with her hands. Chaco made a beeline out of the room.

At that moment Leslie walked in. "Hold everything! What's going on?"

"The master chef and his talented apprentice are baking a cake," Clark said happily. "This is going to be the best cake you've ever tasted. You wait. It might be the best cake in the history of cakemaking. Get a picture of this, will you?"

"It's a magic cake," Melissa said.

"It's a mess," Leslie said, heading for cleaning supplies.

"You might as well wait till we're done," her husband said. He folded in some of the strawberries, then poured the batter into a cake pan. Leslie snapped a picture of them. There was flour in their hair and cake batter on their clothes, but they were beaming. "It smells good enough to eat," Clark said, licking the spoon from the bowl.

"First we have to bake it, Daddy," Melissa said, giggling. With that, into the oven it went, Clark's first-ever cake, made with love and—as they would find out—a little bit of Chaco's magic.

Clark started cleaning up, feeling about as happy as he'd felt in ages. He'd completely forgotten about the politics at the college where he taught anthropology. He'd forgotten about the chores he needed to do. He'd forgotten about all of it, in fact, for a half hour while he baked a strawberry birthday cake with his daughter. He had a feeling it was something he would remember for a long time, and he hoped she would remember it, too. As the wonderful aroma of strawberry cake filled the kitchen, Clark considered that maybe Chaco had supplied some magic after all.

Leslie took her daughter upstairs for a bath. Clark went to check on Matthew. "Hey, buddy, let's have a quick game before dinner."

"I can't right now. I'm reading my book," Matthew said without looking up. "They're fighting the bad guys."

Clark noticed a large action-hero bandage on one of Matthew's fingers. "What happened to you, bud?"

But Matthew was mum. Engrossed in his book, that was his world for the moment, and Clark let it go. "Well, dinner in a few minutes then." He closed the desk drawer. As soon as he left the room, Matthew scampered over to return the jackknife to its rightful spot, glad that his father hadn't noticed. Then he carefully closed the desk drawer. Adjusting the bandage on his finger, he went back to his book.

To avoid detection, Will drove slowly up the bumpy, narrow road with his lights off. He parked where he had parked earlier and climbed out of the car. Quietly closing the door, he began to pick his way toward the house, not using his flashlight. He moved slowly and soundlessly, keeping the profile of an animal. The waxing crescent moon hung over the western horizon like an apostrophe punctuating the stars.

When he arrived at the adobe wall, he discovered that the ladder he had seen earlier was gone. He made his way around to the front of the house, where the gate was closed but not locked.

Silently he let himself in. The house was dark; apparently everyone was in slumber. He avoided the gardener's quarters, instead making his way around the west side of the house, where the garden was planted with fruit trees. Even in the moonlight, he could see oranges.

An open window caught his eye. It was barred with artistic wrought iron *rejas*, but peering in he could see someone sleeping in the bed. He spied a backpack on the chair. It was Martha's. At last, he was close enough to perhaps learn what he wanted to know. He had tracked Martha to the restaurant, following her when she had headed back to the school. He had seen her fly. More than anything, he wanted to find the Lost City. He planned to track Martha all the way. Seeing her at Xochicalco was a coup. He had long suspected that the ancient site held secrets of the future.

He hadn't spoken to her because he thought he had made himself invisible. He was unsure if she had seen him or not. He knew she had seen something, but she may have seen only a hazy form and wondered what it was. That's what he hoped.

The chair holding the pack was about three feet from the window, just out of reach. Will quickly retrieved some electrical wire from his pocket. Unrolling the wire, he created a hook on one end.

He worked quickly. There was no time to waste. On his second try, he hooked the backpack. It dropped to the floor with a soft thud. He ducked down and waited. After a few seconds, when Martha didn't stir, he went back to work. Slowly he pulled the backpack to the window. Then he reached through the bars and took hold. He quickly rifled through it, looking for a calendar or notebook, anything that would give him clues as to what she was planning. But aside from a few snacks and a pen and a change of clothes, the contents revealed nothing.

He swore silently, upset that he had been unable to learn anything except that Martha had not left yet. He would have to continue to watch her. He pulled one more thing from his pocket—a small tracking device. He attached it discreetly to the bottom of the pack. Then, as soundlessly as he had come, he headed back to the school before anyone took note of his absence.

The moon had set; it was very dark. Will stumbled twice and the second time he fell and cut his knee. When he turned his flashlight on to check the wound, his neck prickled with the sensation of someone—or something—watching him. He swung the flashlight around but saw nothing. Still, the feeling lingered, and he stepped up his pace.

In the darkness a solitary animal watched. Although it was a powerful predator, it had no need to hunt, because the prowess required at this time was different. Necessary now was the ability held in the temples of antiquity—the power to enter the realms beyond the merely physical. The jaguar had been called and in turn was calling upon its lineage to journey to the new world. Its otherworldly powers, as they had been long ago, were needed once again.

Martha slept dreamlessly, unaware that the spirit realm was working on her behalf and that the forces were coalescing to make her journey possible. There was nothing she had to do except sleep, because for a few hours, things were being done for her. Her opportune moment was fast approaching, when alignment in the heavens would create openings for opportunity on the earth.

Francisco, aware of these alignments, entered the dream world during the night. He moved out through the landscape of the dream vision to explore worlds unseen with everyday eyes. In this unpredictable realm he needed to move quickly and sure-footedly, with all his senses alert, and so he assumed the shape of the jaguar, as he had learned from his grandfather, who in turn had learned from those who came before him, and on and on, going back in time. In this way, he could navigate low to the ground without drawing undue attention to himself, silently slipping through the realms he wanted to explore, observing and gathering information.

When Martha got up in the morning, she noticed her backpack on the floor by the window. She was certain she had left it in the chair. When she picked it up a piece of wire dropped on the tile floor, making a clicking sound. As she stared at it, it dawned on her that someone had tried to take her pack. She hurriedly dressed and went to find Francisco, who immediately asked the gardener to search the house and the property. The gardener found the gate open, indicating that someone had been inside the grounds.

"It appears that someone is interested in your venture," Francisco said. "As I said, many are interested in what you are doing. Many have tried to do it. My suggestion is that you go home for a day and meet me tonight at Xochicalco after it closes to the public. Why don't we meet around nine? You have everything that you need at this point, and it is best that you leave as soon as possible. I will spend the day building the power for your journey, and I will have everything ready when you arrive."

They sat down to breakfast on the terrace, but Martha felt nervous, wondering who had invaded her personal space. *What were they after?*

Francisco asked if she knew the name of the student she had seen at Xochicalco.

"Will," she said. "He's new. I saw him at the ceremony."

"Let me check with Aurora," he told her. Esperanza brought them fresh-squeezed orange juice and papaya as well as refried beans, rice, and scrambled eggs. It was delicious, but Martha wasn't hungry. She nibbled at it while Francisco talked.

"You know that you can follow the map of the jaguar," he said. "We have talked about that. When you look at it with your inner vision—your third eye—you will see it clearly. It will reveal much information. The more you use it, the more you will learn. That is the way it works."

"I haven't learned to shapeshift," Martha said. "I wanted to know how to do that."

"When you return, we will have a session dedicated just to that. You can bring your friend Ned. It is something he might enjoy."

"But won't I need to know how to do that?"

"You will discover that whatever you need to know, you already know," he said. "It will arise as you need it. Trust yourself. We have everything in us that we need. We have collected knowledge and wisdom over lifetimes, and it is available to us to use. The serpent shows us how to shed our skin—by which I mean the past—but inside the serpent dwells the knowledge to create the new skin. We also have this within us. As we go through the great shift, we are to use all of this, and it is all becoming available to use."

"You sound like Aurora," she said. Then she laughed, remembering that he had taught Aurora. "I still do not feel very prepared," Martha added. "But perhaps I never will."

"It is not so much about preparation as it is about timing. Right now, the timing is right. This is what will make it possible."

Martha folded her napkin and put it on the table. "Thank you for everything you have taught me," she told Francisco. "There are so many surprising things. The world you live in is incredibly different from mine."

"Shamanism is an ancient practice that has existed for thousands of years," he said. "And even though some consider its techniques to be primitive, it has continued to be a part of our world. It was thought that it would disappear as we grew more educated and rational," Francisco continued. "But the opposite is happening. It is growing in popularity, and those who are drawn to it now tend to be well educated. They are people like you. Why do you think that is?"

Martha shook her head. She'd never thought about it.

"It is because you are discovering the truth inherent in it. You are seeing that shamans, who had no books, had an intimate relationship not only with the natural world of plants and animals and minerals, but with the world of spirit and energy. They had an understanding of those worlds that surpasses what we learn in school. Shamans understood that everything is alive and that everything has a spirit. And they knew how to navigate all these worlds and to communicate with them in powerful ways in order to live in balance and harmony."

Martha felt magnetized by his words. Even though his manner was calm, his eyes threw sparks when he spoke.

"Many today want to know how to live in balance and harmony," he went on. "People are drawn to these practices by their desire to know how to connect with their innate healing abilities. They want information. How can they access their connection to the grand scheme of things? What is their purpose? How do they fit in with the big picture? How do they coexist with others? How do they simply get along with their relatives?" He laughed. "That is a surprisingly big challenge. But seriously, many among us are coming to recognize the importance of these teachings and to rediscover them anew."

He leaned forward. "Now I will tell you something not at all surprising. Scientists have found that our bodies are wired to respond to the techniques that shamans use. Shamanic practices stimulate the brain in ways that lead to healing and to feeling better. The reason so many people have lost their way is that we have lost touch with the practices that were designed to help us live rich, whole, interactive lives. Shamanism is a spiritual path that is based on direct experience. It teaches us that all life is sacred."

Martha was spellbound. Francisco had shifted into his professorial persona, discussing his training from a third-party perspective. He flew like a hawk over his own history in order to share the details of it. From this perspective she saw something she too needed: the ability to give herself distance to make sense of experience when she was in the midst of it. As she wondered if she would be able to do this, something within her told her she would.

"Ah, you learn quickly," he said. "We can use the power of hawk to see what we are doing and what purpose it has," he explained. "We can use it to give us perspective. We can fly above our actions, so to speak, look down, and take stock. It is good to do this, it helps us to make sense of everything. This is the beginning of shapeshifting. You become something else in order to see what you need to see."

Surprised at how quickly she caught on to what he was showing her, Martha visualized herself flying above her problems, looking down at them.

"Like everything else, shamanism is evolving," Francisco said. "We are becoming new shamans. The old ways are giving way as the earth evolves and as we evolve with her. Shamanism is ancient but never static. It changes in the way that everything changes. Change is, in fact, the one thing we can be certain of. This is why it is important to always be present and aware. In this way we will know exactly what we need to do, and when we need to do it."

Martha nodded, trying to take it all in.

"We are shamans by nature," he repeated. "Our bodies are wired for it. It is part of our biology. It is who we are." He leaned back in his chair, as if listening to something beyond her range of hearing. Then he continued.

"The shaman's world is based on direct experience with the natural world and the spirit world, and with the stars, who brought us original knowledge and return to us now for the next step of our evolution. There are no instruction books or field guides for this, although there are many who are receiving messages and helping us to anchor this new energy on the earth. The Internet is a marvelous resource." He chuckled. "Who would have thought of such a thing, yet look how it helps to share the information."

Martha seemed surprised that Francisco might use the Internet but he quickly answered her unspoken question. "I don't," he said. "Because the information is already a part of who I am. And when you return, I hope to hear your experience directly." Once again his eyes sparked.

"I can't believe that I might learn something that you don't know," Martha said.

"We are all a part of the puzzle. Our experience on earth is about relationship—the relationship of every single thing to every other single thing, and how we can all coexist. The reason we have come to this evolutionary step is that we have evolved to the place of becoming who we are meant to be. Some day it will be in the history books, if we still have books." He nodded. "Yes, big changes. We are all a part of this change. Some day we will look back and see the evolutionary leap we made."

Martha was awed by Francisco's knowledge. "It seems to me that you are the one who should be making this journey," she said. "You are so powerful, and you have studied so many things. You would know what to do and how to interpret everything."

"Ah," he said. "But I was not given the dream." He was silent for a brief moment. "It is you who were given the dream. The person who is called is the one who must answer."

🎴 14 🎴

The morning class at the Ancient Wisdom School got underway just after breakfast, with Olivia talking about how humanity was evolving. She was more animated than usual, and Sheila and Angela exchanged knowing glances. Obviously, something was up.

"We have always focused on learning the ancient ways," Olivia explained. "But knowing what has been practiced for hundreds of years doesn't tell us what works now. We must expand on the traditions that have been passed down, and we will do this through our own personal spiritual experience." She strode across the front of the room and turned dramatically, as if what she was about to impart was very important. Sheila shook off her sleepiness to pay attention. She had stayed up late talking with Angela and Ned.

"What we are going through now is unique in our history. We have never been through something like this before. We are writing on the palette of our own becoming." She paused, allowing each of them to absorb what she had said. Then, enunciating her words carefully and speaking slowly for emphasis, she told them, "We are instruments of change not only for ourselves but for others. What is happening is that we are creating a new template and a new human."

Sheila looked at Angela with surprise, as this had not been discussed before. Roger, crossing his arms over his chest in a defensive posture, blurted out a question before he could stop himself. "What if we're not that comfortable with change?"

Olivia smiled at him. Of all the students she had taught, Roger struggled the most with feelings of safety. He was more comfortable trying to maintain the status quo, and she admired his courage in making a decision to attend the school.

"First, everything is changing all the time," she said. "We've talked about that. The only constant *is* change. I could pay you a great deal of money to stay the same, but you would be unable to do that. This is why we like to meet this force with impeccability." Olivia surveyed the room and noted that everyone was attentive.

"Why is change so challenging?" Sheila asked, hoping for some clarification that would help her and the others with the process.

"It's because we haven't learned that we have some power when it comes to the subject of change," Olivia replied. "When we are able to stop thinking that change is something that happens to us, and instead begin to realize that we can align ourselves with change in a way that is impeccable, we become comfortable with it. We also become powerful because we are creating." She smiled, then went a step further. "We can even become excited by the idea of change. Of course, this requires us to be in the here and now. It is easy to lose our way by living in the future, thinking about what we want, as opposed to consciously being present with what we are creating. It is at the moment of creation that what we want appears, and creation happens at every moment, with every thought."

She moved across the room. "Are you following this? Do you understand?"

Ned raised his hand. "What I'm hearing is that we can't be worrying about things in the future that we can't do anything about. We need to be focused on what we want to create in order to... well...create it."

"If we always had a teacher, that would make it easier," Sheila added. "It gets challenging when we don't know if we are going in the right direction, or making the right decisions. Will we come to a place where we have a better sense of that?"

"You are each in the process of coming to realize that you are your own teacher," Olivia told them. "Think of yourself as a tree, connected to the earth through your roots and to the stars through your branches. In that same way we are connected to all the wisdom of the past and to all the wisdom of the future. This is why you are also learning about stepping outside of time from Steven. When we step outside of time we step into the place of creation.

We see that we have everything we need. Once you see it, you will understand it. Just remember that everything is a process, and eventually you will get to where you need to be."

∾❧∾

After class Will caught up with Angela as she headed to lunch. "Do you mind if I join you?" he asked. "There's something I'm having trouble with. I wonder if you can help."

"I'm not an expert on any of this," said Angela, with a toss of her long hair. "Maybe you should ask Steven."

"I'd rather ask you," he said with a rare smile. "Besides, then we can get to know each other."

Angela, wondering if he was flirting, stopped. "So what is it?"

"Portals."

"No way," she told him, walking away. For some reason, she felt a sense of suspicion.

But he persisted. "I heard you went to England."

"I'm not supposed to do that again," she said. "Besides, Aurora told us to stay put, remember?"

"I'm not going anywhere. I just want some practice. I want to feel comfortable with them. I thought we could do a couple of short trips just so I can get the hang of it."

"Ask someone else."

"What about Xochicalco?" he asked. "That's close."

"Did you not hear what happened? I got stranded there. I really have no interest in doing that again."

"I'm talking daytime—right after lunch. Please?" He voice bordered on desperate. "It's the only thing I'm not up to snuff on. I'll owe you," he said. "Big-time."

Something inside her told her not to help, but she found herself feeling sorry for Will. She knew the feeling of not being good at something. "I'll think about it during lunch," she told him. "I can't afford to get in trouble. I really want to finish the program here. Besides, I have some paintings I have to do. Those are taking most of my free time."

They joined Ned and Sheila, who had already started eating. "Looks good," Will said as he and Angela went to get their food. As Will helped himself to chips and guacamole, he said to Angela, "No pressure."

She smiled half-heartedly. She was finding it hard to say no. She took her plate back to the table and sat down across from Sheila, who looked at her with a frown. "What's wrong?"

Glancing at Will, who was still several feet away, she quietly said, "Later."

Sheila turned for a quick look at Will.

"What's going on?" Ned asked, picking up on the shift in energy, just as Will pulled out a chair and sat down with them.

"They feed us well, that's for sure," Will said.

"True," Ned replied, realizing he wasn't going to get any answers. "So Will, how are you finding the classes? You and I are the only two new people."

"I'm getting the hang of most of it," Will said. "It's a steep learning curve, don't you think?"

Ned agreed, saying, "Martha's been a big help for me. She catches on quickly. I miss having her here."

"I can imagine," Will told him. "What do you hear from her?"

"Nothing," Ned responded. "It's my understanding that she can't be in touch with us right now."

"Why not? Isn't she with Francisco?"

"Who told you that?" Sheila asked, suddenly alert.

"Uh, nobody... I thought that's where she went. Isn't she working with him?"

"We don't know if she's working with him or not," Sheila said. "Aurora hasn't heard anything since Martha left." Ned was quiet.

Angela stood to leave, saying she had a few things to do before the afternoon class. Sheila followed her.

"Angela, I'll stop by your room in five minutes," Will called after them.

Hearing a knock on her office door, Aurora looked up to find Francisco. Surprised to see him, she asked if anything was amiss.

"All's well," he said as he came in. He handed her a bag of oranges from his trees, their fragrance very present, then placed a hawk feather on her desk, which he had found on the way. "I need to check something with you. Do you have a new student?" He sat down.

"We have two. Ned and Will." She studied him. "You wouldn't be here unless something was up."

He told her briefly about Martha's experiences at Xochicalco.

"Students do go there from time to time," she said. "It is a power center. But if Martha felt odd about it, there must be something to that. Let me see what I can find out."

"What do you know about Will?"

"He was sent to me by a friend of a friend. He did some work with another teacher, and wanted hands-on experience in this country. He knew we'd be visiting sacred sites."

Aurora told him that Will had some emotional blocks that needed to be cleared—like several of the others—and they had begun that work. "I feel he can overcome those. That is what we teach, after all. But some people want shortcuts. They don't want to do their own work. With luck, he will see that the only way, and the truest path, is to do your own work. It is the only path to authenticity." She stood up to place the bag of oranges into a bowl, thanking him for bringing them. "We can follow the wayshowers," she continued, "but ultimately the impetus must come from the internal spark that begins to glow and light our way."

She picked up the hawk feather. "Hawk has a keen eye," she said. "I'll watch to see what I can learn."

"Is he practiced in using the portals?"

"No," she said. "As I understand, he needs work with that. Steven is planning to spend some time with him."

"We had a late-night visitor at the house as well," he said.

Aurora eyed him, speaking carefully. "What can you tell me about this?"

"Nothing really. There are always those who wish to be a part of this who haven't been invited. As always, we must work around them. Now I have a request." He told her of the need to build power for Martha's journey. "But please do this without divulging details of when she leaves." Aurora agreed, telling him she would arrange it for later that evening, and Francisco left as inconspicuously as he had come.

Having a few hours at home was something Martha hadn't planned on. The day was overcast, a contrast to the bright sunshine she'd become accustomed to in Mexico. She hoped it would clear up by the time the birthday party started. She let herself into her house, put her backpack on a chair, and turned on the lights in the kitchen and the family room. Noticing that a lightbulb had burned out, she retrieved the ladder in order to replace it. Then she called her friend Liz to see if she wanted to have lunch. It had been a while since Martha had spent time with her.

"You're back in town?" Liz was surprised. "Why don't we take in a movie later? There's a new one I'm dying to see."

"I'm just here for the day," Martha said. "My granddaughter's birthday party is at five but I could do a matinee."

Liking the idea, Liz picked her up at one and they made it to the theater with a few minutes to spare. As Liz filled Martha in on her latest problems, Martha quietly reminded herself that her friend had not experienced the personal and spiritual growth that she had. Liz therefore was still enmeshed in a reality that told her life was problematic. Martha was surprised about the number of problems Liz had—but it occurred to her that they were the same problems Liz had had for years. She complained about them, but she never managed to resolve them.

It took considerable willpower for Martha not to give Liz any advice, but she noticed that Liz hadn't asked for any. Martha began to feel tired just listening, and she remembered what Francisco had said about people who drain your power. She could feel her power draining out—not a good situation. In fact, it was something Francisco had specifically asked her to avoid.

Perhaps she should have avoided Liz. As the lights dimmed and the movie began, Martha politely shushed her friend, who was still talking over the opening credits.

The movie was a romantic comedy about a man who gets a chance to live one week of his life over. There were several magical things that happened in it, one a scene where the man flew. After the movie, as they climbed into her car and headed out of the parking lot, Liz remarked, "Wouldn't it be fun to fly?"

"It is fun," Martha said. "But it wasn't very realistic how they showed it."

"What do you mean? It looked real to me." Liz was confused.

"That's not really the way you fly."

"You sound like an expert," Liz said.

"Not an expert by any means, but I just know that you don't fly like that."

"When have you ever flown?" Liz's question put Martha on the spot.

"I learned how recently," Martha replied. She kept her tone casual.

"You're funny," Liz said with a laugh. "For a minute, I almost believed you." She headed up the hill to Martha's house.

Martha took another tack. "Have you ever wanted to fly?"

"I dreamed once that I flew. It was really fun. It was the best feeling." Liz's expression grew dreamy as she thought about it, and she almost missed the turn to Martha's street.

"What if you could fly like that in real life? Would you want to?"

"It's not possible," Liz insisted. "So let's talk about something else. By the way, Jen isn't doing hair anymore. We've got a new person. You'll hate her."

Martha decided she needed to draw a line. "Hate is a strong word," she said. "Surely there's something positive you can say."

"Look what she did to my hair," Liz complained. "Let's see you put a positive spin on it."

"Your hair looks good," Martha told her. "I was going to ask you who did it."

"You need glasses," Liz replied. "A weed whacker would have done a better job!" She pulled up in front of Martha's house and let her out. "Listen, don't be a stranger. Let's have dinner soon."

Martha waved and went inside, relieved to hear silence. She felt tired but there wasn't time to rest. Instead she cleared her mind of her interaction with Liz, letting go of the frustration and anger that her friend had emitted. She had begun to see Liz in a new light, and she wondered if their friendship would survive. She wished she could take Liz for a flight around the neighborhood. That would open up her horizons. But Liz had been too close-minded to hear.

How often does opportunity pass us by, Martha wondered. *What opportunities had she missed?* She promised herself to notice opportunities when they appeared and to say yes to them. Then she laughed out loud at the idea that she could possibly handle any more opportunities coming her way until after her journey.

She had an hour, just enough time to take a shower and pull on party clothes. She hadn't called Clark yet because she wanted to surprise everyone when she arrived at Melissa's birthday party.

Clark had outdone himself with the decorations. He'd strung fairy lights in the bushes in the backyard, creating a sense of wonder and magic. He'd hung cardboard fairy cutouts from the branches of trees and draped everything with multicolored crepe streamers, all at Melissa's request. Even the deck was festooned with streamers. In the flowerbed, punctuating his efforts, the dahlias bloomed like a sea of colorful fireworks in red, orange, pink, and yellow. Melissa had invited six friends to help her celebrate and they were talking excitedly. There were several presents stacked on a card table. Matthew was helping his dad cook hotdogs on the grill, and Leslie was putting the final touches on the table when Martha arrived.

"Grandma!" Melissa shrieked. "You came to my party!" She ran to give her grandmother a hug, and Martha handed her a present wrapped in pretty paper.

"Wait till you see what it is," Martha said, bending down to kiss her on the head. "But don't shake it."

"Mom, I'm so glad you came," Clark said. "You're never going to believe it, but I baked the cake. I think Ned's coming," he added. "He said he'd try to make it."

As if on cue, Ned appeared, carrying a large, neatly wrapped box. He was shocked to see Martha. "What are you doing here?" he asked, handing the box to Melissa.

"Later," she murmured. "What did you bring?"

They watched Melissa and her friends carry it to the table, where the girls admired this latest gift as they giggled and chattered.

"Starlight," he whispered.

"Starlight!" Martha exclaimed, quickly putting her hand over her mouth and hoping no one had heard her. "I'm missing so much by not being at the school."

Ned explained as much as he knew. "Chaco has been making jars with starlight in them. Melissa can give a star jar to everyone in her class. Wait till you see them."

"What are they for?" Martha asked.

"Nightlights," he said. "But no batteries required. I don't know exactly how they work so don't ask. But they glow in the dark."

"They're magic," Melissa said, reappearing next to her grandmother. She already knew about the gift. "Chaco said so. He told me that a long time ago people came from the stars."

"The star people?" Martha asked. "What did he tell you?"

"You know, Grandma. They were very smart. They taught us everything. Like how to fly. They know a lot. I want to go visit them."

"Maybe someday you can," Martha said.

"Chaco said I can."

"No you can't," Matthew said, butting in on the conversation.

"I can so," Melissa insisted.

Martha knew she had to distract both of them before the discussion escalated, and she did so quickly by sending Matthew to help his dad serve. She told Melissa they would talk more about the stars later. "I want to hear all about what Chaco told you," she told her granddaughter.

When Ned got a moment alone with Martha, he asked in a low voice about what she had been doing. He felt like he couldn't wait another moment to find out.

"Walk me home after the party and I'll tell you all about it," she said as they sat down at the picnic table.

"The food's ready," Clark said, distributing plates to the children first. There were bowls of potato salad and baked beans on the table, and Martha helped herself to both. She complimented Leslie on how nice the party was.

"Clark did most of it," Leslie said. "He's suddenly interested in cooking. It's wonderful. Wait till you see his cake."

"It's strawberry," Melissa said. "I helped."

"I'm looking forward to it," Martha said.

As soon as they were finished eating, Clark went to get the cake. Ned offered to help. Clark put the candles on it while Ned retrieved some plates from the cupboard. "Ned," Clark said, "I've been wanting to ask you something. It sounds crazy, but Melissa mentioned it, and it's been on my mind. It's probably just her imagination—you know how children are—"

He was beating around the bush so much that Ned didn't know what was coming. He wondered if it had to do with Chaco.

"I know it sounds crazy, but she said that my mom made your car fly."

Surprised, Ned wasn't sure what to say. It was just a few weeks ago that Martha had indeed made his car fly, but he'd never told anyone about it and didn't think he should. Yet he also didn't want to make Melissa wrong. He needed to think fast.

The phone rang while he was mulling this over, and when Clark hung up, Ned decided it was best to tell the truth. "It is true," he conceded. "But can you keep it to yourself for the time being? I don't want my sister to know, since it was her car."

Clark was stunned, but he also felt a surge of adrenalin and excitement at the possibility of something so seemingly farfetched, and he wanted to know everything about it. "When? Where? How?"

"There isn't really time to tell you the story now," Ned said. "But soon. I think it would be good for you to hear about it."

Clark was so flabbergasted that he put nearly a dozen candles on the cake instead of six. When Ned pointed this out, he carefully pulled out the extras and smoothed over the holes in the frosting. Just then, Melissa appeared. "Daddy, hurry, we're waiting!"

"I'm on my way," he said. "Go tell everyone."

Turning back to Ned, he said, "You and I are definitely going to talk again soon. I've had a sense that something's going on, and I'd like to know what." Clark lit the candles and headed for the terrace with its twinkling lights. "There are a lot of things that aren't adding up, and you may have the answers."

Ned hoped that he wasn't going to be in trouble with Martha as he followed Clark outside. Melissa beamed with happiness at her cake as the group sang "Happy Birthday." She closed her eyes tight, made a wish, took a big breath, and blew with all her might. Five of the candles went out.

"One left," Clark said. "Blow again."

Her face clouded up. "Now my wish won't come true."

"Blow fast," Clark said, wanting to avoid a tearful scene at her party. "You have a minute to get them all out."

"But I made a wish about grandma."

"Blow!" Clark's voice got louder.

"Blow!" Matthew insisted, echoing his father. "We want cake!"

"But what if my wish doesn't come true?" The first tear ran down her cheek.

"Ten seconds left," Clark said, looking at his watch. "Ten, nine, eight, seven…"

Melissa blew and the last candle went out. Everyone clapped, and at that precise moment, the air was lit with tiny lights. "Fairies!" Melissa exclaimed as everyone looked.

"They might be fireflies," Matthew said.

"Fairies!" Melissa insisted as her friends giggled with delight.

"Oh my," Martha said, staring as she held her breath.

"They're too big to be fireflies," Ned said quietly to Martha.

Then Matthew pulled something out of his back pocket and handed it to Melissa. She held the small stick, decorated with ribbon, in her hand. "I carved it," he said. "It's a fairy wand. Chaco kind of gave me the idea. I waved it twice to test it. I hope that's OK." He studied her with a frown. "Do you like it?"

Melissa ran around the table and gave him a hug. "Thank you very, very much," she exclaimed. "You're the best brother in the world and I love you with my whole heart."

It was a moment of connection that rippled out to touch everyone. Clark put his arm around his wife, who kissed him on the cheek. Ned put his arm around Martha. The little girls hugged each other. Above their heads, the lights twinkled brightly.

"I'd say this is a pretty special birthday," Clark said. He cut the cake and Ned passed the plates around. Matthew ate his without complaint, discovering that strawberry cake wasn't as bad as he imagined. Martha was impressed and told Clark he had done a wonderful job on his first cake. "I even made the frosting," he announced with obvious pride.

Leslie leaned toward her mother-in-law. "Later I'll show you pictures of what the kitchen looked like when he finished," she said. "There was flour everywhere."

"They made a big mess," Matthew added.

"But you have to admit it tastes pretty darn good," Clark said, happy about his efforts.

An hour later, Leslie had taken the children up to bed. Martha was helping Clark clean up. Ned was out in the yard taking down the crepe paper. "Mom, did I ever have imaginary friends? Look at Melissa. She's got a menagerie. I don't remember having them." He loaded the plates in the dishwasher.

"I don't remember that either," she said. "But Melissa's aren't imaginary. Bob the Bear is a real teddy bear." She emptied the leftovers into storage containers and put them in the refrigerator.

"Now that Chaco's around, Bob the Bear doesn't get as much attention." He covered the rest of the cake with aluminum foil. "Melissa swears that the cat talks to her. I kind of wish I'd had a talking cat when I was a kid."

"Don't you think it's wonderful that children live in a world where that is possible?" Martha asked.

"But as adults we know that cats don't talk. At some point she has to grow up. Did you know that Chaco taught her a song, too?"

"Seriously? How does it go?" Martha asked. Clark started to sing the first verse about the jaguar, but he had no sooner begun than the dishes in the cupboards began to rattle. He turned to look. The whole house was shaking. "Are we having an earthquake?" he asked in disbelief. But when he stopped singing it subsided.

Leslie came into the kitchen. "Did you feel that?" she asked.

At almost the same moment Ned came in from outside. "I think we had a small earthquake," he said.

Martha stood very quietly, not believing what had just happened. She looked at her watch. It was time to go. She gathered her things and thanked Leslie and Clark for the lovely evening. She told them she would see them soon and kissed them goodbye. Ned held the door. Heading outside, she fully expected the jaguar to be waiting for her. She knew he was, somewhere. He was stalking her wherever she went, showing up in one way or another. He had appeared in her coffee, he had shown up in the song. Francisco was right, the jaguar had brought her a map. And now she needed to use it. The jaguar was keeping tabs on her until she did. She could feel him, especially in the darkness, walking with her.

Ned wanted to talk. He reminded her that she was going to tell him how things were going. But with the jaguar stalking her, Martha knew there was no more time to delay. She walked quickly. The clouds had cleared. It was a beautiful evening, but the damp Pacific air carried a chill. She told Ned what she was sensing. "So the jaguar is doing that? Things get stranger and stranger, don't they?" he mused.

Martha shivered, buttoning the sweater she had worn over her blouse. Ned put his arm around her and she leaned toward him. "I have to head back," she said. "I'm meeting Francisco."

"I wish you could stay a little bit. One of these days I want to have some time with just you and me."

"That would be nice, but I can't tonight. I promised Francisco I would be there." She hesitated for a minute, then decided to share what she had learned. "Someone is following me. Francisco wants me to leave tonight."

Ned was alarmed. He asked who it was.

"I don't know," she said.

"Then let's go together to the school. At least I can accompany you that far. It's just a short hop from there. I'll feel better knowing you're with me." Then he grew concerned about the fact that she was leaving at night.

"You're not helping," she told him, increasing their already brisk pace.

"But don't you think it's odd to leave at that hour?"

She admitted that she did, but she told him it had to do with timing. "There's an opening tonight that makes it highly possible for me to do this." A lone dog barked from behind a fence as they passed, adding to the tension.

"Do you have any idea how you'll do it?"

She didn't; she was hoping Francisco would help her with that. "Having him involved makes me feel safer," she said. "I can't tell you why, except that he knows so much and can do so much." Then she remembered the latest news. "He's invited us to do a shapeshifting class when I get back," she said as they turned the corner to her house.

"A what? That sounds like something I don't need to know," Ned said. "I'm happy with the shape I have."

"You might really like it," she replied, "if you give it a chance. Look how much you like flying."

"That's true. I'll think about it," he promised. "No guarantees."

Since their houses were adjacent, they arrived home at almost the same moment. Martha went inside to get her backpack and Ned went to collect his. They met in the backyard. She had changed into her jeans and hiking boots.

He had hoped for an opportunity to kiss her, but Martha seemed focused on her journey. "You'll do good," he smiled.

Unexpectedly, Martha leaned over and kissed him. "Thanks for supporting me," she said.

Ned circled his arms around her. "Any time," he whispered. The warmth of her body felt very good next to his.

But just as suddenly she pulled away. "Oh no. This is exactly what Francisco told me not to do."

Ned frowned. "He told you not to hug me?"

"He told me not to get involved in a relationship. It takes away energy that I need for this endeavor." She shook her head. "Tell me I'm not crazy," she said.

Ned was disappointed, but he remembered what Steven had told him: that it wasn't time. Maybe this was what Steven had meant. "I am still a relative newcomer to all this," he said. "But I don't think you are crazy." He smiled again. "Hey, what just happened is our secret. My lips are sealed." Martha smiled, too. She was beginning to see another side of Ned. "And maybe we can continue where we left off when the time is right," he added.

"I'll be in touch," she said.

"Ready when you are." He took her hand and they stepped into the portal to return to the school.

Ned and Martha kissed in the dark courtyard of the school. "Take off your backpack so I can give you a hug," Ned said. After they put their backpacks down on the nearby bench, Ned wrapped his arms around Martha.

Not far away, Will watched from the shadows. His tracking device was working.

"Now I know why Francisco told me not to do this," Martha said, leaning against his warm body. "Oh no, it's nearly nine. I have to go. It's time to dream the world in."

"I want to be part of your dream," Ned told her. He picked up her pack and helped her put it on, then shouldered his.

"Our dream," she said. "Our dream of a new world. You're dreaming, too."

"Our dream," he repeated. "I'll see you soon." He touched his heart with one finger and then pointed at her in a tender way.

She waved goodbye and was gone.

After a wistful minute of wishing he was going with her, Ned headed back to his room. He bumped into Will as he walked away. "Sorry," Ned said. "I didn't see you."

"No problem." Will didn't stop.

Thinking about Martha, Ned wondered how long it would be until he saw her again. He found a note from Angela taped to his door. "Call me when you get back," it said. Wondering what was up, he walked past her room to see if the light was on.

It was. He knocked softly so as not to disturb anyone else, and she came to the door in her pajamas. "I thought you were going to call," she said. "But as long as you're here, come in."

He apologized for dropping in.

"No problem. Listen, I have news. Francisco was here. Roger was walking past the office and happened to overhear him asking about Will." She sat down on her bed and gestured to the chair, where Ned took a seat. "Why do you think he's interested?"

"I don't really know."

"I think we should keep an eye on Will, maybe stake him out." When Ned asked why, she said, "To see what he's up to. He's been keeping to himself and not mixing with the rest of us. Today he wanted me to show him how to use portals, but I hid out in Sheila's room so he couldn't find me."

"I think we should leave it alone. You know what Aurora said. We already got in trouble once." He stood to go.

"What if it involves Martha?" Angela's question stopped Ned cold.

"What do you mean?"

"I don't know. Do you know where Martha is?"

"I just saw her," Ned said. "She was at her granddaughter's birthday party."

Angela's surprise was apparent. "But we gave her a sendoff. I thought she left."

"She did. But you know Martha, she had promised Melissa."

"Where is she now?"

"She…" Ned stopped, remembering what Martha had told him a few minutes earlier and wondering who was trustworthy. After all, he'd seen Angela talking with Will earlier. *What if she was gathering information for him? And why had Will been wandering around just now?*

Angela studied him. "Where did she go?"

Ned shook his head. "I don't know anything I can tell you. Listen, I need to hit the hay. Long day."

"So you're not going to help me?"

"Let me sleep on it," he told her, buying himself some time. Before long Martha would be on her way. He didn't want to tell anyone where she had gone tonight.

He went back to his room, suddenly realizing he felt tired. He reached into his backpack for his toothbrush. But as he rummaged around for it, he found something completely unexpected: a brand new pair of some very feminine underwear. *How in the world had that gotten in his pack?* He upended the pack, dumping the contents on his bed. Out tumbled a lot of things that were not his. He stared at them for almost a minute before he realized they were Martha's. Somehow, he had given Martha his pack when she left instead of hers.

Panic set in. She would need these things and she might not realize she didn't have them until… He didn't want to think about what might happen. No wonder they had both been told not to start a relationship yet. It had already created a problem. He stuffed everything back in the pack and hurried to the portal. He would have to find Martha. He hoped it wasn't too late.

But as he passed through the courtyard, he ran into Steven. "Ned, can you help me get the word out? We're having a ceremony in ten minutes. It's important. We're going to be building power for what Martha is doing."

Ned's stopped in his tracks, torn about what to do. Martha's pack was on his shoulder, but he could hardly turn down Steven's request. Not after all the time Steven had been spending to bring him up to date on his studies.

"Sure, Steven," he said. His heart sank. Thinking he could slip away after the ceremony got underway, he hurried to knock on doors.

That evening Francisco walked out onto the dry land near his house and called in the council of his ancestors. He needed instructions on what he was to do next. The energies were shifting and changing on a daily basis. What he needed to do was also changing. Tonight his council came from the realms beyond earth. Some came from the stars. Some came from places he didn't know about.

The council gave him a clear message. He was not to go with Martha, despite his desire to do so. He thanked them for their message. He had done this work too long to be upset, or to react with any emotion at all. He had surrendered control years earlier. He was here to do what was required to bring about the shift in consciousness. His own desires and wishes were secondary to that, and he knew better than to interfere. In fact, he had something else to do while she was gone. The energies needed to be anchored and held. He would notify the others around the world—in Africa, Asia, Australia, Europe, and the Americas—who were each working in their own way to bring about the shift.

In addition, Cuernavaca and its surroundings needed to be strengthened. This area, long a power center, had had some of its pathways disturbed by development. Aurora and the students would help him with this endeavor.

He looked up at the dark sky, suddenly feeling an energy so strong that it dropped him to his knees.

We are beings of light. We come to assist as you experience an energetic rebirth as powerful as original creation. Know that the heart of humankind must open to aid in accessing the doorway into the higher realms of self-awareness. The power of your hearts is being activated.

As Francisco, prostrate on the ground, rolled over and looked up at the stars, he was gripped by a powerful wave of emotion that opened his heart in a way he had never experienced.

As you open to the coming changes, your true nature shall be revealed and you will be asked to embrace the essence of love within you. You will learn to utilize the gift of your sacred power. This is a time of deep transformation. Indeed, it is the evolution of consciousness as you know it.

Feeling the changes taking place within, Francisco grew still. This was more real than even he had expected.

Be with us, he prayed silently. *Be with us as we put one foot in front of the other and embrace our new selves. Be with us as we emerge new. Infuse us with the power to complete this work that has been so long in coming, and as we transcend our limiting stories and histories and become creators of our destinies. We are ready and willing.*

As he lay on his back on the hard ground, he realized that none of his teachings could take him any further. From here on in, he would need to make it up as he went. The ancestors had brought him to this point. Now they would bid him goodbye as they heralded him into the next world. He was one of the new shamans, being born into a new time. It was up to him and to the others making this transition to know what to do.

Time had gotten slippery. The rules were being rewritten. Everything was changing. The rug was being pulled out from beneath the current structure. All things would realign. When the dust settled, what would it look like? Making his way back to the house, Francisco wondered about all of this. The long-awaited time had finally come.

And it was true what the ancients had said: *we are the ones we are waiting for.*

※ 15 ※

The moon was not yet up when Martha arrived at the ancient city of Xochicalco. And because there was no electricity for lights on the isolated hilltop, the site was deserted and dark. Martha stood quietly and looked around, trying to imagine what the city must have been like hundreds of years ago when it was populated. The night was warm, but the questions that came into her mind made her shiver: *Could this happen to our cities? Could it happen to the town where I live? What makes a place a thriving mecca full of architectural wonders and then reduces it to artifact and rubble?* In the distance, coyotes called, and the sound intensified her feelings of discomfort.

The excitement she felt at being poised to take her promised journey was tempered with the vulnerability of being alone in this powerful place, which still held the energy of times past. Her experience with having seen it come to life made her cautious. At first she stood near the front of the Temple of the Feathered Serpent. With her finger she traced one of the carved quetzal feathers that adorned the serpent, thinking of the beautiful, multicolored feather that had directed her to the Cloud Forest House not all that long ago. The endangered quetzal, so revered in ancient times, was still having an impact, its power passed down—symbolically and tangibly—through the ages. Or maybe its power was being passed down *until* the time when it could have an impact… That idea gave her goosebumps.

She wondered where Francisco was and decided to wander around to look for him. The minute she took a step, he spoke, saying, "Right here." Startled, she swung around. He sounded very close, but she was unable to see him. Her eyes strained in the darkness.

"Ah, right next to you," he said. A moment later he materialized, explaining that he had been waiting in another dimension. "I believe this is the one you will want to use to begin your journey."

"Then you will have to let me know how to get there," she said.

"Your intent is what will propel you. Intent is the basis of manipulating this reality. Our reality is quite malleable. Remember what I told you. Intent is a force in the universe. We line up with it to cocreate."

Martha had learned the basics of how to use intent at the school. It was the way she navigated in the portal system. "So I will intend to move into that dimension?"

"Use your intention to go to your destination. Intention creates direction. Use the map that the jaguar gave you. Follow jaguar through the dimensions."

Francisco seemed like he was barely there. As he spoke, a mist formed around him in the shape of the jaguar. Martha was fascinated to see it, as it seemed to circle him and then disappear into him. She nodded, listening to what he was saying, even if she didn't completely know how it would work for her.

"Also, you will be moved by your will. The will creates momentum. Remember the way I showed you to focus through your power center. You will move your desire through your will and in that way bring it into being." The misty jaguar rose up around him again, then faded. She was unable to tell where it came from, or where it went. It was eerily realistic.

"Direction and momentum," Martha repeated, "using intention and will." She made mental notes, wondering if there was anything else, especially anything more concrete that she could use, like a real map or a guidebook. The coyotes cried again, and fear nibbled at the edge of her courage.

"People fear change more than anything else," Francisco said, looking more luminous than solid. "Yet change is the one guarantee of your growth and evolution into who you wish to be. Learn to embrace change and use it to your advantage."

Martha began to worry about how much change she would face on her adventure.

"Simply be ready to go with whatever shows up," Francisco said. "There are things your mind will not be able to understand. At these times you must trust yourself to do what feels right. You will know. This is powerful energy. Listen to it and use your inner guidance."

She nodded, losing her momentum again. "And you think I should go tonight? I mean, is it night in the other dimensions? I think it would be better to get a good night's sleep and leave during daylight, so I can see." Her nervousness had begun to show. The darkness was getting the best of her.

"There is an opening now," he said. "And the opening calls in the readiness. It is what you have prepared for." He surveyed the area around them as if he were checking something. "Time is running out. You will bring back necessary wisdom."

The words rang in her ears. *Necessary wisdom.* She wondered what she would learn.

Then, lowering his voice, Francisco added something even more profound. "You will encounter Quetzalcoatl. Be prepared for that."

It was one thing to meet him in a dream, Martha thought. It was quite another to meet him for real. All at once she felt like she was in over her head.

Francisco's voice took on an urgency that she had not heard before. "You must leave before the serpent coils." He gestured at the carved reliefs on the wall behind them, and the mist of the jaguar swirled. "If the serpent coils to strike, it will be too late. We cannot wait that long. You are new to this and you do not yet realize how momentous this is. But for the keepers—those of us who have passed this information down for hundreds and hundreds of years—this is as big as the pyramids themselves. It is monumental. The reason we have preserved the ancient wisdom traditions is for this very moment." He gestured broadly with his hands, as if cradling the world in them.

"The serpent already struck me once," Martha said.

Francisco drew back as if he himself had been struck. "Then now is the time. Quickly."

Suddenly overwhelmed, Martha's courage flagged. Trepidation took hold. "Are you sure you can't go with me, at least part of the way?" she asked. Her heart sounded like a drum in her chest, and her knees grew weak. She felt woozy and light-headed.

"What is your most courageous dream?" he asked. The energy of his words revived her, and Martha remembered her purpose. "This is what you must follow. It is your internal compass. Can you feel it?"

Martha nodded.

"You are where you need to be," he told her. "And when you are ready, you will simply let go."

With that he disappeared.

Martha was stunned. *Let go?* She felt like she had been pushed off a cliff. She was in freefall, and her anger flared. It was not at all what she had expected. At the very least, she had anticipated being sent off with an invocation or a prayer, as he called on his powers to clear the way.

"I thought you were going to go with me," she called after him, but her words found nothing but emptiness. He had vanished, leaving her quite alone. Not even the mist of the jaguar remained.

Martha stood in the darkness in a state of disbelief. She had no idea which way to turn. She looked around uneasily, not feeling safe. She had not pictured this. She had thought her travels would occur during the daytime when she could count on natural light to show her the lay of the land. At no point had she envisioned being alone in the middle of nowhere in pitch-blackness. *What if the ancient city came to life again?* It gave her the willies to think about it. *Where was Francisco when she needed him?*

She began to panic. She had no idea what to do, and the more she focused on her fear, the more panicked she became, until sheer fright spread through her veins like hot liquid. All she could think about was her predicament. *Why did she agree to do this? How could she possibly succeed? What if she never returned?* She was walking in circles, her mind playing like a broken record of failure scenarios. As much as she had learned, she still felt like she really didn't know very much at all—certainly not enough to do what she was supposed to do. Her heart was racing and she wanted to scream for help.

After a few minutes, she remembered to use the calming techniques she had learned. Slowly she accepted the fact that she couldn't rely on someone else to take care of her or make decisions. She was on her own, the one thing she had most feared. Even though she felt like she was adrift in a small boat on a dark lake, she still needed to row. Her very survival was at stake.

Because she knew what her fear was, she wanted to face it. She wanted to feel comfortable being on her own, even if it wasn't by choice. But as much as she pretended to be OK, she didn't feel safe. This had been a problem for many years, and it made her overly cautious. Simply put, she wanted to feel safe navigating the world without having to worry about or second-guess every situation. She had always held back out of fear. *How freeing it would be not to do that!*

She followed that thought, realizing that this was her opportunity. For once and for all, she could part company with fear and embrace adventure. She had been given the opportunity for a reason. It was time to stop asking why she was chosen and instead go forth into the unknown. It was time to trust her internal guidance and native wisdom.

She shook off some of her shakiness, but the panic hunkered in her chest. She acknowledged it like a familiar friend, remaining present with the feeling of wanting to run, taking slow, deep breaths. Even with her mind insisting *this will never work*, she stayed her course.

After a few moments, the fear dissipated, and she experienced an enormous sense of relief. Just as Aurora had told her, embracing it instead of fighting it or trying to flee helped—and she was happy she had remembered to do that.

Taking a deep breath, she felt more clear-headed and confident. One by one, she began to go through the steps that would launch her journey.

I have everything I need, she reminded herself. *I am ready to—*

Not far away, she heard something move. Turning quickly she saw nothing, but in the darkness her eyes played tricks on her. The longer she stared at something, the more it seemed to be moving. It was as if everything had come to life, creating a world of shifting shadows. She heard another sound from another direction and turned toward that. Once again, panic set in, filling her mind with fearful possibilities as she imagined things that weren't there. This time she took charge more quickly.

Quietly she shouldered her backpack, knowing she had packed it carefully. It was growing late, and even though she would have been quite happy to crawl into a comfortable bed to sleep, she pushed those thoughts aside. *I'm going for it,* she thought. *Francisco's right, I am ready.*

The scream sent her over the edge. It was a hair-raising animal scream as primal as any she'd ever heard, and she froze in her steps. Then, trying to make herself invisible, she flattened her body against the wall of the temple. She held her breath and listened keenly, not wanting to move or draw attention to her position.

As she racked her brain for what could have emitted the eerie scream, it slowly dawned on her. *Jaguar!*

Only the jaguar could have made such an unearthly sound, which seemed to have been amplified by the darkness as well as the structures surrounding her. As she calmed herself enough to think clearly, she realized the sound had come from the area of the ballcourt below.

The primordial scream had awakened a primal instinct, and she moved toward it.

Its echo spread in waves through the depths of her soul, rousing within her something that was both ancient and ancestral.

It pulled her as powerfully as a magnetic force. It was irresistible and she moved almost against her will. But after a moment she realized it was her will propelling her. This was the direction of her intent. She could feel it. She was responding to a call to action, and the call was familiar. In her mind a random thought surfaced. *What if she was walking into the jaws of a live jaguar?*

Cautiously she moved closer still, and the closer she got the more her courage grew. She was finally embracing her fear of accomplishing—solo—a feat of such magnitude. She was emerging into a possibility she had never yet investigated. She felt triumphant, and the feeling bordered on invincible.

It was something she had not felt in a long time. It converted her sense of purpose into movement, and she strode across the ground, moving toward the evolutionary call of a new timeline.

As the ceremony to build power got underway, Ned knew his only opportunity was to act quickly. Students were milling about as Steven and Roger built the fire. Ned moved into the shadows at the far end by the portal. He realized he was using this portal by himself for the first time, but his options were limited. He knew that Martha needed her backpack. It was time to put inexperience aside.

With one more glance around, he stepped into the portal, repeating the name of the site, Xochicalco, under his breath. A moment later, he was there, and he was so surprised that he laughed out loud. But almost immediately he grew quiet in order to get his bearings. He had to find Martha.

His heart sank as he realized he didn't have a flashlight; it was in his pack, which Martha had. He wished for the bright, reflective face of the moon. Instead, an immense sea of stars twinkled overhead, silhouetting the temple and creating a ghostly landscape. He shivered.

Because he couldn't see well in the dark, he strained to hear. He thought about calling Martha's name, but then decided against it. *She could be anywhere.* He began to feel his way over the rough terrain. It made sense to move to the highest vantage point in order to survey the site. It was deathly quiet, and there was no sound other than the slight scuffing of his feet on the ground. He sent out a telepathic message, hoping Martha would hear. *Martha, where are you?* He waited, but the silence was so deafening it roared in his ears.

He focused on his task. Martha had talked to him about the method she had learned for making things happen. It had to do with thinking about what he wanted. He wished he had paid more attention, but it was not something he had believed in at the time. *Where was she?* At the top of the hill, he stopped to catch his breath because he was not used to the altitude.

This was where he had been the other night with Angela, when they were lost. Now, even though he knew where he was, he still felt lost. His actions were not creating the results that he wanted. Once again, he was spinning his wheels. He might as well be driving uphill on snow-covered streets for as much progress as he was making. He thought briefly of his hometown, St. Paul, Minnesota, where right now it was the height of summer and the grass probably needed mowing again.

Ned had retired recently from a fulfilling career as an engineer and he had always considered himself capable and hardworking, willing to do whatever the job required. It was one of the keys to his success. But on this deserted hilltop in central Mexico he faced a conundrum. He didn't know what to do. He was unable to rely on any of the skills he had used in his life to achieve competence. It was a helpless and uncomfortable feeling. He was a beginner again, yet it was unfamiliar to be in that position and to not know where to turn. His skill set for this particular work was not where it needed to be. Perhaps he should have consulted with Steven.

He searched for several minutes, growing more and more frantic and forcing himself to move even more quickly over the ground. At first he was optimistic about finding Martha, but he gradually decided that he was clutching at straws. He sent one more message, this one slightly desperate. *Martha! Where are you?*

His feeling of desperation grew, along with a sense of guilt. It was his fault that Martha didn't have her backpack. Without meaning to, he had jeopardized her journey. He dreaded explaining that to the others. He wrestled with what to do. He had already been in trouble for his adventure with Angela. He couldn't risk further repercussions. Yet at the same time he felt great concern about Martha.

After a few more minutes, Ned gave up and decided it was time to head back to the school. As he turned to leave something caught his eye, and he bent over to pick it up. It was a smooth stone, carved in the shape of a donut. He couldn't make out the details in the dark, but he put it in his pocket to look at later.

As he turned to go, he heard footsteps. Certain that he had found Martha, Ned stepped around the corner of a temple, just as someone moved around the far end of it. Ned quietly followed, and at the next corner he saw no one, so he turned to go the other way.

Scarcely breathing, he hurried along the wall. Then he waited, listening. Again he heard movement, and this time it was coming toward him! He stepped out from behind the temple and ran smack into Will. *Will had been following him!*

There was a moment of confusion as things got sorted out. They were both startled, but as recognition set in, the questions started.

"What are you doing here?" Ned asked.

But Will, equally surprised to see him, wanted to know the same thing. "What are *you* doing? I thought you were..." He stopped, not wanting to implicate himself by saying Martha's name.

"This place is closed," Ned told him, reluctant to show his hand about why he was there.

"I know it's closed," Will said, his voice edgy. "Otherwise there would be lights and people." They had reached a stalemate. Ned kicked the ground as Will eyed him closely. "You must be doing something if you brought a backpack."

"I could say the same thing," Ned said.

Will was disappointed as he realized he was tracking the wrong person. For whatever reason, it appeared that Ned had Martha's backpack. *Was Martha nearby?*

Ned wanted to keep an eye on him. "Were you following Martha?" he asked.

"Was she here?" Will glanced around as he realized that she had been here.

"I'm going to head back," Ned said. He wanted to get back before the ceremony ended.

"Me, too. After you."

Ned looked around one last time, ruing the fact that he hadn't found Martha. Evidently she'd gone. And although he wanted to know why Will was there, he didn't push. After all, he didn't know Will's motive, and they were in a desolate place.

The two headed back together, keeping an eye on each other but also silently relieved to have companionship.

The ceremony at the school was well underway when Will and Ned returned. They slipped into the group and were quickly caught up in the rhythmic energy fueled by a steady drumbeat. The students were singing a song designed to give Martha power on her journey. They stood two or three deep in a circle around the fire. Over and over they sang the words and the energy continued to build until it was palpable. Feeling it, some of Ned's worry lifted. He joined in the singing and began swaying with the others. Their voices were steady and strong. The energy grew around them. The flames of the fire flared and Ned imagined the power from the group going out, making its way—as he had been unable to do alone—to Martha. After a few minutes, he sensed that it was really happening, and he sang with all his heart.

With a growing sense of confidence, Martha had begun to follow the jaguar. She couldn't see it, but she moved toward the lone primal scream. And while even that was just a memory at this point, the leftover resonance inside her created a pathway of energy that she was able to follow. There was no physical trail. What she was tracking was the ancient memory that had been awakened inside her.

She noticed the energy of support building around her. Momentarily she thought of the ceremony being held at the school and wondered if that was what she was feeling. She began to walk in a rhythmic way, and sing a song to herself, a song she had learned at the school. Her heart expanded and she felt stronger. It felt like the others were with her.

She came alive in a new way. The memory that had awakened created a sense of balance within her. Her own instincts aligned with the vibration she was feeling. She became the jaguar. Her feet padded over the ground, which felt familiar, and her movements were fluid and supple. Down onto the ballcourt she went, padding on the dark turf with a sense of recognition. She went across and over and down the hill into the wild land as if she had done this many times. Surefootedly, she followed the jaguar.

She had a sense of coming home. It was a feeling that was somewhere between joy and peace. The closer she got, the stronger it became. *I am moving toward my center,* she thought, *into the heart of everything that is.* By focusing on that, she moved more deeply into it. For a moment she felt like she was turning inside out. There was a strong tugging at her chest, but it passed.

She had crossed into a dream, yet she was awake. In the dream landscape, she moved easily, without worrying about the dark. In the east, a light came up. At first she thought it was the moon, but it was the sun. With more light, she was able to see where she was going. She was in a rugged, fairly dry terrain much like what she had been in earlier. She had no idea if she was going in the right direction, but she continued to follow the magnetic pull that drew her. In the distance she saw buildings, perhaps a small town, and she grew excited, thinking perhaps she could stop and rest. She would also be able to find out where she was, from whoever was there. But after a while she realized it was a mirage.

For a time she loped, and then she let a fast trot carry her down an open hill. She recognized this land.

This is the map of the jaguar, she thought, without realizing how she knew that. It was the map Francisco had described. He had told her that it contained everything she needed. After a time she came to a spring bubbling up out of the ground. She took a drink and decided to rest.

She was surprised the sun was coming up. It was disorienting to be moving into daylight when she thought it was the middle of the night. She looked at her watch, but it had stopped working at nine o'clock.

Briefly, she thought of Ned, who popped into her head. It made her wonder what he was doing, so she sent him a telepathic greeting. For a couple of moments she wished that she could communicate with him and the others at the school. But she quickly returned to the business at hand, knowing it was important to stay present and connected. She did not want to get lost in a daydream.

The energy that had pulled her this far had faded, and she wondered which direction she needed to go. She moved first into the south, but she seemed to be retracing things she had already passed. She remembered what Francisco had said, that south was the direction of the past, of looking at where she had been. Turning west, she immediately saw the jaguar not far ahead. She ducked instinctively behind a rock. This was the closest she had been to it. Francisco had given her no instruction on what to do if she suddenly found herself this close. She took a deep breath and then ever so slowly, in order to see what it was doing, she leaned out to check on the cat. The jaguar was staring right at her.

16

Everyone, it seems, wanted to learn to fly. The other students, having heard about Martha's expertise, asked Olivia when she would teach them.

"The best time to learn," Olivia said, "is when you are ready. At that moment it becomes nearly impossible not to fly."

"But can you teach us?" Sheila asked.

"I can teach you, and whoever's ready will learn. Unfortunately we can't speed up the process."

Under his breath Roger, whose ability was still overshadowed by his pessimistic worldview, said, "I knew it. I will never master flying."

Sheila, sitting at the other side of the room, leaned forward in her chair, eager. "How do we know when we are ready?"

"You will recognize your readiness," Olivia told them, "when you begin to feel an undeniable sense of lightness, as if you are about to lift off."

Sheila felt shivers up her spine, and she grew giddy. "I've had that feeling," she announced. "A few days ago, I had an overpowering feeling that I was about to float away. It felt great! But at the time, I had some work to do, so I focused on my work instead."

"We'll start with you then," Olivia told her.

Sheila was shocked. She looked at the others in disbelief. Excited, the students stood up to go outside, but Olivia did not want to risk any mishaps. "It is best to do this indoors," she said, "until you learn to control the flight." She explained to them that they might accidentally get hung up in a tree, land on someone's roof, collide with a moving vehicle, or drift further than intended. "Any of these are possible when you are learning. One of the most important things Martha did was to learn indoors, and then to practice indoors," she added.

Roger groaned, looking very uncomfortable. "I don't think I will try flying," he said. "I don't like heights. With my luck, I would drift off and end up on Mt. Popo." Several of the students laughed uneasily at the idea that this was possible.

"Use your personal discretion," Olivia told them. "Some of you may not be ready. It is an advanced skill."

But Sheila was eager. "How do I start?" she asked.

"First, I'd like all of you to move to the perimeter of the room with your chair," Olivia said, "to give us some room. Next, please observe quietly, without talking or making noise, so as not to distract the person learning." She instructed Sheila to stand in the center of the room. "Remain as calm as you can," she told her. "Relax and breathe normally. Now close your eyes and focus. You will know when you are ready when you feel very, very light. That's good. You've got it."

Olivia moved around Sheila, making movements with her hands. Sheila lifted ever so slightly off the ground. "Open your eyes," Olivia instructed, "but remain calm. Staying calm is perhaps the most important part."

As she opened her eyes, Sheila immediately put her arms up for balance. Then she began to grasp for something to hold onto, creating a flapping motion so common to beginners. She began to lose her balance, and in a split second she was hanging sideways in the air. In an unfamiliar element, she was like a fish out of water.

The room went dead silent. But Roger, unable to contain his concern in the face of what he was witnessing, shouted, "Somebody catch her!" Then he leapt into action, grabbing hold of Sheila in the way a teacher might support a child learning to swim, with his arms under her torso. She was so startled she grabbed hold, wrapping herself around him sideways. They went down in a heap.

Olivia stepped forward to help them up. They were a tangle of arms and legs, but fortunately neither of them was hurt.

"Whew! That was close," Roger said, finally getting to his feet. "It was lucky that I jumped in to help when I did."

But when all the faces turned to him with expressions of surprise, he clapped his hand over his mouth. He realized that what he thought was a heroic gesture had made matters worse. Not only that, but he had disrupted Sheila's trial flight right at the moment she became airborne.

Olivia took him aside and spoke quietly. "Roger, would you feel more comfortable waiting outside?" Her tone bore no judgment. "Sometimes it takes a while to adapt to a new idea such as this. You are welcome to watch through the window."

Flustered, Roger quickly promised not to interfere again. "I totally want to learn this," he said. "I will follow your instructions one hundred percent. I won't perform any more rescues." With his thumb and forefinger, he made a zipping motion over his lips, and then he locked his arms together over his chest suggesting that would make him unable to interfere with anyone else's flight.

Sensing that Roger had learned something important, Olivia agreed. "All right then," she said, nodding. "Let's begin again."

Sheila knew what to expect this time, and she was able to remain calm and not flail her arms. As she began to float, Olivia explained how to control her direction by thinking where she wanted to go. "You can also use your body to determine direction," she said. "In the beginning, just float. We won't use any speed."

Sheila drifted around the room, hardly believing she was in the air. She wanted to shout with joy. But instead she focused on not running into anyone. This was especially tricky at corners, when she needed to make corrections in her direction and consciously choose to turn. This involved a new way of thinking about body movement. She made three circles around the room before Olivia helped her land.

"That was unbelievable," she said when her feet touched the floor. "It's better than anything I've ever done." She was wide-eyed and euphoric.

"Do you feel like you have a sense of how to do it?" Olivia asked.

"I hope so," Sheila told her. "Because I can't wait to try it again."

"Practice the process indoors a few times until it comes naturally to you and until you can control what you are doing. When you're ready, we will practice outdoors." Sheila couldn't even imagine what that would be like.

"No one is to leave the school grounds flying," Olivia told them, sensing their impatience to practice. "We have a convenient location here, but it means that we must be considerate of our neighbors. We can't be upsetting them by flying over their houses. We also cannot jeopardize what we teach here by being irresponsible. And I don't have to remind you, I hope, that we are close to the central plaza, which is often full of people."

They all agreed to this. For the next two hours, everyone got a turn, even Roger, who was able to leave the ground for 30 seconds before he erupted in laughter and couldn't continue. Afterwards he sat in a chair in the corner, so overcome with glee that all he could do was giggle. When Olivia asked him if there was anything he needed, he just shook his head. Then he erupted again in uncontrollable giggling.

Ned found it hard to focus. He kept thinking about Martha and the fact that she didn't have her backpack.

"Ned?" Ned looked up and found Olivia looking at him. It was his turn. "You're a million miles away," she said. "What's up?"

"Sorry," he said. "I was thinking about Martha." He seemed worried.

"Why don't you talk with me after class," Olivia suggested. "But first the business at hand. Martha has taken you flying, hasn't she?"

Ned nodded. "When I first met her. It just happened," he said, thinking about the unbelievable flight he made with her above the river.

"Yes, she had just learned, as I recall. You must have been astonished."

"I was flabbergasted." His eyebrows went up as he remembered his surprise. "I didn't believe it was possible. But suddenly there I was, airborne and holding on for dear life." He paused and his head drooped. "But because of me, we didn't get very far."

"Well, let's get you activated. I suspect you want to be able to keep up with Martha. She certainly isn't one to wait around for anyone."

Ned was caught off-guard by the sudden sensation of lightness that came over him, and the next thing he knew he was drifting past Sheila, who gave him a thumbs up.

"Turn," Olivia called as he approached a corner. But because he wasn't focused, he ran smack into the wall. He hung there for a moment, until Olivia pulled him away. "Remember to think about where you're going," she reminded him. "It's like riding a bike. You're in charge of direction." Ned handled the next corner well, managing a turn. After a couple more passes around the room, he landed next to Roger.

"Isn't it great?" was all Roger could get out before he giggled again.

A few minutes later, Ned stayed behind while the others headed off for lunch. Olivia came over and sat next to him. "Is there something you want to share?" she asked.

Ned hesitated, as he still wasn't ready to share what had happened.

"When you're ready," she told him, sensing his angst. "And feel free to speak to the person you are comfortable with—Steven, Aurora, or myself." She looked over at the open window, noticing the voices coming through of the others enjoying lunch. "You must be hungry," she said. "I won't keep you. But if I may say one thing—you must release Martha from whatever it is that you are holding onto. This will only interfere with the work she is doing. It doesn't really matter what it is, as long as you let it go."

"Do you think she's OK?" Ned asked, letting his insecurity get the best of him.

"I do," Olivia said. "It's important to believe that and to hold it in your heart. You will be helping her in that way." She gently waved a fly away. "Our power building ceremony last night was very powerful, by the way. Did you feel that?"

Ned, put on the spot, looked away. "Yes, although I had to leave for a few minutes," he said, sensing she already knew that. But she didn't press him.

"There's always a lot going on at these sessions," she said. "Far more than we can keep track of." She smiled. "Level 1's especially," she noted, "are practically bouncing off the walls wanting to try their new skills. They are drawn to real-world practice. And because that is part of the learning curve, Aurora and Steven and I tend to stand back."

Hoping to escape, Ned stood up to leave. "The flying was great. I can't wait to practice," he said.

But the guilt he was harboring was apparent to Olivia, and she brought it up because it needed to be handled. "Why don't you eat some lunch and then Aurora and I will help you release it. Guilt is something that slows our progress. It serves no useful purpose on this path, so the sooner it can be released, the better. It will interfere with your new skills," she added.

Ned agreed and left. He looked at the others, who were laughing and talking amongst themselves. Roger was flapping his arms, obviously recounting the story of his brief flight. For one moment, Ned wished he could feel as lighthearted as they did. He turned and went to his room.

Sitting on his bed, holding Martha's backpack, he wondered what he could do to get it to her. There had to be something.

Suddenly Chaco jumped through his open window and onto his bed.

Ned didn't know if it was his imagination or if he had just heard Chaco speak. But he had heard something, and he was almost certain that it was the cat. This was a first for Ned, and he didn't quite know what to do. He stared at Chaco.

¡Ay-yay-yay! Chaco flicked his tail. *Yes, you heard me. I'll handle it.*

Ned shook his head in disbelief.

¡Ay caramba! Chaco stared back impassively. *"I'm not here to waste time. Do you want to do this or not?*

Ned watched the cat's mouth, which never moved. Still, he had somehow heard what Chaco had said, and he decided to go with it.

"It's heavy," Ned told him, not quite believing that he was having a conversation with a cat. It made him giddy to realize that this was what Martha had experienced, too. But at that time, he hadn't understood it.

¡Ay-yay-yay! I'm not going to carry it. Chaco sat on the bed and began to clean his face. He had just had lunch with the others.

"But how will you—" Ned didn't even get the question out before a surprising gust of wind hit him in the face, taking his breath away. The papers on the nightstand blew across the room and the oil painting of Mt. Popo hanging on the wall rattled ominously. The paperback book he had been reading earlier dropped to the floor with a thud. Ned immediately grew serious. "All right. If you can somehow teach Martha's granddaughter Spanish, you can certainly handle this. It's just that I have never…you know…worked with a cat…" Not sure how to relinquish control, Ned maintained his hold on the backpack. "I'm not sure about the logistics."

The second blast of wind almost flattened him. It toppled the nightstand, blew the pillows off the bed, and left the painting dangling at a precarious angle. Straightening his shirt, Ned pulled himself together and made a quick decision. He put the backpack on the bed next to Chaco. "Here. It's all yours." He stood up to leave before Chaco could call in a full-blown tornado. With one last look at the cat sitting next to the backpack, he walked out.

Seconds later, remembering his manners, he turned back to say thank you, but when he poked his head in the room, Chaco was gone. Ned walked in and looked around. There was no sign of the backpack either. Shaking his head, he straightened the room.

Then, realizing that his appetite had come back, he went to join the others, who had vanished. Suspecting they had all walked to the central plaza, he filled a plate with food and sat down at one of the tables to eat. He checked his watch. It wasn't time for the afternoon class. He still had almost a half hour. He allowed himself to feel a sense of relief and even happiness because Chaco had apparently taken the backpack to Martha.

Reaching into his pocket Ned pulled out the item he had found the night before at Xochicalco. It was the first time he had looked at it in the light of day. Brushing the dirt off, he turned it over in his hand. It was a yellow stone about two inches wide, carved into the shape of a small donut. He wondered if he should turn it in to the museum.

He was holding it when Aurora passed by on her way to the afternoon class. She stopped abruptly. "Where did you find that?"

"I—uh—found it—uh…" Ned wanted to avoid giving her the details, but before he could finish, Aurora asked if she could look at it. He handed it to her. As she studied it, a strange look came over her face.

"Where?" she asked again in her calm but compelling way.

This time Ned answered without hesitation. "Xochicalco," he said, offering his idea that it might be a relic.

"It's far more than that," she said.

"I was going to turn it in," Ned told her.

"It is important that it gets to the current keeper as soon as possible."

Ned was intrigued. "Do you know what it is?"

Aurora sat down across from Ned at the table, and he was struck by the power of her presence now that she was so close. He had never noticed this before. "You are growing in awareness," she told him. Her eyes sparkled as she thought about how often her students surprised her. "That is the reason you were able to find this, especially at night."

Ned, who hadn't yet mentioned finding it at night, felt an odd sensation in his body. It was a mixture of excitement and trepidation. He was now associating with people who knew the truth, even if it wasn't spoken. "How did this come into your possession?" Aurora asked. "I imagine there is an interesting story."

With a sinking heart, Ned began to talk, finally revealing the details of what had taken place. Aurora listened without interrupting. Finally, when he was done, Ned asked what she meant by the current keeper.

"Martha hasn't told you?"

He shook his head no. "I've only known Martha about as long as you have," he explained. "But I do know that she is in my life for a reason, and I felt a connection to her from the get-go." He shook his head again, this time slowly as a sign of not quite believing what was happening. "It just keeps getting more and more interesting."

"I gave Martha an amulet when she first found me in the Cloud Forest House several weeks ago. But part of it was missing. It has been missing for a very long time," she murmured, turning the small piece over in her hand.

"And this is it? How do you know?" Ned felt a sense of excitement take hold.

"I can feel it," she told him. "Eventually you will recognize the feeling you get when you know something is true. You will simply know it. It will be very clear. There will be no doubt." Her message was so vivid that Ned understood what she meant at a visceral level. "That is the same recognition that I have now with this piece I am holding…. The world of energy is alive."

"So this belongs to Martha?" Ned was astonished. "But she's never seen it? What does it do?" His curiosity getting the best of him, he reconsidered his futile attempt to return the backpack. It appeared that something unexpected and good had come from it.

"Here's what I can tell you," Aurora said. "Information used to be encoded into amulets, much like the way we put music on a disk nowadays. The information would activate or be downloaded when the person touched the amulet. The one that Martha has works with the current keeper to maintain the lineage of the ancient arts. It is also involved in keeping them new. We are using the information we were given long ago, but new information is also coming through all the time. The process is never static."

"I see." Ned frowned, suddenly worried again. "So how can we get it to Martha? She must need it."

"I don't know," Aurora said. "All I can say is, there is a reason *you* found it."

Now Ned felt truly puzzled.

"We need to put this in a safe place." Aurora stood. "Will you trust me with it?"

"Of course," Ned said. "But I'd like to keep it for one more night, now that I know what it is." He folded his hand around the piece when Aurora handed it back to him, already concocting a plan. There *was* a reason he had found it.

He headed back to his room. He had about ten minutes before class started. Lately, he'd been wondering if his own powers had been growing along with his awareness. The classes had helped him begin to see the world in a new way. And he needed to finally test himself.

He hadn't done anything this radical since he was an engineering student, and his excitement surged.

During class, he found it hard to focus. But because he thought Aurora might get wind of his plan telepathically, he put it out of his head. He didn't want to be stopped. So he listened while she talked about the upcoming transition and what it meant for all of them. "We are anticipating that this will happen soon," she said.

It meant that very soon the things that they had been practicing would become the way they lived. "You won't even recognize yourselves after these changes," Aurora told them.

After class Ned went directly to his room. He told the others he was going to skip going to dinner, prompting Sheila to offer to bring him some takeout. She could see he felt a sense of urgency to take care of something, and she wondered what it was. He had been unusually quiet all afternoon. "Do you need any help?" she asked. But he declined her offer.

All he said before he waved her off was, "Just some business I have to attend to." Eager to begin, he went to his room and closed the door, making sure it latched. He moved quickly to where he had hidden the yellow stone. He pulled it out and put it in his pocket, then exited his room and went to the portal in the courtyard.

The air was thick with the scent of flowers he couldn't identify. He spotted an interesting beetle on the adobe wall, but he didn't take time for a closer look. Instead, he glanced around. As he had hoped, everyone else had gone to dinner. He was alone, and he had two hours to carry out the plan he had formulated. He pulled out the stone and held it in one hand. "Let's do it," he said just as a truck backfired in the street. Startled, he turned toward the sound, losing his concentration for a brief second. That's when it happened. What should have been a normal portal experience was something else entirely.

Ned was practically knocked off his feet by the acceleration. He had not expected that, and he instantly wondered if he had made a mistake. But there wasn't time to worry. He held onto the stone with all his might. It reminded him of the time he and Martha had accidentally driven off the road high above the river, and the car had plunged downward, crashing through the branches of trees. He had held onto the steering wheel for dear life until there was silence. For a moment he wondered if the car was caught in the treetops, and then they discovered it was floating high above the ground. Somehow Martha had been able to make the car fly, saving their lives in an exhilarating way.

Ned felt out of control like that now, but he had nothing to hold onto but the stone. He was not sure where he was headed. Everything was a blur. He was moving so fast he couldn't tell what was up from what was down. It took his breath away. He had never even imagined something like this was possible. He saw a jaguar. He saw Martha. He saw a vast expanse of arid land punctuated by brush and outcroppings of stone. The images were surreal. He wished he could control what was happening to him.

Like an intense, vivid dream, the experience ended abruptly. Ned screeched to a stop and found himself in the courtyard of the school. He had no idea how long he had been gone. Blinking rapidly, he tried to understand what had just taken place. He felt winded and weak in the knees, but very relieved to be back.

But his relief was replaced with shock when he discovered that he no longer held the stone. Crying out "No!" he dropped to his hands and knees to look for it, but his search turned up nothing.

He had wanted to help Martha. He had also wanted to prove that he was capable in the unseen realms. He had failed on both accounts. Silently, he began to beat himself up, even questioning why he had come to the school. *Was it just to be around Martha? Maybe he didn't belong here.* As doubt took hold, he momentarily forgot what Steven had told him about doubt, that it could ruin everything if he let it in.

"Ned?"

Glancing over his shoulder, Ned saw Sheila, standing just a few feet away, holding some takeout food. There was a quizzical expression on her face.

"Did you lose something?" She came over next to him as he stood up.

"I lost a stone that I found," he said. "It was for Martha." He brushed himself off as he continued to scan the ground.

"It must have been important. You look like you're in shock."

"Very important," he said. He rubbed his face with his hands, trying to restore his equilibrium.

Sheila helped him look for the piece for a few minutes, but when they couldn't find it she suggested they eat. "I have to tell you what happened. We can look again after dinner."

Ned, still trying to process his experience as well as the repercussions it might have, was lost in thought.

"This food smells really good," Sheila added, more to herself than to him. He followed her to the tables on the portico by the pool, patting his pockets with his hands, still hoping to find the stone. He didn't feel hungry, but he sat down, hoping that going through the motions would restore a feeling of normalcy.

"This is called *comidas corridas*," she said, pulling out some traditional Mexican foods as she practiced her Spanish. "I hope you like zucchini flower soup and tortillas."

Inhaling the aromas, Ned realized he was hungry. He poured two glasses of water. "I want to get your take on what happened," Sheila said, relaying what had taken place a short time earlier in the central plaza when she and the others went to eat: A small, dark-haired woman had approached them with a prophecy that had given Roger a sense of foreboding.

"What was it?" Ned was not paying much attention but he wanted to be polite.

"She said the teaching inside the stone is being awakened. She said it in Spanish, but Roger translated. Do you think it means something?"

Ned asked her to repeat it and then frowned. "What stone did she mean?"

Sheila fretted. "We don't know…. What was the stone that you lost?"

"Just a stone for Martha," he said. "She wouldn't be talking about that." But he wondered. *Could she possibly be referring to that stone?* He had to admit that the timing was uncanny.

They ate for a few minutes without much conversation except for commenting a couple of times on how delicious the food was. Ned, who was trying to formulate another plan, also thought about how everything seemed to be coalescing. *Maybe converging was a better word.* He asked Sheila if she had noticed.

"I can definitely feel it," she said. "It feels like everything is coming together. It's like Aurora said in the first class. We would all have a piece of the puzzle. All of our paths are heading to the same place. We're each contributing something unique."

Martha locked eyes for several seconds with the jaguar, during which time neither of them moved. She had leaned out from behind a rock to catch a glimpse of it, not expecting it to be so close—and certainly not expecting it to be looking directly at her.

Its beauty was remarkable. The gold eyes were liquid suns. The dappled coat was sleek and thick, rich orange spangled with black stars. It was grace and serenity packed into a muscular frame. The jaguar was placid, having perfected two arts: stillness and waiting. There was neither hurry nor fear. Martha hesitated to move. She wanted to stroke the fine fur. She wanted to speak to it as she spoke to Chaco. But this was a jaguar, she reminded herself. Its paws were enormous, and she could only imagine the claws. She knew the animal was not only strong, but extremely fast and agile.

She thought about pulling back as slowly as she had moved forward. She wished to simply disappear out of its viewing range. But the cat would still be aware of her scent as well as any sounds that she made.

Since her choices were limited, she began a slow-motion retreat. She held her breath, picturing what she wanted—to follow the jaguar to her destination at a safe distance. She hadn't considered that she would get this close to it. *Perhaps she was tracking faster than she had realized, or maybe her destination was nearby. Was that why the jaguar had stopped?* All of these things went through her mind.

As she pulled back, something caught her eye. It was a round stone lying in front of her. It was so unusual that she bent to pick it up, forgetting momentarily about her situation. Unbelievably, it was the stone she had seen in her dream.

She held it, wondering where it had come from and how it had happened to end up here, seemingly in the middle of nowhere. She tried to remember what she had known about it in her dream.

And then the jaguar leapt.

17

Popocatepetl, the majestic snow-capped volcanic mountain east of Cuernavaca that towered over the Valley of Mexico, rumbled to life early in the morning, spewing a plume of vapor and ash that could be seen for miles. As word spread through the school, there was quickly talk of this being evidence of the impending shift. "This is exactly what we heard would happen," Sheila told Angela and Ned as they arrived at breakfast on the covered terrace by the pool. She felt unnerved by the proximity of the 18,000-foot peak.

"It is spooky to have it so close," Angela agreed. "I hope we don't get an earthquake." She fidgeted with her fork as Aurora explained to the group that the energetic shifts were making them all feel jittery.

"There may be other energetic disruptions on the face of the earth," Aurora continued. "There may be earthquakes and volcanic activity. But just know that we have been doing the inner work in order to prepare for change, no matter how it manifests in our physical realm. These changes, especially the ones happening inside of us as we shed the old paradigms that haven't worked, are all bringing us into the new energy and helping us to make the quantum leap. There is immense energy flowing in now, and we have to open ourselves to connecting with who we truly are. We have to open ourselves to remembering why we are here. We came to be a part of this shift. This is an opportunity such as we have never seen."

Steven began to talk about the mountain. Popocatepetl was as an active volcano with a long recorded history of eruptions. Its name, given to it by the Aztecs, meant "smoking mountain." Most people called it by its affectionate nickname, Popo, which belied the immense power stored beneath it in the depths of the earth. "The ash clouds from eruptions can obscure the sun and make breathing difficult," Steven said. "But the wind is moving it away from us today."

As they ate scrambled eggs and *bolillos* and slices of melon, Aurora explained that Popo was a force to be reckoned with, but cautioned them all to be calm. "You are the wayshowers, those who are paving the way for others to follow in your stead. Your courage, your determination, and your trust in your abilities have brought you to the precipice of this new reality. We will all be going through change, but it is important to stay centered and to not let fear get the upper hand."

"How far is Popo from here?" Roger asked. "Are we in danger?"

Steven reassured him that they were safe. "It's about forty miles. But we could get rained on with ash, depending on the wind. We need to be aware of the potential."

Before they went to the morning class, Aurora added one more piece of information: "Remember to remain grounded. As the new energy comes in, you will feel it moving in through your crown chakra. The energy and light will fill you, and then you will notice it expanding around you. The most important and powerful work that you can do right now is to anchor the new light into your bodies and into the earth."

As she stood up to leave, Roger asked Aurora about the comment the woman in the central plaza had made to them, that the dream within the stone was being awakened. "Does that mean something?" He shared that it made him feel uncomfortable.

A look of concern came over Aurora's face. "When did this happen?"

"Last night," Roger said. Seeing her expression, he was convinced that the prophetic message was not good.

But after a moment Aurora's countenance changed. "We haven't talked about this yet. I guess now is a good time, since apparently it is happening." There was hushed silence around her and everyone waited in anticipation of what she would say. But it was something unexpected.

"I know I have told you that you have been our most challenging group thus far." She smiled, looking around at all of them. "But you are also the most rewarding because you are willing to move at the brisk pace that is required of late." Several students exchanged knowing glances, and Roger looked at Sheila with raised eyebrows. "I think these go hand in hand," Aurora continued, "and I thank you for your willingness to move quickly." Chaco appeared and sat down at one side of the group in a sunny spot. He closed his eyes but his ears were cocked. He was clearly paying attention, too.

"Now we are going to begin to put into use everything you have learned," Aurora said. Several students murmured, wondering exactly what this meant. "It means the pace will get even faster, but I know you are prepared."

Roger felt lightheaded. He leaned back in his chair. Every time he had a sense of catching up, he was faced with another quantum leap. "Oh dear," he said quietly to Angela. To him, the others seemed to have a sense of mastery, but he wondered if he would ever feel confident about this work.

"Ages ago," Aurora continued, now making reference to the prophecy, "information was encoded in the stones at sacred spots so that it could be preserved. The vibration of the earth was dropping at that time, and it was essential that this wisdom was not lost. It was said that the wisdom would become available to us at some point in the future, when the vibration of the earth began to rise, and when the vibration of humanity would rise with it. That is what has been happening for the past several years, and we have come to the point where this information has become available." She paused. "Martha has gone to bring this back to us."

"Have you heard from her yet?" Sheila asked.

Aurora shook her head. "No, but we didn't expect to hear anything until she returned. This message that you were given tells us that she will be returning soon. It is wonderful confirmation of everything that we know. It tells us that everything is on schedule."

Roger wondered if there had ever been any dropouts from the program. He decided to ask Steven privately. The stress of the day's events was taking its toll.

All morning the students checked on the status of Popo, which smoldered in the distance, while they wondered if there would be more activity. No one mentioned Martha, but everyone was thinking about her. No one knew what would happen next.

In the morning class Aurora talked more about what was going on, telling them that the earth was experiencing potent bursts of solar activity that were bringing new energy and information to them in the form of light. "We're undergoing a lot of change," she said. "Most of you are noticing this in the form of physical symptoms. Our bodies are being rewired for this shift. It has to be done little by little to allow us to have time to adjust. But it is an intense process, and I encourage all of you to take it easy. Don't feel you have to push yourselves too hard."

"Is that why I've been feeling tired?" Sheila asked.

"Yes, it's common to experience fatigue, as well as strange aches and pains. You may feel like you can't focus very well on what we're doing. You may not be able to sleep. Just be kind to yourselves." She looked around the room before continuing.

"At the same time," she said, "there isn't time to dawdle. We are in the midst of an evolutionary leap and it is going to happen relatively quickly."

Roger took a deep breath to steady himself. "What if we don't get this part of it right?" he asked.

"I have a lot of faith in what we can accomplish," Aurora answered. "We are being divinely guided, and there are many beings watching over us. We need only do our part. All of you, by being here, are doing your part. The work that we are doing will help others to make this shift as well."

Integrity was crucial, she said. "If we are going to manifest the vision that we have for this world, if we are going to fulfill our soul purpose, and if we are going to create authentic lives for ourselves, then we must act with integrity. Our thoughts, our actions, and our words need to be aligned. What is going on inside must match what takes place outside." She asked them all to take a moment to consider this.

"It is important to mean what you say," she went on. "If you say or do things that are out of alignment with what you believe, you will feel uncomfortable. You may even feel angry or upset with yourself, and be tempted to project this onto someone else."

She surveyed the room to see if they had questions. "You will be ineffective if your thoughts go one way and your actions go another. It is important to live from the place of alignment. When you are aligned, you will see your ability to cocreate with source energy and with each other grow."

When there were no questions, she continued. "We also talked, in the first class, about how each one of you has a piece of the puzzle. I know you've been thinking about this. This piece, which you hold, is your unique gift. It is why you are here and it is what you came to share. As we transform, we become authentic so that we can bring our gifts to the world. This cycle is supporting people in doing that. Each gift is a piece of the puzzle, or a strand in the fabric of the universe. Each strand is essential, and each gift must be given to the world. In the past we may have been reluctant to share our gift because we were afraid of being judged. So we held back. But now is the time. You will begin to feel the importance of sharing your gift."

Roger turned to Sheila and shrugged. "I don't know what my gift is," he said. "I really don't."

"Maybe it's your willingness to learn," Sheila suggested. "You have overcome a lot of resistance since you started these classes. Maybe you're supposed to share how you did that."

He shook his head. "I wish I knew."

As the morning class ended, Aurora announced there would be a surprise in the afternoon class. Momentarily everyone forgot about Popo; they turned to each other with questioning glances. *What was the surprise?* Ned's wish was that it had something to do with Martha, but he didn't want to get his hopes up. "We'll meet in the courtyard after lunch," Aurora told them.

As the students stood up, the room began vibrating. The water in the pool outside the classroom began to slosh. Sheila, who was still seated, felt her chair shaking. The jaguar mask, which hung in the back of the room, rattled against the wall, and Aurora looked at it, hearing a message that she didn't share.

For a few stunned seconds, everyone tried to make sense of what was happening.

Aurora's voice confirmed the worst. "It's an earthquake. Everyone outside," she instructed. They filed out as quickly as possible and assembled in the courtyard away from any walls. The shaking continued for about two minutes. Olivia hurried over to join them as soon as it stopped. Everyone was accounted for except for Steven.

"Where is he?" Sheila asked. "Shall we look for him?"

But Aurora told her Steven was away from the school, taking care of some business.

"Do you think he's safe?"

"I hope so," Aurora said. "I believe we will hear from him soon."

Ned put his arm around Angela, who was close to tears. "I've never been in an earthquake," she said. "That was so scary."

Olivia and Aurora began a quick check of the school to discover if there was any damage. The gardener joined them. Everything appeared to be fine, except that the phones were out. Will reported that he couldn't get a signal with his cell phone and several of the others discovered the same thing.

An aftershock rattled the doors. Aurora told them to stay in the open courtyard until everything settled down. "We can have lunch," she said. "But don't go to your rooms yet."

They picked at their food. Angela wondered out loud about Martha. "Let's assume she's alright," Sheila said. "For all we know, she didn't even feel this. I mean we have no idea where she is, right?"

After about forty-five minutes the gardener came to say that the television was reporting there was some damage in Mexico City. The earthquake had registered 6.8 on the Richter scale. He brought his small television set out to the courtyard and plugged it in with an extension cord and the students gathered around to watch the live news reports. The gardener went out to the street to survey the neighborhood, but came back several minutes later to say there was no noticeable damage in that area. He'd spoken with a delivery truck driver who said the main road into the capital was closed.

The television reported that telephones were out and that several buildings in Mexico City had collapsed. Rescue efforts were underway. But details were sketchy and there was lots of mayhem and misinformation.

Noticing that the students were growing more anxious, Aurora asked that the television be turned off, saying that there was much to do. After warning them that there could be more aftershocks, she gave them permission to go to their rooms if they needed anything. "We'll assemble in the courtyard in ten minutes," she said. She and Olivia disappeared into the office.

"We've long suspected that these kinds of things would begin to occur," Olivia said a few moments later, in the privacy of the office. "But it feels disconcerting." She sat down in a chair and looked at her friend. The two had known each other for several years. Olivia had studied with Aurora and then been hired to teach at the school. But they had yet to go through a major challenge.

"Let's hope that this is an isolated incident," Aurora replied, sliding into the chair behind her desk. "You and I have to remain calm, no matter what. The students are still new to some of these practices, and they will need our support."

"But we don't know what it will be like to go through the shift. This has never been done." Olivia put her hands over her face, closed her eyes, and took a deep breath, as if she needed a moment to regain her center.

Aurora could see that she was worried. "It's true, we don't know. But at this point, the transition is already underway. Our only option is to go through it. And for my part, I am excited about this. I believe I am here now specifically to be a part of this, and to help others with moving through it. I believe that's why you're here, too."

Olivia pulled herself together, shaking off the doubt that had momentarily taken hold. "You're right. I know that's true. It's just that, for a minute, I began to lose my momentum and my…trust in the process."

Aurora frowned. "It should feel very natural at this point. Are you saying it doesn't?"

"I'm not sure," Olivia admitted. "But it's been a long time since I've felt any doubt."

Aurora considered what to do. She counted on Olivia's steadfastness and breadth of experience, as well as her wisdom and courage. She knew that if Olivia's confidence flagged, the students would pick up on it.

"Perhaps you should stay in the office," she suggested.

"I'm feeling better," Olivia said. "I just needed to regain my spiritual equilibrium."

"Are you sure?"

Olivia nodded, but as she and Aurora stood to go out to the courtyard, she wasn't completely sure. She was sensing something that made her uneasy, but she didn't know what it was.

"We have to remember," Aurora said, "that Martha will be back at any moment. I believe that she will have the missing piece."

But what if she didn't, Olivia wondered. *What then?*

Five minutes later, everyone was clustered in the courtyard. They were on edge, knocked off balance by what had transpired during the morning.

Olivia spoke first. "As the energetic floodgates of this transformation open," she said, "there will be much shifting and re-arranging in the physical world and in our physical, emotional, mental, and spiritual bodies. There may be some turmoil. We must be prepared for change. Whatever is not in harmony with your heart cannot be ignored. This impacts everything you do, from your relationships to your work. We must allow our life situations to transform. Just know that as we open to this experience, we are all being supported and guided." She knew that she was talking as much to herself as them.

Aurora, sensing this, took over. Her own awareness was heightened, and it made her calmer than normal. "We had planned a surprise. We are postponing that until we can assess the extent of what has happened. We would like to spend the afternoon answering your questions and practicing what we will need to do. We have been teaching you all the basics of the ancient wisdom in order to prepare you for moments such as the one at hand. I welcome this opportunity to test everyone's readiness."

Because the students were so rattled, Aurora needed to shift them into a more effective state. She reminded them to connect to their power centers, and one by one she assessed them to see that they were able to do this. Both Roger and Angela needed help.

"We learned about this as Level 1's," she reminded them. "You power center is located in the area of your third chakra. I want you to consciously move your focus from your head to your power center. Because in your heads, you are simply accessing old patterns of worry and helplessness." She instructed them to sense from their power centers and asked them what they could feel.

"More calm," Sheila said. "Definitely less worried."

"I want you to remember what we are doing," Aurora said, backtracking because she sensed they had not heard her the first time. "We are studying the ancient ways in order to create the new world. What we are going through is what we have been working toward." Several students nodded in affirmation. "We'd like to answer any questions you have at this point, in order to put you at ease and to make sure you are comfortable with everything you have learned."

Roger's hand shot up in the air. "What if—?"

Aurora stopped him in mid-question. "We won't be dealing with what-if questions because those are asked from a place of fear. You will need to rephrase what you are asking."

Roger thought for a moment. "I guess it's starting to hit home what all of this means. There's a reason I came to the school, and that was to learn about shamanic ways. I feel like I have grown and changed. But can you give us some feedback about…how we look to you. Do we look ready?"

"That's a much better question, because you are asking from a place of balance and perspective. You know you have changed, and you want to know how much. How many of you can tell how much Roger has changed?" Aurora asked.

The students answered her question with applause. Roger smiled to see all the support. "That really makes me feel good," he said, turning to acknowledge those around him. "Thank you."

Aurora continued. "As we learn the ancient arts, it sets in motion a process of personal growth. The ancient arts were designed to make us grow emotionally and spiritually, to shake us awake, and to move us out of our so-called comfort zones, which actually aren't very comfortable. But most importantly, they were designed to create a connection with Spirit. The connection with Spirit is something our soul longs for and remembers. By connecting, we discover that Spirit is alive and well within us. Once you know that, you are ready." Aurora looked at Roger to see if that answered his question.

"I've felt the connection for brief moments," Roger said. "But it hasn't lasted."

"Those brief moments are important," Aurora said. "That's how it starts. Gradually you will begin to have a more general sense of the connection. You will feel how much a part of you it really is."

Roger cocked his head and narrowed his eyes. "In the meantime," he said, "do I look ready?"

"You do," Aurora said. "But you may not know you are ready until the moment you step into action. We can spend a long time preparing, just to make sure everything we think we need is in place, but at some point, we need to move to action. At that moment, you will be surprised to see how things click into place. It is miraculous really, how beautifully it works. When you step into action, what you need arises the moment you need it. And that is something you will discover when it happens to you. You can't learn it. But once you try it, you will realize you have that ability."

Sheila raised her hand. "I feel like I am right at that point. That captures it exactly. I hadn't put it into words yet."

"What sometimes happens," Aurora said, "is that we keep one foot in the old world while we put one foot in the new world. We don't quite trust that everything will work when we make the leap, so we are hedging our bets. It means there is still some fear of letting go, some concern of how everything is going to manifest in your life. That keeps you straddling two spaces rather than moving fully into your new direction."

"I feel like I've made the decision in the deepest part of me to move forward," Sheila said. "But it does feel like I am moving into the unknown, and that maybe not everyone is ready for that. Perhaps I will be there alone."

"We're all headed in the same direction," Aurora said. "You may be surprised that when you come fully into the new space that there are others there as well. Remember to focus on what brings you happiness, what brings you joy. And also, remember to breathe in that essence of who you are, because you know who you are. You know how strong and focused and centered you can be."

Angela was next. "I feel like I am still having to deal with some negative people," she said.

"Everyone is in the process of evolving," Aurora said. "We can choose whether to spend time with those who feel negative to us and we can choose whether we let them determine how we feel. It is important to remember that you can release your own feelings when they are negative. In other words, if you notice that you are feeling negative about something, change that. Let the negativity go. Begin to think of something else. Distract yourself with something fun. Learn what thoughts make you feel good. For instance, thinking about ways you are blessed will help. These can be simple things. You might feel blessed because the sun is shining, or because you have beautiful vegetables to cook for your evening meal, or because a flower has a wonderful fragrance. These are the ways the natural world shares its beauty, and if we open to it, we will see how fortunate we are to experience this. The more you focus on what you enjoy, as opposed to what you don't enjoy, the better you will feel."

"I see that," Angela said. "That's very helpful."

"Make it a part of your practice to enjoy things," Aurora said. "Eventually you will find you are doing it quite naturally."

As they wrapped up their session, Aurora mentioned Martha again. "We do not know when Martha will be back but we must be as prepared as possible when she arrives," Aurora continued. "She is the messenger who will bring us the missing pieces. The more prepared we are, the more we can be ready to move into what she shows us."

"But still no word?" Sheila asked.

"No," Aurora conceded. "But the minute we do hear something, we'll share that with you." She did not mention to them what she and Olivia had recently discussed, that there was a possibility that Martha might choose not to come back once she experienced her personal transformation. They had known that was possible, but they decided to keep it to themselves. It was uncharted territory, and they were all learning as they went.

As they headed out of the courtyard, the ground shook with a new tremor. Angela grabbed hold of Will, and as she did, an envelope fell out of his back pocket. Will didn't notice. Ned, walking behind him, bent to pick it up so that he could hand it back. But the words written on it caught his eye. In the confusion, no one noticed that he put the envelope in his own pocket. A minute later, having moved away from the others, he pulled it out to look at it more carefully. Written in pen on the outside of the small envelope were the words "Martha info."

Ned felt his heart stop. Then anger flashed, but he quickly realized that anger would not be much help to him. He glanced over his shoulder. The others were still milling about and talking, and Will was talking to Angela. Ned opened the envelope. Inside was a piece of folded paper. His heart was racing as he pulled it out. He stared at it for several seconds, not believing what he saw.

The sheet held Martha's personal information—including her home address and cell phone number. Someone had written, "Here is what we know. We are tracking her cell phone with GPS.

Enclosed is tracking device." *Why did Will have this? Had something happened to Martha? Should he tell Aurora? Or handle it himself?*

All these questions raced through his mind as Ned mulled over what to do. He put the envelope in his pocket, staring at Will. He wished he hadn't given Chaco the backpack to take to Martha. Will probably had put the tracking device on it.

A moment later, Aurora announced that the surprise had arrived. The door to the office opened, and Steven walked out with Mary Bole. As the students gathered around, he introduced everyone. He had gone to England, he told them, to bring her to visit the school. They welcomed her warmly, as they had all heard the story of Martha's portal mishap that ended in an unintended visit to Mary's farm. They knew Angela had tried to bring Mary to the school as well. And they knew that Mary wanted to come to the school because of Martha.

"I wish Martha was here," Ned said. "I know she would enjoy seeing you." He tried to keep an eye on Ned through the corner of his eye.

"I heard a little about what she's doing," Mary replied. Looking around with a mixture of trepidation and excitement, she was eager to have a tour.

"Mary will just be here tonight," Steven said. "This is her introduction." As Sheila and Angela took Mary by the arm and began to show her around, Steven asked Roger to fill him in on the earthquake. Will headed to his room.

Aurora knew it was important to get the stone from Ned for safekeeping. Pulling him aside she asked him quietly to bring it to her. "It's very important that it's safe," she said. "Can you bring it to the office before dinner?"

Ned nodded. As she walked away he realized he would have to come clean and tell her he lost it. But first, he wanted to know what Will was up to. He had decided to follow him to find out.

When Will slipped out of the school a short time later and headed for the central plaza, Ned did, too. He stayed far enough behind to not cause suspicion, but he had to hurry to keep up.

Ned ran a few paces as Will turned the corner, but by the time Ned arrived at the corner, Will had vanished. There were several people on foot, but no sign of Will. *Had he gone into one of these buildings?*

As it turned out, Will had gotten into a car. He ducked down as Ned went by, then started the car and pulled out. He had Martha's cell phone, which he had found in Ned's room. That meant, of course, that Martha had Ned's phone. He planned to call her using her own phone, hoping she would think it was Ned.

☷ 18 ☷

When the jaguar leapt, Martha's life flashed before her eyes. It was a spontaneous, visceral response, well beyond her control. While the cat's beautiful, outstretched body appeared to go into suspended animation, Martha's history on the planet went into fast-forward. She saw the events of her life clearly, yet she watched from an altered state. Gratefully, she was not afraid. Instead, she felt at peace. A calm came over her. It was like watching a movie on a big screen. Everything was crystal clear. She was not in her body, which gave her a sense of objectivity.

As her life review approached the present, Martha saw herself being rapidly transformed. She witnessed the evolution on a holographic diagram. In the center was her physical body. Around that was her mental body, then her emotional body, and finally her spiritual body. Changes were taking place in every field. She observed the fact that she was a product of what she believed. She was shown that the beliefs were held in her cells. As the beliefs changed, the subatomic particles making up her cellular structure changed. Bit by bit, her density gave way and she began to radiate light. All this happened within the blink of an eye, until Martha was looking at someone very new, someone she didn't recognize. *So this is what it feels like to die,* she thought. She was relieved that she hadn't experienced any pain.

When the process finished, she saw her own beauty for the first time. It shimmered like hundreds of candles, leaving her in awe. *How had she never seen this before?* She stared at herself as if she were a fragrant rose in full bloom, because she had never seen herself objectively. For several seconds, she simply soaked it in, absorbing its essence. Her heart opened with love, the kind of tender, caring love she had given others but never herself.

She experienced what it felt like to love herself. *How beautiful to be the recipient of self-love and to appreciate the beauty of her essence.*

She was relieved as well to be free of the worries she had carried for so long within her. Not in any rush, she waited, idly wondering if she would receive instructions about what to do. She was back in her body, but in her mind's eye she held the image of her beautiful new being, so full of light it sparkled. *What would happen next?*

She had always known what to do when she was alive. She followed all the rules she had been taught. That meant being responsible, working hard, and nurturing her family and friends. She kept appointments, volunteered her time, and remembered birthdays. And when she didn't know what to do, she cleaned the house or worked in the garden until she had clarity. But here, there was no furniture to dust or weeds to pull. In fact, there was nothing for her to *do*—all she could do was *be*....

It occurred to her that someone might come for her, and she looked around in anticipation. But as she did so, it dawned on her that she was still alive. She looked at her hands, then her feet, and she moved her body this way and that to make sure that everything worked. I am alive, she thought. *Really, truly alive!* She actually felt more alive than ever before.

And then she noticed the jaguar had vanished. She had no idea where it had gone but it didn't seem to matter. She still needed a moment to adjust to her very new self. She was definitely changed, and she pulsed with a vibrant energy. She was almost giddy due to the feeling that resulted from the weight of her past having been cleared. It was hard to believe she had carried that with her for so long. Guilt over things not done or not done right, shame over supposed inadequacies, anger at injustice, it was all gone. While she remembered the facts of her life, the emotions associated with them had been released. The incorrect assumptions she had made about people and events were released. Judgments were replaced with simple facts, and she was left with an immense feeling of relief. Her heart felt expanded and warm.

She noticed that she felt blessed by those same life experiences. Though some of them had been extremely challenging, they were the chariot that had brought her to the present moment in a fluid and judicious way. With the benefit of hindsight, everything made perfect sense, which astonished her as she considered it. She felt a new harmony with everything around her. She was as pristine as a meadow of wildflowers that had grown up out of the decaying undergrowth. She found herself reluctant to leave this spot, in case her past would come sweeping back. But it didn't.

She looked at the rock she was standing behind, feeling a strong connection to it. The connection extended to take in the bush next to the rock and the ground beneath her and the sky above. Everything was beautiful and alive. She felt intimately connected to all of it, with no sense of separation. There wasn't any difference between her and each of these things. We are the same, she thought. *I am made of air and mineral and water, sparked by the same force that gives life to all.*

She had entered a state of absolute contentment. She looked around her as if she were seeing the world for the first time. The sky was bluer than blue and the sparkles and spidery cracks on the rock were beautiful. She soaked it all in, bit by bit, wondering why she had been oblivious to this before. A window on the world had opened, showing her a very new view. There were flowers on the bush and she breathed in their delicate fragrance. A hummingbird flew up, stopping just inches from her face as its wings whirred. As she felt the vibration, joy surged through her.

She was as happy and complete as she had ever felt. There was nothing she needed. *Was it really this simple?* She allowed herself to marvel. *This was heaven on earth.* All she needed to do was enjoy it.

Martha forgot about finding the Lost City. It no longer seemed important. She also stopped thinking about how she would get back. There was no rush. She wanted to enjoy being where she was for as long as she possibly could.

And then she remembered what Aurora had told her. They would be transitioning from doing to being. They would focus less on what they accomplished and more on experiencing what was happening. They would notice the birds singing and the shapes of the passing clouds and the song of the wind in the grasses and trees, like children. They would experience the beauty that surrounded them, the living artwork of the natural world as well as their own creative power as they brought into being what they thought about. These words floated into her consciousness as if from another reality. *This was what Aurora was talking about.* It suddenly hit home and she understood what Aurora meant.

Realizing she needed to know more about her surroundings than what she could see from where she stood, the idea of an aerial survey popped into her mind.

A moment later she became eagle. She found herself soaring over the spot where she had just been standing. The jaguar rested in the shade. She surveyed the area, making wide, effortless circles.

Beneath her, to the east, was a jungle of trees. Rising up out of the canopy she saw a stone structure. She flew closer to investigate, discovering a pyramid nearly covered by vegetation. She dropped down for a better view, landing carefully on the top. From this vantage point she could see more clearly. There were other structures below, and she began to navigate down the steps. They were so narrow she had to walk sideways.

She was startled when her cell phone ring, because she had purposely turned it off before she left. Midway down the stairs, she stopped to fumble in her backpack. Pulling the phone out, she was puzzled to see that the call was from herself. *How could that be?* By the time she answered, there was no one there. The phone seemed different, but perhaps it was because she was in an altered state. She stared at it for a few seconds, but for some reason she had forgotten how to make a call. She turned it off and put it away, deciding instead to sit and eat a sandwich. Eating would help to ground her. As she went to open the pack, she noticed that the small silver hummingbird that Ned had put on the zipper was missing. Dismayed that she lost it, she reached in the pack for her lunch.

That was when she discovered that the items in the pack were not hers. One by one she pulled them out, piling them beside her on the step. There was a flashlight, a compass, a small battery-operated radio, a change of clothes, and a kit with toiletry items. And they all belonged to Ned. Recalling her last interaction with him, it slowly dawned on her what had happened. Ned had handed her the wrong backpack.

Unfortunately, that meant she had no food. But as she put things back in the pack, she found two energy bars in the side pocket, the same ones she had given Ned for an emergency. She also found a ham sandwich. She wasn't fond of ham, but she hungrily ate it and then devoured half of one of the energy bars. The rest she saved for later. She opened a bottle of water and drank some of it.

She realized she had no clean clothes to change into. Ned's were too large, but they would have to do. She was surprised that she wasn't upset; instead, holding up his blue jeans, she was overcome with hilarity. There must be a reason this had happened. For the life of her, she couldn't imagine what it was. But at some point perhaps it would be clear. Or maybe not. She realized it really didn't matter.

Then it dawned on her that the phone call had been from Ned, because he obviously had her phone from her backpack. This made her laugh all over again. Her clothes wouldn't begin to fit him, although he had the option of going to the store to purchase what he needed. But there wasn't time to worry about this latest snafu. At least he had packed a new toothbrush.

Shouldering the pack, she continued her descent. The site was overgrown but intact, and stepping back from the pyramid she had descended, she realized it was shaped like an enormous seated jaguar. It had to be the Temple of the Jaguar, which Francisco had described to her. That meant she had found what she was looking for. She had followed the jaguar to the Lost City.

She had lost all sense of time and seemed to be moving in and out of dimensions. That was also something she couldn't worry about. In the past she had been a great worrier. But both Aurora and Francisco had helped her to see the futility of that. Worry changed nothing, and it made her feel powerless. It was better to be present with whatever she was doing.

Despite being alone in a remote location, she was enjoying the experience. She had to admit, if she thought of this as an adventure vacation, it was amazing. She could never have arranged a trip like this through her travel agent. Or even through the Internet. For years she had envisioned a vacation in Mexico, but she had not imagined something this remarkable.

Of course, it wasn't a vacation. She had work to do. She had promises to keep. She had not forgotten about that part of it. But part of her was musing about something entirely new: the idea of not going back.

It shocked her when she first thought of it. *What if she stayed?*

She wasn't even sure why the idea came to her but it did. She noticed that ideas were drifting into her consciousness that didn't seem to be her ideas. They seemed instead to be part of the intuitive process, ideas that were being given to her via the guidance system that Aurora and Francisco often talked about. She had an overwhelming sense that if she decided to stay, everything she needed would come to her. She could begin to live a simpler life.

Her surroundings were lush. Wandering around she discovered a banana tree, and she plucked a ripe banana from a huge bunch that was mostly green. A bit later she discovered a spring that fed a fountain. Exploring without thinking about a schedule, she felt as if she had stepped outside of time, and thus had all the time in the world. For whatever reason, there didn't appear to be any inhabitants of this paradise.

Her next discovery was an avocado tree. She picked a beautiful avocado and put it in her pack for dinner.

She began to wonder about the information she was supposed to take back to the school. If this actually was the Lost City, and she was certain it was, then somewhere there was information for her. She didn't have a clue about how to go about finding it. No one had given her any instructions about what to look for. For some reason, she had assumed that whatever she needed in terms of information would be given to her. So far, that had been the case.

She couldn't remember the details of her dream, and she didn't have her journal to look it up. There was nothing to do but look around, she decided.

She knew it would be smart to explore as much as possible before it got dark so that she wouldn't have to use the flashlight any more than necessary. She began a cursory inspection of the buildings. The site was smaller than Xochicalco, although it was hard to tell the full extent of it, given how overgrown it was. *Where were her answers?*

When she turned on the phone to see what time it was, she saw that she had a message. Or maybe it was a message for Ned. In any event, there was no way for her to check it, as she didn't know Ned's password. She turned the phone off and put it away. As soon as she did, she realized she had forgotten to check the time. *Perhaps it didn't matter.*

She decided to walk around the Temple of the Jaguar. She wondered if the jaguar she had followed was still around, or if it had left now that its work was finished. She certainly would feel better knowing. In the interim, she decided she would sleep at the top of the temple, where she had initially landed, under the stars. It would be safe up there.

Encircling the base of the temple was the stone serpent. Martha kept her distance as she followed it around the base, just in case it decided to come to life. The bas-relief carvings were similar to those she had seen at Xochicalco, and at one point she was tempted to touch them, but she stopped herself. She would do that tomorrow. She turned the first corner, then the second, finally returning to where she had started. The trip around the circumference was uneventful.

For dinner she ate an avocado, a banana, and the rest of the energy bar. She wished she had the nuts that she'd packed in *her* backpack, which Ned had, but she was happy that she had found some fruit.

While it was still light, she prepared her makeshift bed atop the temple. She put Ned's big sweatshirt on for warmth, and she was surprised at how comforting it felt. Overcome with sleepiness, and she fell into a sound sleep before the sun went down.

In the night, as the world turned, a bright star rose. Martha slept dreamlessly as the star climbed higher. When it was overhead, a beacon of light beamed straight down on her, traveling through the donut-shaped stone that she wore around her neck, and into her heart. The beam was highly energized and set up a vibration within her.

Awakened by this, Martha thought at first that she was experiencing an earthquake, but when she put her hands on the huge temple stones beneath her she felt nothing. Placing her hands on the area of her solar plexus, she realized that the vibration was internal. It spread throughout her body in an ever-expanding circle. By the time it reached her throat it had become so strong that she sat up. Ned's phone read three-thirty.

The light streamed into her, and it was so intense she thought she was going to explode. Her cells danced wildly, sparked by the increased vibration. Her internal electric circuitry hummed and buzzed. Wrapping her arms around her, more for comfort than warmth, she stared up at the star, larger and brighter than any of the others around it. It seemed like a spotlight. There were no thoughts in her mind.

Slowly the first light of morning arrived as she sat atop the pyramid. She was still thrumming with energy, which continued to course through her.

She heard someone speak to her, and the voice was materializing not through her ears, but inside her heart. It was beautiful, personal, and familiar, like someone she knew and loved from long ago, from another time. Something within her recognized it. It came from the star, through the light.

The beacon of light streamed down from the sky and into her heart. In fact, as she looked at the light streaming down, she became aware of the connection that had been established. She felt it in her heart, as if a line had been stretched from the star to her heart.

"This is the new earth," she exclaimed, looking around. She knew this deeply within, and she said it over and over, letting the truth of it sink into her cells, to make it familiar. "This is the new earth!" A thrill of excitement went through her, and as it did, she wanted nothing more than something reassuring from her routine world—a cup of tea.

She opened Ned's backpack, looking one more time to see what it contained. She found a small thermos that she hadn't noticed before. She pulled it out and opened it. From the aroma she knew it was Aurora's new blend, the one that wasn't named yet. She decided not to think about how it might have gotten in the backpack. The important thing was, it was still hot, and she poured some into the lid and took a sip. A name floated into her awareness—she would tell Aurora later. She drank a cup as the day dawned.

She felt cradled in a bubble of energy that contained everything she needed. She had a strong sense of being present, not worried about anything from the past or the future. She heard another message: *You live in a state of perfection. Everything you need arises at the moment you need it.* She felt blissful and alive and happy—ever so happy—to be on the earth at this moment in time. "Life is perfect," she said out loud, meaning it.

She was spinning the fiber of a new way of living, and she focused on feeling this more distinctly. Her thoughts were moving out to create what she was thinking about. The tea was a perfect example. She thought about it and it appeared. She wasn't sure how it had happened—that was part of the mystery, Aurora had told them. And it wasn't necessary to know in order to be able to do it. Yet she was reluctant to trust that the new energy was so magical as to provide tea when she wanted it, or whatever else she needed. This went counter to what she had learned growing up. And yet that is what had happened. *Was it possible? Could she believe it?* Francisco had told her this would happen.

The universe was actually conspiring to help her in so many ways, perhaps in all ways, she thought. The enormous restructuring she was going through was making her see the world with a new perspective. She had turned on her own axis to a new vantage point. It was like seeing the back of the moon for the first time, or the earth from a space shuttle. She could feel the power of the shift. It was a momentous occasion, the dawning of an epoch. The cosmic soup had been stirred into action. The old ways of being were being left behind. She could sense the new earth.

She was dreaming like Quetzalcoatl, to bring a new world into being.

Don Francisco's words drifted into her awareness. *You are dreaming the new world. No one knows exactly how this will look. Remain flexible and courageous. Hold love in your heart. Meet the new world with the dream that you have for it. Be the dreamer. Remember, we live in a collaborative universe.*

And then she remembered something he said that had shocked her: *We will be made new, from our head to our toes. We will walk with new bodies on a new earth.*

After a couple of hours she descended the pyramid to determine what else she needed to do. Exploring a bit more, she came to the large stone from her dream. She stood in front of it, scarcely believing her eyes. There was the carved figure of Quetzalcoatl, the one that had unfolded and come to life in her dream. Only this time it was real; she was standing before it in the flesh.

A moment later, Quetzalcoatl stood next to her. "You have come," he said.

She nodded, so struck by his regal presence that she couldn't speak.

"By coming here, by accepting my invitation, you have activated the ancient dormant energies that can now align with the energies from above, from the sun and the stars and the galaxies beyond this galaxy. You are the intersection point, the point where these energies can come together," he said.

The resonance of his words rippled through her.

"By your coming here, so now can the energy of a new time take root and grow. It can feed those who have known there was something more. A new way of being on the earth can begin."

As he spoke she was filled with light. "We usher in a time of love and abundance. We awaken the gifts within each person. Let the rejoicing be heard," he called. "Let the lies and the negativity fall away. Let the eagle and the condor soar." She was soaring, too, on the wind created by his words.

"May all hearts be joined in the rhythm of life. May the earth, who sustains and nourishes us, know that her beauty is deeply appreciated. May all people be blessed by the new ways as the dawn of a new age lights the land. Welcome the day; we have so long waited for it. The earth will rise anew from the dreams of so many."

His prayer carried Martha into the new time. While not many people had arrived yet, they would be coming. They would join her to create communities based on abundance of heart and spirit.

A moment later, Quetzalcoatl folded silently back into the bas-relief. His message had been delivered, and he could retreat to the world of stone that had preserved his essence for so long. The old had been made new, and the way had been paved. The bud of the ancient dream was in bloom.

🎴 19 🎴

Standing next to the Temple of the Jaguar, it dawned on Martha that she had stepped into a self-fulfilling prophecy. Not so long ago, she had come here in her dream. Now she was in the same spot—but in the physical realm—to bring what was needed into the world. Her dream was actualizing as it blended with her reality. The experience was disorienting, because she felt like she had already been through it, but she focused on the work at hand.

She touched the carving of Quetzalcoatl in farewell, knowing that while she would leave the stone representation of him there, she would carry his living message with her in her heart, where it bloomed like a bird of paradise.

The new energy surrounded her like a soft, billowy comforter, its embrace so encompassing that she wanted to stay. *It feels like home,* she thought. And yet it was more than that.

There was an effortless feel to it, like nothing she had encountered before. The longer she stayed in it, the more she liked it. She felt no sense of worry about the future; rather, she had an enormous sense of being present, and during this "presence," she observed that everything took care of itself. It was very different from the measurable, material world that she had been taught was the only reality.

In the old world, there was not much downtime. Everything was based on how much someone did, and there was never enough time to get it all done. It created a never-ending treadmill of duties and obligations.

This new energy felt good, and it made her very happy. She was drinking in the world and being sustained by its beauty. In fact, she was a part of that beauty.

Only one thing was absent—her family and friends. It was clear to her that this energy was meant for sharing and creating community. That was the next step, and she was excited about that opportunity.

Still, the energy of simply "being" as opposed to "doing" overcame her and she found herself sitting and enjoying her surroundings. She watched a small beetle move across the ground. Not far away, a horned lizard sat in the sun. Song sparrows flitted in the nearby grass. Overhead, making high, lazy circles, was a golden eagle. A family of quail ran by, keeping to the cover that camouflaged them. There was a large indigenous population, and at this particular moment she was a part of it.

It was morning at the site, yet there was a timeless, placeless quality to it, as if all the labels had fallen away and what was left was simply the omnipotent pulse of nature. For the first time, Martha felt truly a part of that.

A movement a few yards away caught her eye, and Martha turned to see what it was. At first she was unable to tell, because it had gone into a long shadow cast by a nearby building. Squinting in the bright light, she shielded her eyes with one hand, straining to see.

Sitting in the shaded area was a small animal. When she leaned forward for a better look, it emerged from the shadow and trotted toward her, tail held high.

"Chaco?"

¡Ay-yay-yay! Of course. He seemed ready to kick up some cosmic dust.

She was astonished. "How did you get here?"

I have my ways, just like you.

Martha was so happy to see him that she decided it didn't matter how he had gotten there, even though she was curious. *If he knew the way, why hadn't he shared it?*

He stopped about four feet from her, just out of reach. *We each find our way.*

"Are you saying anyone can find this?" She leaned back against a rock.

It is open to anyone who follows the path to the new time.

Martha felt her head begin to spin. She had become so engrossed in observing the wildlife that she had momentarily forgotten about her journey. *But of course, there were animals here when she arrived,* she thought. *There were plants and trees and insects, the sun and the moon and the stars, just no humans.* As she became aware of this, she also realized she hadn't noticed it before. It made her wonder what else was she missing.

We have always known the way. Chaco sniffed the air, detecting an interesting scent, then sat down nearby.

"That makes sense," she said. "Apparently we humans were the only ones who got off track."

So it seems. He stared intently at something unknown off to the right.

Martha, who saw nothing, sighed.

A long time ago, you knew the way.

It fascinated Martha that Chaco was able to remain fully present and observant of his world, yet also carry on a conversation with her. "How do we find it again?" she asked.

The process is underway.

She studied him. "I have to take the answers back, yet I sense I have not found them all."

They are all here. They are in the stone. They are in the stars. They are in your heart.

His words gave her goosebumps as she remembered what had happened to her already this morning. "We're all being awakened," she said, "simultaneously."

Let the cocreation begin. He stretched out on the dusty ground, as if he had just completed his work.

"That seems to be the key." She wished she could stretch as easily as he did.

You're on the edge.

The hint of a frown formed on Martha's face. "The edge of what?"

¡Ay-yay-yay! Everything. You're embracing the mystery. The pieces are about to fall into place.

It was an electrifying idea, and Martha leaned forward, absorbing this latest information. *As close as she was, she still wasn't there. At what point would it make sense?*

Chaco's eyes were closed as he soaked up the morning sun. *At the moment you surrender to everything that you know.*

She was surprised. "I thought I had done this."

Every...thing.

"I see." She didn't see, but she didn't know what else to say. She was at the end of what she knew to do.

Chaco rolled over, taking a dust bath, as Martha sent a silent prayer skyward, surrendering and asking for help. It was easy for him, she thought. He didn't have to undo an ingrained, unwieldy, and unsustainable belief system and figure out a new way of being. He didn't have the pressure of telling everyone what he had found.

And then, in her mind she saw a picture of what was coming. It flashed in front of her eyes in a visceral way. The graphic image was very real, and it had answered her prayer. Instantaneously, like a lightbulb turning on, it came to her what she needed to do.

She rummaged through the backpack for pen and paper, jotting down some notes so as not to forget, and holding in her mind's eye for as long as possible the image of what she had seen.

That's it. Chaco stretched out to his full length. *See, not that hard.*

She had been shown a vision of the new world. She stood at the edge looking in. It showed a new way of being. She searched for words to describe a process she saw—a seamless fusion in which what was needed was provided as the need for it arose.

But Martha still didn't know how to make the leap from where she was to what she had just been shown. "It involves a new way of seeing and being and experiencing the world," she said, puzzled about why he thought this was easy. "The rules are different."

Exactamente. He stood up and shook himself off, letting dust and dried bits of plant matter fall to the ground. Then he walked away.

"Wait. Where are you headed?" She was enjoying his company and the companionship of someone to talk to. And she was also hoping her would be of additional help to her. But he turned, briefly looked back, and with a quick *adios*, kept going.

She watched until he was out of sight. After wondering briefly how things were going at the school, she brought herself back to matters at hand. It was time to discover what other secrets the site held. Indeed, it was time to uncover the rest of the information she had been sent to find, so that she could return to the school.

───※───

Angela and Sheila gave Mary a second tour of the Ancient Wisdom School before breakfast, in the light of day, showing her things she had not seen the night before. After breakfast, she went to the morning class with them. She was overwhelmed, but eager to enroll in the next Level 1 session.

"You'll all be level 3's by then," she said. "You'll be so good at everything."

"Maybe not all of us," Roger said. "Some of us are on the slow track. I should probably start over. Then I'd know what it feels like to be advanced."

Sheila laughed. "He does alright for himself," she told Mary. "He even did some beginning flying."

"Flying!" Mary was blown away by the idea. "I am certain I will like that. How do you do it?"

"You'll learn soon enough," Angela told her. "It's best to go a step at a time and to learn the basics first."

"I can't believe you had an earthquake yesterday. That must have been so frightening. I've never experienced one."

"Very," Angela replied. She was still shaken by the event. "I don't want to go through another one. You're lucky you came when you did."

Aurora came into class and they immediately fell silent when they saw how serious she looked. "Does anyone know where Ned is?" she asked.

"Maybe he overslept?" Angela said, her voice rising to form a question.

"He's not in his room. Steven went to check. And what about Will? Has anyone seen him?"

"Not since last night," Angela said, wondering what was up. "He was here then."

"Olivia is going to teach the class this morning," Aurora said as Olivia walked in. "Steven and I need to find out what's going on." With that, she left, wondering if, once again, things were spinning out of control. Ned had not brought the stone to her, as promised. But more concerning was the fact that neither he nor Will was around.

Heads turned to follow Aurora as she left, and Olivia knew their focus would be disrupted as the students worried about what might have happened. Mary was concerned that her return to England might be delayed. Steven had promised to take her home after the class, and she didn't want her husband to worry. Everyone was feeling on edge in the aftermath of the earthquake. After trying for a few minutes to get them to focus, Olivia gave up and dismissed them. She felt somewhat frazzled herself, with the tension of recent events taking their toll.

⁂

When her cell phone rang, Martha was startled. She had turned it on to check the time. Thinking it was Ned, she answered. But it was Carol, Ned's sister, calling from the Caribbean where she and her husband Joe had gone on a long-awaited cruise. She wanted to speak to Ned.

"I can't believe your call got through," Martha said. "I'm in kind of a remote spot."

"What's Ned doing?"

"It's a long story," Martha told her. "We accidentally got our phones switched, so I've got his, and he's got mine. You can try calling him on mine." Martha gave her the number. "Are you enjoying the cruise?"

"We are having a blast," Carol said. "Especially Joe. You know how he dragged his feet about this. He's already talking about taking another one." Carol sounded unusually happy, and Martha was glad. *Perhaps something inside her had shifted and she had been able to let go of some of her negative feelings. Ned would certainly be delighted with that.* "Life's too short not to have some fun," Carol said. "Good to talk to you."

After they hung up, Martha mused about Carol's apparent metamorphosis, and she wondered what had taken place to create that. On a whim, she tried to call Ned, but when the call didn't go through, she went back to exploring the site, looking for clues to the wisdom she was supposed to take back to the school.

Will was driving when he heard Martha's phone ring. He pulled off the road as he answered it. He was in luck; surely it was Martha checking in with Ned.

"Ned? It's Carol."

"Did you want to talk to Ned?"

"Who's this?"

"A friend of his," Will said. "He loaned me his phone."

There was a pause as Carol considered what to do. "Well, just tell him that I called then," she said. "I'll talk to him when we get back. Where is he?" She had tried to call him at the house with no luck.

"He's down here with me," Will said.

"Down where?" Carol asked.

When Will told her, Carol had no idea what he was talking about. She asked him to say it again.

"Cuernavaca?" Will repeated, this time as a question to see if it would ring a bell.

It didn't. Carol asked where that was. She was shocked to hear the answer. "He's in Mexico? Since when? Doing what?" She turned to tell her husband that Ned was in Mexico.

"He's at the school," Will said. "Listen, I can't speak for him. Either he'll call you and fill you in or he won't. It's not my business. But I have to hang up." Feeling short-tempered, he closed the phone, checked his rearview mirror and pulled back on the road.

Carol tried to call Martha back but got no answer.

A few minutes later Will pulled up in front of a resort hotel on the outskirts of town. He checked his text messages to find out if his partners had been able to track a location for Martha based on Ned's cell phone. The answer was no. There was nothing indicating she was anywhere in Mexico or Central America.

Will was frustrated. He was running into one dead end after another.

As a last resort, he decided to call Martha. He couldn't believe it when she answered.

She assumed it was Ned. "You sound different," she said.

"Probably a bad connection," he said. "Where are you?"

"I'm not sure," she said. "But I made it. And you're not going to believe it, Chaco was here."

"Chaco," he muttered, wondering how the cat had been able to go there. "Do you have any idea where this place is?"

"It feels like Central America," she said. "But I really don't know. If you saw how I got here, you'd understand."

He immediately asked how.

"I'll tell you when I get back," she said as a growing feeling took hold that the caller wasn't Ned. "This is Will, isn't it?" she suddenly said.

There was silence at the other end and then the call was disconnected. Feeling uneasy, Martha turned off Ned's phone and put it away. So what had happened to Ned, she wondered, and why did Will have her phone? As she mulled over this latest development, she had a new sense of urgency to complete her work. Obviously, she needed to return to the school as soon as possible.

At the same moment, Will, realizing time was of the essence, made a U-turn in the rental car and headed back to the school. He had one last chance to find where Martha had gone, and that was through the cat. He looked at Martha's phone, debating about whether it was of any use to him at this point.

Aurora and Steven were in the office, brainstorming about what could have happened to Will and Ned, when the phone rang. A man had found a cell phone and wanted to return it. After getting some details about this, Aurora gave him directions to the school.

She hung up the phone and looked at Steven. "The man who just called saw someone throw a cell phone out of a car," she said. "To make a long story short, it appears to be Martha's."

Steven drew back in surprise. "That doesn't sound good."

For a moment the two looked at each other in silence. "Perhaps he will have more details when he gets here," Aurora said. "He is on his way."

Steven took a deep breath, nodding his head as he considered what to do. "What are you getting about this?"

"We've been going on faith that Martha is on track," Aurora said. "I still feel that way, although I am sensing that something isn't right."

"I am too," Steven said.

"But there are a lot of unanswered questions right now, and we do not know where Ned and Will are. Something's not right," she repeated, this time with more urgency.

She was distracted by voices outside in the courtyard, and when she stood to look, she found that most of the students were milling around. "I need to see what's going on," Aurora said. As she headed to the door, Olivia appeared to tell her she had dismissed the class.

"We're all worried," Olivia said by way of explanation. "No one could focus."

Galvanized by this, Aurora took charge. She went out to the courtyard and asked everyone to collect. As they gathered around her, she put Sheila and Angela in charge. "I want you to organize another ceremony," she said. "This one will be to focus energy to guide Martha back." She quickly checked her watch. "We'll start right after lunch."

Steven followed her out, and she suggested he use this opportunity to take Mary back to England. "You have about an hour," she said. "When you return, you can help with preparations for the ceremony." Mary, surprised she was leaving so quickly, went to get her things. She said a heartfelt goodbye to Sheila and Angela.

After making sure that everyone had something to do, Aurora went back into her office for a few minutes. She wanted to call on her allies from the world of spirit.

But her phone rang again. Thinking it might be important, she answered. It was Martha's son, Clark, asking if his mother was there. He hadn't heard from her since Melissa's birthday party.

"She's not," Aurora said.

Clark explained he had tried to call her and had ended up talking to someone who had found her cell phone. "Yes, the phone is being returned shortly," Aurora told him.

"But where's my mother?"

"We expect her back," Aurora said, without being specific about when. "May I have her call you?"

But Clark persisted. "I'm concerned that something has happened to her. After all, she's in a foreign country by herself, and it has recently come to my attention that there are some things going on that I...didn't know about. We just found out from her neighbor—Carol—that she's in, as she put it, a remote location. Carol talked to her a little while ago. My mother didn't tell me any of this. Do you know where she is? Carol said Ned is missing, too."

Aurora asked for clarification, making Ned repeat the detail about Carol having talked to Martha, and she asked if Martha had said anything else. But he had no other information, and Aurora could tell he was frustrated. "Let me see what I can find out and call you back," she finally said, puzzled about what she had just learned.

❧❀☙

Clark hung up, not having learned anything about his mother. She had given him very few details about her trip and it suddenly occurred to him that he should have asked. He sat down at the kitchen table and slumped in his chair.

Melissa tugged on his sleeve to get his attention. "Daddy, don't worry. Grandma is OK. Chaco told me."

"What? How would Chaco know anything?" He had reached the end of his patience. "Sweetheart, Chaco is a cat. Cats don't talk. They eat, they sleep, and they chase mice. That's it."

Melissa's face clouded over, primarily due to his impatient tone. Clark immediately regretted having spoken so abruptly. He did not want Melissa to be upset. "What did Chaco tell you?" he asked in a much softer voice, putting his arm around her.

"You have to promise," Melissa said.

"Promise what?" Clark asked.

"To believe." She gestured in a dramatic way, putting both of her small hands out with palms up. He could see that she believed this with her whole heart.

After a few seconds, Clark reluctantly agreed.

"Chaco went to see Grandma."

"When?"

"He just got back. See? She's fine." She leaned her head on her father's arm.

"Where is she?"

"In a very special place. It's called the Lost City. I want to go there, too."

Clark mulled that over. "Where is it?"

"I don't know, Daddy. Ask Chaco."

"And where is Chaco right now?"

"In my room. But don't bother him. He's asleep," she said. "You can ask him when he wakes up. I'll be right back." Melissa ran out of the room as Leslie walked in.

This was all too much for Clark, who put his face in his hands. "I don't know what's going on," he told his wife.

"Neither do I," she said. "I think when your mother comes back, we need some answers."

"Why is this happening?" he asked, sinking into self-pity, but there was no answer. Leslie had gone to check on Melissa. Clark continued to stew, but after a few minutes an odd sensation came over him. He grew lightheaded and warm, and he wondered if he was getting sick. Lifting his head out of his hands, he found himself staring at Chaco, who was sitting directly in front of him on the table.

Buck up.

"What?"

You heard me.

Dumbfounded, Clark stared at the cat, who stared back without blinking. Neither moved a muscle. Clark wondered if he had actually heard the cat talk, or if he had simply imagined it. The remaining option was not so desirable: he was going crazy. Heat surged through his body.

¡Ay-yay-yay! Chaco walked over and swatted Clark in the face. Shocked, Clark jumped back.

"Are you talking to me?" he asked point-blank. His face was flushed; perspiration beaded on his forehead.

Now why would I do that? Chaco jumped off the end of the table.

"Wait," Clark said.

Alright, if you think you can hear me, I'll tell you what you need to know. Your mother is a courageous woman who is doing something remarkable for humanity. Now stop whining. And remember the promise you made to Melissa, to believe.

Clark stared with a shocked look on his face as Chaco sauntered out of the room. For several minutes he sat at the table without moving, not knowing what to think. When Leslie reappeared, she asked him what he was doing. "The kids need their baths," she said, "before we go. How come your face is so red?" She left again to pack for their weekend trip to visit her parents in Portland.

"Baths. Right." He stood up. On the table where Chaco had been sitting was a small silver trinket. When he picked it up and cradled it in his hand, he discovered it was a hummingbird.

Clark, who taught anthropology at the local college, had studied the indigenous cultures of the Southwest. As things began to click into place in his head, he hurried to his computer. Doing a quick search on the meaning of hummingbird in ancient cultures, he found this: "The hummingbird is a good reminder to the shaman. We can find solutions to our questions and learn to better understand our purpose when we step outside the usual and open our vision to the world of spirit that surrounds us."

As he mulled that over, a dragonfly photo on the same page caught his eye. Earlier, as he sat outside reading a professional journal, a large blue dragonfly, iridescent in the sun, had landed momentarily on his knee. He'd never had one land on him before, and instead of brushing it away, he had simply watched it, wondering why it had chosen his knee for a landing pad. "The appearance of a dragonfly," he read, "can set you free of the limiting thoughts or beliefs that have been a strong influence in your life."

Clark closed his eyes, wondering once again what was happening. He still felt strange, yet he couldn't put his finger on exactly what was different. *Limiting thoughts... Why was it so easy for Melissa to believe that Chaco talked to her, and so hard for him? Why was he so unwilling to let her believe that cats could talk?* He shook his head, trying to shake off the sensations that had overtaken him. As an academic, he valued an intellectual approach. Even as a boy, he had been more like Matthew, interested in the facts. Shutting down his computer, he asked himself a question he had never considered. *Were there things going on that he couldn't see because of his training?* The question shimmered on the surface of his awareness, causing his skin to prickle as he headed upstairs to handle the children's baths. He knew the answer, but he wasn't ready to admit it.

When Sheila saw Mark come into the courtyard of the school, she hurried over to him, excited that he had come. "I'm so glad you decided to check out the school," she told him. She hadn't seen him since their conversation in the café on the day she was looking for Martha.

"You're not going to believe what happened," he said. "I wasn't going to come. But then I found this." He held up a cell phone, but Sheila didn't know what that had to do with the school until he explained that it evidently belonged to one of the students. "When I checked the phone numbers in it, I found one for the school. So I called. Turns out, this belong to someone named Martha."

"Martha." Sheila's face went white. "Where did you find it?"

"Near my hotel," he said. "Actually, I saw someone throw it out of a car."

Worried, Sheila led him to the office, where they found Aurora. "I think something has happened to Martha," Sheila said, introducing Mark.

"I have just had a report that Martha is fine," Aurora told her. "Evidently she lost her cell phone." She thanked Mark for returning it.

"I think I am supposed to come to the school," Mark said as he gave Aurora a quick synopsis of how he had learned about the school and then found the phone. "Someone is giving me a message."

Aurora smiled. "It wouldn't surprise me that another student has come because of Martha. In some very surprising ways, she has been an ambassador for the school. We look forward to seeing you."

As Sheila escorted Mark out to the entrance, he stopped in the courtyard. "Do you mind giving me a tour? This place is awesome."

"Not at all." Sheila smiled. "I can't stop thinking about how you found the phone. Aurora is right about Martha—she is quite the recruiter. She brought Ned, then Mary, and now you."

"You sound like you know I'm going to enroll."

"Everybody who gets to know Martha enrolls," she said. "She's kind of...contagious. Wait till you meet her."

"Can't wait. I've already talked to her neighbor Carol. Carol is the one who told me it was her phone. She called right after I found it. She asked if I was Will. Evidently she had just talked to someone named Will. He must have been the person driving the car."

Sheila turned on her heels and made a beeline to the office to share this information with Aurora. Martha hadn't lost her phone—Will had taken it. No wonder Will was missing.

Will slipped into the school a few minutes after Mark arrived. He took a quick look around, then ducked into his room where he could watch for signs of Chaco from the second-floor window. All he needed to do was capture the cat.

✠ 20 ✠

There are events in every life that cannot be explained rationally, and this was one. Martha would never be able to explain her experience in a way that made sense to most people. And yet those who had learned to listen with their hearts would understand and be changed by it. They would absorb her words in an effortless way and make the knowledge a part of their essence.

It had become clear to her that the wayshowers were making a path into the new world. There were others doing what she was doing in other places, all around the globe. She sensed that she was a part of that amazing work. She was grateful, as well, that no machete was needed to clear vines. This was energetic clearing; it was as draining as physical labor, yet it could be done in a recumbent position, while watching clouds overhead or stars in the night sky.

Martha lay on her back, staring up at the stars. Her head was propped comfortably on Ned's backpack and the warm air bathed her bare arms. She felt happy, almost deliriously so. Outside of time, there was no schedule. There was nowhere she had to be, nothing she had to do. She tried to remember the last time she had aimlessly enjoyed gazing at the stars like this, wondering why it hadn't been a higher priority. What silly things we priortized or felt we needed to do, she thought, when there were grander experiences like this available. How many times had she gotten caught up in doing things and forgotten to notice the beauty of her world? But we were all guilty of that. We had all hopped on the train that hurried us through busy and self-important lives. We all allowed ourselves to get carried away by inconsequential matters. These thoughts drifted through her mind as she lay on the ground enjoying the ebb and flow of divine alchemy. The powerful energies had settled, and she had begun to adjust to the feelings and sensations of aliveness that they created.

What she was noticing now was this: in the grand scheme of things, nothing was important save for the connection she forged with herself in the universe. She had visited this earth—and other habitats as well—many times, and the common thread, the thread that connected everything, was her inner truth. She had become very aware of her self-knowing. She could feel the part of her that was immortal—her soul. And in the instant that she felt it, she tasted timelessness. She entered the still point of presence, which expanded to become a spacious, encompassing moment that stretched out forever.

She saw her soul wending its way through this experience and that, as timeless as the movement of the stars. Its journey was eternal, yet at this particular moment in time and space it was experiencing awareness through her physical presence on earth. Behind that pinpoint of human awareness was infinite awareness. She could sense that now.

Soon she would return to the school, although she felt little urgency to do this. Whatever had shifted inside her left her feeling content with simplicity. Her past had fallen away. Her striving had gone with it. What she was noticing now in an effortless way was beauty and joy. It seemed to be all around her. *What if I stay,* she wondered, *instead of going back?* It was an unexpected question, but it danced on the surface of her awareness like a water strider on a pond.

She realized that staying was one of her choices. In the Book of Martha, she could decide. She was the artist with a blank canvas, a tin of brushes, and a palette of luminous rainbow colors. In this new world, everything glowed as if lit from within.

Even if she returned, she knew that she wouldn't tell so much as show. She would embody the energy that she was experiencing in order for the others to be able to experience it in the way that she was. Perhaps, she mused, she would even bring them here.

But for now, she wanted some more time to herself in the new energy field. She wanted to learn how to operate in the new dimension. The rules were new, and there was more transparency than she had ever experienced. Everything that wasn't representing truth was falling away, and she saw that it would be essential to embody truth. In other words, actions and words would need to align. Anything that didn't match her vibration would fall away. As she gave up the conventional approaches she had learned, she would need to honor her inner wisdom and trust it to guide her. She sensed that she would be giving up parts of her old life. She was happy for her grandchildren, and glad that Melissa could so easily see the energies that existed outside the familiar third-dimensional spectrum.

After he lost track of Will, Ned searched for nearly an hour, wandering around the central plaza in case Will had gone there. Finally he gave up and headed back to the school. But on his way he encountered a short dark-haired woman who spoke to him in Spanish. "Sorry," he said. "I don't understand." As he moved to go around her, she took hold of his arm to stop him. She gestured to a young boy, who came and stood next to her.

"She said, we are in the great awakening," the boy said. He had been drawing with chalk on the sidewalk and he held a piece of chalk in one hand. He seemed shy, stealing a quick glance at Ned. He moved to go back to his drawing but the woman put a hand on his shoulder, speaking again. Once again the boy translated. "What was forgotten, is being remembered."

Ned, still wondering where Will had gone, tried to move past them.

"She wants to know, do you have the round stone?" the boy said. The woman stared at Ned, her eyes as dark as obsidian.

Ned studied the two of them. *How could they possibly know about the stone he had found?* He debated about what to say, finally telling them he didn't have it. He looked at the drawing the boy was making on the sidewalk of a yellow sun over a mountain, or was it a pyramid? There was a figure next to the pyramid. Ned started to feel queasy.

The woman spoke again and the boy translated. "Does your friend have it?" Her voice was urgent, and she seemed to be insisting that Ned knew something.

"I don't know where it is," he uttered, shaking his head. "Tell her I really don't know anything."

But the woman persisted. "You must find your friend," the boy insisted. "Tell her to talk to the stones."

"But where is she?" Ned asked.

"In the place where the stones speak." The answer seemed to come from far away, and Ned wondered if he was hearing things.

"Where is that?" Ned was at a loss.

"You must find it," the boy told him, translating again. Then suddenly he darted off, chasing a dog.

"Wait," Ned said. "I need more information." He suddenly remembered what Sheila had told him, about the message she and the others had been given. It was something about the stones having information in them. Ned felt overwhelmed. He was worried about Martha, he didn't know where Will was, or where he had lost the stone that he was supposed to give to Aurora. And now he was supposed to find Martha? He had no idea where to begin.

He stared at the boy's drawing, wishing it held some clue. As he looked at it, it came to life. The small stick figure turned into Martha, and she was standing beside a real pyramid that towered over her. "Martha," he said in surprise. She looked up.

"Can you hear me? Talk to the stones," he said, his words coming out in a rush. "They have information. It's inside them. They can tell you what you need to know."

Behind him, the dog barked. Ned turned to see the boy disappear through a blue door, and the dog bounded after him. The woman was gone. He found himself quite alone on the street, standing above a chalk drawing on the sidewalk.

Confused, Ned walked away. He made a quick decision, not to go back to the school and face Aurora. He didn't want to tell her he had lost the stone. He had no idea how to begin to find Martha, or how to get the message to her. Pondering what he should do, he turned to walk back to the plaza.

His first concern was Martha, because he wanted to help her. He asked for a sign, some indication of what he should do. At the corner a bus went by. On the destination sign above the windshield, it read Taxco. Immediately he thought of Francisco, and his hopes soared. If he could find Francisco, he could consult with him about how to help Martha. Without further ado, he headed in the direction of the bus station.

Puzzling over what information she was supposed to take back to the school, Martha heard Ned call her name. She looked around, half expecting him to step out of the shadows like Chaco had done. He wasn't there, but she could hear him saying something. It sounded like "Talk to the stones."

"Which stones?" she asked.

The voice sounded so much like Ned it was uncanny. Yet it was coming from inside her head. She waited to hear more, but there was no more, just that brief message. She wasn't sure if it was helpful or not. Talk to the stones.

By this time she had navigated the entire site looking for clues, but she began to walk around again. She went first to the Temple of the Jaguar. The stones around the base were ornately carved with symbols and pictures. She had hesitated to touch them, in case they came to life. But this time she simply spoke to them. "What do you have to tell me?" she asked. "I have come to find out."

The reply was almost immediate. *We have waited for this time. We have held the information. We are the Keepers of the Wisdom. Who are you?*

They spoke in one voice, which seemed both timeless and ancient.

"My name is Martha." She waited, but they did not speak. She wondered if perhaps she needed a special name or a password. None of this had come up during her time with Francisco, but she did not come this far to be foiled at this point. She asked her inner guidance what to do, but all she heard was, "Tell them who you are."

She began again. "I am Martha. I am she who has followed the map of the jaguar through time and space to arrive at this place. I have trusted the guidance that brought me here, and I have come in search of the wisdom that you hold." She paused before adding one more thing—what Quetzalcoatl had said in her dream—that seemed crucial. "I am one of the dreamers of a new earth." Then, not knowing what else to do, she down in front of the stones and waited.

The response came quickly. *The gateway has opened for dreaming. The time that has been spoken of is here. As the stars align, as the vibration of humanity increases, the information can emerge that we have protected. Long ago when those who held the wisdom chose to keep it safe, we were named the keepers. We have kept the wisdom in order to share it with those who are dreaming the new world.*

For some reason, it seemed like the most natural thing in the world for the stones to be talking. As they spoke, the wisdom held for so long in the stones became hers. It came to her like a song, infusing her being with joy.

This new time is a gift given in antiquity to the people of now. It was held until the time that humans were able to make the shift. You are ready now. There are enough who are ready that this can be created. It begins in your hearts. You will find the feeling of love in your hearts.

This will spread into the rest of your body, changing your cells and your organs, changing your very structure. Those who are ready will change, and the change will spread like fire through the land. The old systems will fall and the new ways will arise.

You are the instrument of change. As we share the wisdom with you, it becomes who you are. And then you share it with others, and they become it as well. In this way the evolution takes place. There is no teaching, only the preparation of the soil so that the seed can take root. These seeds make a new garden, a new earth, a new time. As we share them with you and you share them with others, the unfolding begins.

The seeds of love sprout in your heart and spread through your being. There is nothing for you to do save for allowing. Surrender to the energy of Source so that it may flow through you. Drink from this river to create what you need. Energy becomes manifest through you. Your physical bodies transform the energy of love into what you need. This has always been available but it has never been possible on earth. Each of you will create using your divine gifts, and this will sustain each of you, and in this way all will flourish.

Martha felt the vision she had had when Chaco was there solidify and take root within her. She understood it now. She pulled out the piece of paper she had been making notes on and wrote:

These are new times. Follow your heart. Love from the place of needing nothing. Love because it feels good. Love because it is the best thing you can do for yourself.

The stones began to hum with a vibration that penetrated Martha's awareness. Her whole body tingled with the sound. The sound took her not only to new heights, but to new clarity. She kept writing:

You are here to experience heaven on earth. What's keeping you from this? Listen to the song that you carry within you. What do you want to create? We are breaking new ground for a new world. Envision your biggest dream.

The wisdom poured forth from the stones and from Martha as the cocreation began. Freed from the stone, the seeds of the new time were being spread, carried energetically by the vibration, which could now be heard. Around the earth, the stones in the sacred temples and pyramids began to sing. The awakening, which had begun earlier, went into high gear. In small towns, in big cities, in rural areas, this person or that stopped to notice an unusual sensation of joy rising in them. It seemed to have no cause, but it made them stop and marvel for a moment at the beauty of the natural world—a tree, a flower, a bird, a bumblebee, a waterfall. They noticed that something seemed different. The sky was bluer, the grasses were greener, their hearts were lighter.

Martha packed up her things to go. She felt eager to share. The new energy pulsed within her, and she glowed with the beauty of having shed the density of her past. She felt youthful and she walked with a light step. In this place where the past met the future, she had found the seeds of the new earth. It was the wild card. By creating a new beginning, she would anchor a new dream. She had changed, and she would stay changed. She had discovered and fallen in love not only with everything around her, but with herself. And all it had taken was a leap of faith.

A small, heart-shaped stone caught her eye, and she picked it up to take to Olivia. That was it then. She was ready. Giving thanks to the stones and to this place for holding the wisdom, she shouldered her pack.

🕸 21 🕸

Martha was reluctant to leave the new world that she had found. She had acclimated to its rarified air and she reveled in the heightened awareness. She felt at home. Yet she understood that she needed to share what she had learned. Finally the decision to go rose up in her effortlessly, and she knew it was time. Even though she wondered about returning to the denser energy of the old world, she missed her friends. She knew she needed to help anchor this new energy on the earth. This was the way it would arrive.

For a few more moments, she let herself be surrounded by the new energy. It had permeated her being and filled her with beautiful light and love. "One more minute," she said at least five times. She picked some bananas and avocados to take back, then climbed to the top of the pyramid. She planned to return the same way she had come. With one last look around, she leapt into the air, looking forward once again to flying. But she plummeted to the ground.

Shaken, she picked herself up and sat down on the bottom step of the pyramid. She had assumed that going back would be easy. She wondered what was happening.

¡Ay-yay-yay! Chaco sauntered around the corner of the Temple of the Jaguar, stopping to scratch his head on the stone.

"Chaco!" Martha gave a big sigh of relief. "What if I just follow you?"

He sat down about fifteen feet away and looked at her. Then he eyed the pack, so laden with avocados that it bulged at the sides.

"I know it's heavy," she said in explanation, "but I want everybody to taste a little bit of the new earth."

Then you may be here awhile. He got up and turned to leave.

But Martha was determined. "I know I can do this," she said. She was filled with new clarity, and her focus had become unwavering. "The people who built this were masters of energy," she said. "They have shared their wisdom with me. I came here to learn these things, and never again will I act in a way that undermines me or my power." Once more, she climbed to the top of the pyramid.

Seeing that her resolve had returned, Chaco left. He knew where and when he was needed, and where and when he was not. Attending to only essential business made his life very easy.

Standing atop the pyramid, Martha knew the truth that was held in her heart. She carried the light of the new world in every cell of her being, in every word, in every gesture, in every action. She coursed with a new vitality and her dreams were within her creative power. She was able to do what was necessary. She had stepped through a doorway. Moments later she soared above the treetops, beginning her journey back.

She returned first to Taxco, hoping to see Francisco. But he was away and expected back in two days. Esperanza invited her in, and much to her surprise Martha found Ned sitting on the terrace. He nearly toppled out of his chair when he saw her. They were both full of questions. She wondered what he was doing there, and he wanted to hear about everything she had experienced. They talked for a half hour over fresh lemonade that Esperanza prepared for them. To Martha, it tasted even better than she remembered.

She left a note for Francisco, and then she and Ned took a bus to Cuernavaca. Exhausted from not having slept well the last couple of days, Ned dozed off. He slept for most of the trip, giving Martha a bit more time with her thoughts. Retracing the route that she had followed days earlier with Francisco, Martha noticed how different her surroundings seemed. She became aware of the fact that she was moving through the old reality by choice. She was no longer a part of it. This was what Francisco had talked to her about that first day. She understood now what he meant. Having moved into the new energy, it was her home now, and she carried it with her.

As the bus bumped along the highway, she knew that she was very different from the woman who had made this journey a short time ago. She could feel the ways that she had changed. Perhaps most noticeable was that she had stepped out of the density of the third dimension. She was lighthearted, and everyone smiled at her, especially children.

In no time, they arrived at their destination. The bus dropped them off downtown, and she and Ned walked from there. Ned offered to carry her backpack. "By the way, it's your backpack," she said as they approached the school. "I had to make do with a ham sandwich and your big T-shirt."

"Wow, this is heavy," he said. She explained about the avocados.

He apologized wholeheartedly for the mixup with the packs, and he told her that Chaco had promised to deliver her pack. "I thought it was taken care of," he said, puzzled. "I wonder what he did with it."

¡Ay caramba! It's under your bed. Chaco had materialized at the sound of his name, and with a flick of his tail he sauntered into the school, so as to lead this very important procession. Ned and Martha looked at each other and then burst into laughter. "And I thought he could work magic," Ned said, following Martha through the entrance.

"More than you know," Martha replied, watching the cat ahead of them with his tail held high. "Believe me, he has some stories to tell when he's ready."

Ned told her he thought he might be in trouble with Aurora for having left without explanation. He still hadn't shared the details of following Will or hearing the prophecy. "I'm glad I'm coming back with you," he said. "That may counterbalance things for me."

"I'm sure it will work out," she told him.

Entering the Ancient Wisdom School, she realized that everything was the same, yet it all looked completely different. It glowed with a soft light that showed its truth. Everywhere she looked, she saw beauty. The transition had begun. The students were beginning their evolution into the new time and it was evident around them. It had been here all the time, but she had been unable to see it.

Now that the vibration of the earth as well as so many of her inhabitants was increasing, the shift was imminent. The momentum was in place. And even though there were those who continued to live as if nothing was happening, it was only a matter of time before they too realized that incredible change was taking place.

Martha hesitated at the entrance, knowing the moment she stepped inside she would be met with questions. The first thing she heard was drumming. The powerful ceremony to bring her back was just concluding. She took a deep breath and walked into the courtyard with Ned, moving toward the circle of students. Chaco had already made his way to the center of the action to make an announcement. *She's back. She found Ned. All's well.*

As heads turned to look, the students suddenly spotted Martha in their midst. Angela was the first to shout her name. Then Olivia and Aurora and Steven and the others called to her as well. They clustered around her, wanting to hear the details of her adventure.

Aurora stopped a few feet away and surveyed her, taking in the energy that emanated from Martha.

"So you did it," she said. She studied her happily for another moment. "And you're going to be able to share with all of us how we can too can do this."

"I have so much to share." Martha's face lit with a smile. "The shift is under way and we're all a part of it. If we are here on earth, we're taking part."

"I can't wait," Aurora said. "Come, sit. Can we get you something to eat or drink?"

"First, let me hug each one of you," Martha said. She moved through the group sharing heartfelt hugs.

Sheila was the last. "Girlfriend, you look fabulous. You are simply glowing. Take me where you have been. I want some of what you are feeling." She introduced Martha to Mark, who had stayed to take part in the ceremony. The minute he saw her, Mark knew he would be attending the school. She emanated a vibration of love.

Happy to see everyone, Martha couldn't stop smiling. "We'll all be glowing when we're done," she said.

They made a circle of chairs in the courtyard and she began her story.

"A long time ago we were given great knowledge but we lacked the power to keep it as our own and it was lost to us. Now we have the opportunity once again. We are returning to our own beginning, our greatness. A portal has opened to take us into our own potential. All we have to do is make it our intention to step through it. This time we come as masters. We leave behind as much density as we can and bring our mastery into the new energy. We use our gifts to create beauty. The new energy is joyful. Within it we become present. Or needs are met as they arise. The circle of life has brought us to our new beginning." The words poured out of her. She wasn't even sure where they came from. She hadn't realized that the circle of life was a symbol for Quetzalcoatl, but she suddenly understood that it was.

She described arriving at the Temple of the Jaguar, saying that the trip had been like a wide-awake dream. She told them about making the connection with the stars and the massive infusion of energy. "In the wee hours of the morning, I was buzzing with energy. All I wanted was tea. But I had Ned's backpack instead of my own."

"How did that happen?" Sheila asked.

"Just a mixup," Martha said with a telltale smile at Ned, who felt relieved that Chaco had not taken the backpack to Martha after all, because it would have been a beacon to Will. "I discovered I had the wrong backpack when I got there. Initially that meant I didn't have the things that I needed. However, what I needed began to appear, and I soon realized I was creating what I needed with my thoughts." She went on to describe finding the thermos of hot tea in Ned's pack.

"That's incredible, "Angela exclaimed.

"I certainly didn't pack it," Ned explained, and he shrugged his shoulders in an exaggerated way to say he didn't know where the tea had come from. There were titters of excitement as students thought about the manifestation exercises they had practiced. Suddenly they could see the real-world applications for this work. It wasn't just about creating chocolate in a classroom because Steven or Aurora asked them to. It was actually creating what they needed, at the moment they needed it. The responsibility of this began to sink in, and several nodded with new understanding.

"As it turns out, the tea in the thermos was Aurora's new blend," Martha continued. "It was a perfect match for that moment, and I savored it. Before I left, Aurora told me that she hadn't named it, and as I drank it a name floated into my consciousness. It seemed to sum up what I was experiencing. It was so apt that I want to propose it to Aurora."

"Tell us." Aurora leaned forward in her chair, delighted with what she was hearing.

Martha spoke as if the words were the beginning of a poem. "Quetzalcoatl Dreams," she said. "Your blend is a new tea for a new time. As I drank it that morning in the predawn hours, everything began to coalesce. The energy from the stars, from the amulet, from the pyramids—it all came together. I began to experience how Quetzalcoatl was dreaming a new world."

"It's bagged and ready to go," Aurora said, "for whoever is ready. And yes, when I collected the herbs for that blend at the Cloud Forest House, I was following the guidance I had received." She stood up, moving toward several jars of sun tea on a table. "I made a batch earlier," she said, "so that we can all try it." She and Steven and Olivia began filling cups to pass around.

A few minutes later, Martha continued. "What came to me then, and I haven't yet put this in words, so bear with me, was… how to dream like Quetzalcoatl. I realized that Quetzalcoatl had been with me from the beginning of my journey, guiding me—or maybe nudging is a better word. I did need a push here and there." Martha exchanged smiles with several students who had also needed a nudge at one time or another.

The students, who had been waiting for this moment for quite a while, were fascinated by what she was telling them, especially when Martha explained that Quetzalcoatl had made an appearance.

"He actually showed up?" Roger was flabbergasted. "How did that happen? What did he look like?"

"Some of this I'll tell you later," she said. "But there is one more thing I wanted to share now. At one point I was sensing the new energy and observing how beautiful it was. I was noticing the perfection of everything. Every moment unfolded in perfection, creating a series of interconnected, exquisite moments. The air was silvery. Everything seemed new. I was aligned with everything and everything was aligned with me. Especially the animals. They were showing themselves in a new way, with a sense of their awareness of my awareness."

She looked around to make sure they were following her. No one moved a muscle.

"I heard another message. It moved into me and through me. *The force of creation comes through our hearts. We are the force of creation.*" She looked out at them. "*You are the force of creation. I am the force of creation. We are meant to use this force to create our lives.*"

The courtyard was silent as everyone took this in.

"This is the way we create our world," she said. "It's not done in our heads. We do it by using the living energy—the creative force—that moves through each of our hearts. We have arrived at the time where this is finally possible." She looked around at the people she had come to know and care about as darkness fell.

"We simply live our dream, expressing it at every moment. We live it as completely as we can. This means we trust it, we don't doubt it, and we especially don't doubt our power to create it."

With these words, Aurora broke into spontaneous applause, and it was followed by applause and delighted laughter from the others. The joy was contagious.

"I have to get this out while I can remember it," Martha said. "We live our dream day in and day out. It is our responsibility. And one day we will simply notice that our dream has become us, and we have become our dream."

She could feel questions beginning to form about how to do this, but she said she wasn't going to answer questions until later. "For now, just be with it. Try it. Don't talk about it or discuss it. Just be your dream."

She said they would talk more at a later time. "Remember, we are the force of creation. It moves through us and we can shape it. We must shape it to create the new world."

As she finished, she smiled at all of them. "One last thing. We are not only on the brink of something magnificent, we are a key component."

Aurora told them that in a half hour, they would all meet on the open portico overlooking the pool for dinner. As they moved quietly away to begin to practice what they had just heard about, Aurora came up to Martha. "You have become a teacher," she said, "an inspiring one."

"I surprised myself," Martha replied. "I wasn't thinking about teaching. I just wanted to share my experience."

"Exactly," Aurora told her. "That is a powerful way to teach. You do it naturally, without effort. It is clear why this was your path."

"Was?" Martha asked, sensing something unspoken in the phrasing.

"Ah." Francisco came up next to them. He had been standing quietly in the background. "That is your choice."

Martha suddenly felt like she was back in square one. "My choice," she repeated, not following what they were telling her.

"You can choose whether to stay or go. If you stay you can teach others how to discover this energy and how to live on the new earth. If you go, you will live your dream on the new earth," Francisco said.

For the first time, it hit Martha what he meant. She had returned from the new energy in order to share her experience with everyone at the school. But she didn't have to stay.

For the next minute she didn't speak as she let that sink in. "I'm not going to decide right now," she finally said. "But I see what you mean. I see that we will be building communities on the new earth. I can go and be a part of that."

"Yes, your dream is what you make it."

Aurora listened quietly to this exchange, making her own decision. This was her dream, having the school. It was needed, and it would continue to move people into the new energy, especially now that Martha had shown them all how to do that.

"Ah, yes," Francisco said, affirming her choice.

"And you?" she asked.

"I will continue to move about," he said. "I like to travel. I will not have a permanent home. My soul is temporarily housed inside my skin. It too will travel one day."

Martha considered her own dream. She was tied to the physical world through her son and her grandchildren. But otherwise, there was nothing holding her. Her mind raced with ideas.

"One last thing," Aurora said. "We've finally put the pieces together with Will. He is a dream stealer, someone who wants what others have but is unwilling to do the inner work to get it. He wants to take shortcuts and take what others have rather than find it for himself. But as we know, the dream is available to anyone who follows the path to their own truth. With luck, he will discover that path. Each one of us is given the opportunity."

"I finally realized it was Will who was following me," Martha said. "But I knew he wouldn't find me. His vibration was too low. But the energy of being followed kept me focused on my task. I knew there wasn't time to waste, even when I was enjoying the beauty of the new world. It helped to remind me that I needed to return to share what I had learned."

"He represents the old energy," Aurora said, "that there wasn't enough for everyone. It is good to see that disappearing. And it is wonderful to have you back, sharing your vision."

✦

When Ned found her later, Martha was stretched out on one of the padded lounge chairs by the pool. She was deep in thought, staring at the profusion of red bougainvillea on the wall lit by the outdoor lights.

"There you are," he said, sitting down next to her. "It's great to have you back safe and sound." When he saw she was wearing the stone he had lost, his story tumbled out.

She put her hand on the stone, explaining that she had found it at a crucial moment.

"I was upset that I lost it, especially after Aurora told me how important it was. I just wanted you to have it, and I'm relieved beyond measure that you found it."

"Nice work," she said. "That's another thing we will never have a rational explanation for. Does Aurora know?"

"Not yet," he said. "I owe her an explanation. As you can imagine, I wasn't looking forward to telling her I lost it."

"These are experiences that teach us—or challenge us—to be the new humans," said Martha. Still in teacher mode, she was surprised to hear the words emerge. "This is a cycle of transformation to become who we are as opposed to who we think we should be. It's to reveal the person your soul came here to be: your authentic self."

"I'm not sure I know who that is," Ned said, puzzling over it. "But I'm learning. For a while I felt there was something missing in my life, but I didn't know what it was. I didn't think I would ever find it. But now I have an inkling that I will." He looked at her for a moment. "I do think my part of the puzzle was finding the stone. And because I found it, I feel very connected to the wisdom that came through. I think a long time ago, I knew something about this. That's a new feeling."

Martha smiled. "I believe you're right. It's funny how things work out, and how one thing leads to something else. When we follow the thread, we can arrive at our dream."

He reached over and touched her arm. "Any idea where our community will be?"

"You can help me build it. Francisco said he plans to come and go. I may do that too for the time being. I want to show you where I went," she added. "The more I think about it, the more I realize we can create it wherever we are. What will be different is us, who we are."

"I don't quite know how it will happen, but we aren't going to be the same," he said. "I've had that feeling for a few days."

Sheila and Angela appeared.

"We want you to be a part of our community," Martha said.

"We were thinking the same thing," Sheila said. "Here I thought we'd all be saying goodbye when school ends, but now we can dream a community into being."

"Don't forget me," Roger said, walking up. "I've got basic manifesting and basic flying under my belt. I'm actually starting to feel like I might be able to hold my own."

"Do you know what your gift is yet?" Ned asked.

"No, but Sheila gave me one idea."

"Don't say it yet. We're not supposed to tell them until tomorrow. Those were Aurora's instructions," Ned said. "I'm eager to hear what everyone says."

"My gift appeared when I least expected it," Angela said.

"Mine too," Ned told her. "But it also appeared when I embraced my fear. I'm beginning to think that the more we go down the road we've been afraid to go down, the more we find how wonderful life is."

"Guess what?" Sheila said to Martha. "The man I introduced you to lives in Tucson and he's decided to enroll in the school. He'll be a Level 1 in the next session."

"Mary will be in his class," Angela added. "Remember Mary Bole? She said to tell you hello. She came for a tour and got to meet everyone, right after the earthquake."

"Earthquake!" Martha could hardly believe it as they began to tell her the events of the last thirty hours. So much had happened for everyone.

In the morning, Martha decided to make a quick trip home. There was a lot to discuss with her son, she discovered, as Ned had brought her up to date on what Clark was asking about. She promised the students to continue telling them about the new energy when she returned the next day.

Heading toward the portal in the courtyard, she turned and waved. Then, out popped a phrase she hadn't expected, but after she said it, she knew it was just right. "See you all in the new world."

LaVergne, TN USA
07 December 2009
166236LV00001B/4/P